The Twilight People

To Gary

From Patrick

The Twilight People

by

Patrick Feenan

Spiderwize

The Twilight People

Spiderwize
Office 404, 4th Floor
Albany House
324/326 Regent Street
London
W1B 3HH
UK

www.spiderwize.com

This is a work of fiction. Names, characters and incidents are products of the author's imagination. Any resemblance to persons living or dead is entirely coincidental.

The views expressed in this work are solely those of the author and do not necessarily reflect the views of the publisher, and the publisher hereby disclaims any responsibility for them.

This book can be purchased from many online bookstores such as Amazon.co.uk

ISBN: 978-1-908128-03-4

Dedication

I was inspired to write this manuscript, one day, while I was sitting talking to my two grandsons, Sean and Dylan Winters. We were discussing what sort of books they liked, and they replied, Fantasy Fiction, Dinosaurs and other talking-animal stories. My eldest grandson, Sean Winters, is into writing fantasy stories in a big way, and he completed his first four years ago, when he was just six-years-old.

Sean's fantasy story is about, well... I will let you see the story for yourselves. I would like to dedicate this manuscript to all three of them, including my thirteen-year-old granddaughter, Shannon Feenan, who lives in Sunderland, in North-East England, and she is, according to her, a "Macam".

Patrick Feenan

Table of Contents

Acknowledgement

With many thanks to Doctor Eamon Phoenix, the author of the *On This Day,* daily articles in Belfast's *Irish News* newspaper, for his kind permission for me to use a map taken from his historical book, *Two Acres of Irish History.* Also, many thanks are due to Sean Nolan, the editor of the *Ireland's Own* magazine, for his permission for me to use the diagrams/drawings of the ancient creatures featured in the book, and taken from his website. (Part of People Newspapers Limited).

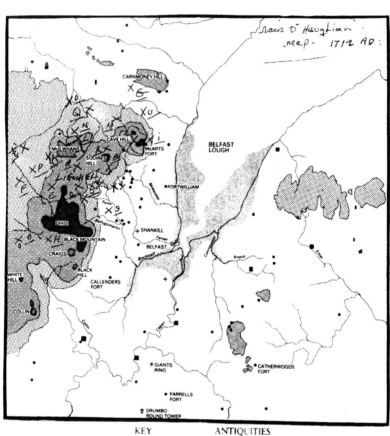

Maurs Ó Haughian
map. 1712 AD.

KEY

- ■ above 400m
- ■ above 300m
- ▨ above 200m
- ▢ above 150m
- ⊔ mud or sand

ANTIQUITIES

- ⋔ cairn or dolmen
- ▯ standing stone
- • earthworks rath or fort
- ■ motte
- ✛ site of church
- ▰ site of castle

Introduction

T hroughout the history of ancient Ireland, many strange and wondrous legends have been passed down through the generations. Creatures who levitated, disappeared and appeared in a blink of an eye, and who transmogrified, changing into different shapes and appearances. These were the Little People, or leprechauns, who could reputedly talk to the animals of the night, especially the wise, White Owl.

Legend speaks of how the leprechauns robbed Spanish soldiers and sailors after the failed Spanish invasion of 1588, when over one hundred galleons went to fight and only twenty-four had survived the battle, making a run for home via the west of Ireland and the tip of northern Scotland. But they had never made it to Scotland, with all twenty-four galleons running into a fierce storm off the coast of County Mayo, on the Irish coast, where they crashed onto the rocks there and all the crews and soldiers accompanying them died.

Another legend tells of a ghostly highwayman, Naois O'Haughan, who had reportedly hidden his treasure somewhere on the mountains around Belfast, N. Ireland. After he'd been hanged by yeomen in Carrickfergus Castle in County Antrim, he had returned from his grave to still hold-up stagecoaches afterwards, and to harangue and terrify stragglers travelling along the roads on a misty or foggy night as they'd made their way home. His and the leprechauns' treasure had never been found for over three hundred years, until three ten-year old boys and their fathers had decided to start the search, but as time had gone on, they'd gotten more than they'd bargained for, as malevolent and violent ghostly beings had pursued them relentlessly. When the searchers had been in dire trouble, they'd gotten help from unusual sources, a long-dead monk, who'd haunted their old village, and a derelict monastery,

xi

long-ago abandoned, without them requesting any help at all. Other help was to come for them in the shape of twelve American airmen, who'd lost their lives when they'd flown into Cavehill Mountain while flying their B-17 heavy bomber on their way to take part in the Allied invasion of Europe in 1944.

This is their story.

The Haunted House

A FEW DAYS BEFORE HALLOWEEN there was a boy called Sam delivering the evening paper when he came to a house which had an address unknown. The house was awfully old and dilapidated and surrounded by leafless trees with a dark black bark. When he tossed the paper onto the front steps the paper was flung right back at him— and then he realised there was something strange about that house.

He went up to the front door when he was delivering the paper. When he knocked on the door the door opened and the step he was standing on lifted him up and slid him into the house. When he was in the house he didn't see anyone at all and then he saw something moving. It had a strange boxed-shaped body and a strange lampshade-like head, and then he saw what it was! It was part of the house's furniture—the drawers for a body, the lamp for a head, and then it started coming towards him and many more strange creatures like it.

He ran as fast as he could through the house. He finally found a way out but then all of a sudden the house started moving like the furniture inside and then he finally realised the house was alive! He ran as fast as he could through the neighbourhood until he came to a cliffside at a building site, and then when the house had him cornered he jumped into the crane and when the house went to grab him it fell off the edge and shattered to pieces.

Sean Winters
7th February 2006

The Twilight People

WHEN THE DEAD OF NIGHT is terrifyingly still, save for the rustling and hooting in the trees by the wise, White Owl, when the moon has a luminous eerie, orange glow; then, strange and unearthly creatures may be all around. You had better watch your parents and your siblings carefully, and love them.

On such a strange, misty, silent night, you, your friends or your family may be unlucky enough to meet the Banshee, or the ghostly and beautiful red-headed Rosaleen and her minions, that paranormal trickster foe...

But if you ever do, then hold your nerve, and pray for the poor and the needy, or for those who may be in despair, as you may be in despair soon for whatever terrible reason, especially yourself, in the perceived safest of places or situations that you may find yourself in.

In their strangest and alien domains that these creatures move in, around the time of darkness, between the shadows and even the raindrops, you should be very wary and afraid, very afraid.

If you or your friends or family get a glimpse of them, don't stare into their eyes, ever, or it may be your turn to die, on account of those flaming red eyes of evil. For you may be spirited away, and may die violently, never to be seen again by your family, school friends, or neighbours.

Prologue

The Ghostly Guardians of Cavehill Mountain

T HE CAVEHILL MOUNTAIN that had overlooked the northern outskirts of Belfast in Northern Ireland had always held a terrifying fascination for me and our entire primary school class of ten-year-olds. Our old village of mostly whitewashed houses, two up and one down, was situated from about three miles from Cavehill, as the crow flew.

Our houses had outlived their usefulness since the three mill owners in our area had sold them to private landlords who had neglected to carry out even the most basic of repairs on them. The houses had been built for the hundreds of mill workers who had flooded into Belfast to work in the mills by the mill owners, from the rural areas at the end of the nineteenth century. The houses sometimes housed families of ten, eleven or twelve members, and some people, mostly children, had to sleep four or five to each bed.

Even in the summertime the hovels had been cold and damp and during heavy rain showers the rain would run down the streets in torrents, because our village had been constructed on a steep hill under the shadow of the Black Mountain, to the west. A fast river had risen in the hills above the village, running down through Kennedy's Race, the village itself, and on for another three mills to turn the waterwheels that would operate the spinning and weaving looms.

Three artificial dams had been constructed and were breeding beds for the wild brown trout that had filled many a breakfast, dinner and supper table in our village, along with the watercress plants that had grown naturally along the riverbank. The Black Mountain was a favourite hunting-ground for the local hunters who'd owned greyhounds, whippets and Jack Russell terriers, and the Irish hare and rabbits were plentiful. A deep chasm had formed over thousands of years, eaten away by the river that had cut a path through it, while on each side of the twelve feet wide and two-foot deep river there grew walnut trees that we'd often strip at the end of the summer to crack open the walnuts to eat the kernels. We'd called it the Wee Jungle, and we'd often go there when we'd played truant from Saint Vincent de Paul school.

This chasm had lain between the Black and Wolfhill Mountains, Wolfhill being the alleged last place in the whole of Ireland where British yeomen had shot and killed the last wolf. During some nights people would imagine at the present time, the howl of a distressed wolf high on the hills above the village, but other old wise people in the village said that it was a banshee warning us that when somebody died it was always the banshee warning the village that there would be three deaths in a row.

Our homes were part of Wolfhill Mountain, having been built from the solid, grey granite that had been hewn out of Wolfhill Quarry, then cut into square blocks with hammers and chisels. Red bricks had been laid around our doors and window frames and some people had said our houses "were so strongly built they could withstand an atomic bomb blast", an event not considered unlikely since we'd be a target of the Russians on account of a main transmitter that was "sat on top of Divis Mountain" that also overlooked our Village, and indeed Bangor Blue slates had topped off our houses.

Our attention and curiosity was now turning to Cavehill Mountain, always mysterious because it had seemed that it had been forever covered in a blanket of mist, as if a cloud had fallen out of the sky and the often high, strong winds had forgotten to blow it off again—and, indeed, it seems it was always hanging there. On a rare day, usually in the summer, the Cavehill had looked like a burial mound for a great giant, the gravediggers having forgotten to bury the giant properly, leaving the forehead and long straight nose above ground. Locals had christened this mound Napoleon's Nose, after Napoleon Bonaparte, the former emperor of France. But local legend had ordained that there was more mystery to the mountain than Napoleon. Ghosts had been seen of Naois O'Haughan, a highwayman who had held up stagecoaches in that area adjacent to Cavehill and our village. Local folklore that the extended O'Haughan family had lived in Skerry, in Ballymena, around thirty miles from our village. After the Plantation of Ulster in 1606 and the following years, the O'Haughans were evicted from their land where they'd farmed hundreds of sheep on forty acres of hilly country.

During the Second World War of 1939-45, an American Air Force B-17 bomber had crashed into Cavehill Mountain during the usual thick fog. The plane had been on its way to take part in the bombings of the Normandy beaches before the allied landing there on June the 6th, 1944, when it had crashed into the mountain on June the 1st. All twelve crewmen had been killed and it had been rumoured that a strange fluorescent light had been seen swaying to-and-fro just before the plane came down.

The airplane crew had probably thought that the imaginary lights had been an airport runway because the entire city had been blacked out in fear of other German air attacks. Perhaps Naois O'Haughan had thought that the plane had been British as he'd sworn revenge on the British soldiers who'd hanged him when he'd been captured. He would wait until a mist had descended on our area, then would sit on the Hightown Road, adjacent to the summit of the Cavehill Mountain, before swinging a lantern to-and-fro as a stagecoach reached him, shouting, "Stop and deliver your valuables!"

O'Haughan had been a teenager when his family had been evicted by planters from Scotland and the north of England, and while his family had moved away from Ballymena he'd stayed on, wreaking revenge for his family's treatment. He is reputed to have had a safe house, and a sweetheart, on the Wolfhill Road, and while his ill-gotten gains of gold and silver coins, gold snuff boxes and jewellery would have been worth hundreds or maybe thousands of English pounds, that would have been worth a million or more pounds in today's prices.

Long after Naois had been hanged in Carrickfergus in 1720 by British soldiers, it had been rumoured that his ghost would later still harry and rob the stagecoaches of French Huguenots that had traversed the same route, from Belfast to Antrim Town—the Huguenots who had settled in Ulster to found linen mills. They'd been hounded out of France by King Louis the XVIII, who had ordered the murders of ten thousand of them in a single night, in the 16th century, men, women, and even tiny children. Afterwards, armed guards with muskets would be posted up beside the stagecoaches drivers, as they'd travelled up the present-day Antrim Road, then nothing but a dirt track. The coaches would then turn left up the Hightown Road before turning right onto the Horseshoe Bend, passing our village high above them, on to the Seven-Mile-Straight and on to Antrim Town and further afield.

But more terrifying local legends had been mentioned of other strange happenings on that mountain and its surrounding areas—like ghostly monks, leprechauns, and a little, seven or eight-year-old girl who would stand and smile at people in the early hours of the morning as they made their way home, she being dressed in old-fashioned clothes—a white, Victorian style, frilly dress, a white bow tied around her long blonde hair and white socks up to her knees. She would run off laughing if challenged, when people had asked her, "What are you doing running about at this time of the morning?"

Another tragic sighting was of a young mother who had committed suicide one dark night, at the beginning of the twentieth century, by jumping into a local mill dam; when she was pulled out the next day her young baby's arms were wrapped around her neck, the baby also dead.

Chapter One

Our First Encounter with Abbot John

A FEW YEARS BEFORE THE AMERICAN AIRMEN had been killed on Cavehill Mountain, and when my mother had been my age, my mother had told me stories around our wooden, blocks fire, about her schooldays, because my father had not been able to get a job, except during the winter if it snowed—and we couldn't afford to buy coal—for Belfast Corporation. She'd gone to the same school as me, Saint Vincent's Primary.

"During the war," she'd said, "the people in our village would lie out in the surrounding fields, for safety, joined by hundreds and thousands of other people from north Belfast. They would listen as the German air force, the Luftwaffe, would come screaming over our village on the way to bomb Belfast.

"The German planes would use the Cavehill and Divis Mountains as markers, and the people could see the blackened faces of the German crews in their cockpits, lit-up by a blue light and who'd been just fifty feet above them.

"On those nights the heavy industries in Belfast would take a heavy pounding," she said, "and each night, just before the Germans had showed up, they would hear the terrible wailing of a banshee and the crying of a wolf that had echoed around the Ligoniel hills."

My father would laugh heartily at this, saying that what she'd heard "was probably the drunk next door beating his wife as usual on a Friday night after he'd spent all his money at the pub, and the howling of the wolf was probably the drunk, after his wife had retaliated, beating him back with her frying pan."

My father had never been superstitious, had not shirked from walking under a ladder and had never gone to church. But mother would still talk on, despite him, telling me and my brothers and sisters about the German bombings and how when the fuel from the incendiary bombs ran down the sewers in downtown Belfast, thousands of rats would run up the sewers to our village, a distance of five or six miles. When my mother had told us that I wondered why the ghost of highwayman, Naois O'Haughan, didn't shine his lantern on Cavehill to bring the German planes to drop and waste their bombs on the mountain. Then I realised, the Germans hadn't hanged him, it was the British, and he'd probably been standing on the mountain doubled over with laughter as Belfast burned.

One September evening, after the school summer holidays were over, me and my two friends, Jim and Peter, had decided to play treasure hunters after watching the movie called Treasure Island, starring Robert Newton as Long John Silver. We had decided that by hook or by crook we would find the treasure of the highwayman, starting first in Carnmoney Cemetery in Glengormley.

We had waited until it had gotten dark as we took our time making the journey on foot from the village, via the Horseshoe Bend, the Hightown Road and the Upper Antrim Road, hoping to find the grave of the highwayman when we would dig it up to see if his treasure had been secretly buried with him by his sweetheart from the Wolfhill Road. We'd arrived at the cemetery at around eight p.m., climbing over the six-foot-high metal railings, looking around to see if the watchman had been around, but he had been nowhere to be seen.

I'd borrowed my father's snow shovel and Jim had borrowed his father's bicycle lamp. But no matter how hard we'd tried we couldn't find the highwayman's grave. Perhaps after he'd been hanged, I thought, his body may have been put down a hole somewhere else and was covered with quicklime; it may have been just a local rumour that he'd been buried there.

We'd decided to return home as Jim had shone his torch on his watch and it had read eleven o'clock. But Peter had disappeared, being there behind us one minute and not there the next. "Peter! Peter!" we'd shouted, oblivious to the fact that the watchman might hear us.

Peter had worn extra thick-lensed spectacles and was blind as well as fat, with a shock of red hair, while Jim and me had been fair-haired and were lanky. Peter, if he'd leaned on a house, wouldn't have seen it in front of him. His absence was unknown to us, as Peter had trailed behind us. He hadn't seen a newly-dug grave that had been readied for a funeral the next morning. He'd fallen down it, hitting his head on a small, protruding rock at the bottom, and while he came to and was scrambling out of it, Jim and me had ran, thinking that a dead body had resurrected itself, us cautiously going back when we'd heard the voice in the darkness saying, "I've lost my friggin' glasses! Where's my friggin' glasses?"

After we'd hauled Peter out of the grave and dusted him down we decided to make our way home, not bothering to look any more for the highwayman's grave because we'd been spooked and the rows and rows of graves went on and on, as if for miles. Even by the light of the bicycle torch we couldn't find Peter's glasses and he was hysterical anyway, swearing that something had grabbed him by the ankle and had pulled him into that grave—and he said that he'd heard a deep, gruff voice saying, "What you are looking for you won't find here—now begone!'

And a howling of a dog had screamed all over Carnmoney Hill, making us even more nervous, but Jim had said that it had sounded like a wolf that he'd heard and seen once, in a Saturday morning, matinee movie, in the Forum cinema in Ardoyne, just a mile from our village.

Eventually we'd reached the Hightown Road again after deciding that enough was enough. After we'd reached the flat section after our plod uphill, we'd breathed a sigh of relief as the rest of the trek was all downhill towards our village; but Peter had to hold onto my coat tail because, although he'd been as blind as a fruit bat while wearing his specks, he'd been even worse without them. There hadn't been another single person or even a car on that road, and the only sign of anything stirring was a dull, red light, atop of a radio transmitter on a hill to our right facing Cavehill mountain.

As we'd chatted to each other we'd noticed that a firstly thin, then thicker mist was descending all around us, not unexpected as the Cavehill Mountain was over eighteen hundred feet above our village and we were very high above sea level ourselves. McArt's Fort was to our left at the summit of Cavehill although we couldn't see it because of the mist and darkness. While visiting it once with our school we could see that it had consisted of an old rath, or ring fort, that had been ringed with small boulders that were 150 feet wide from north to south, and 180 feet wide from east to west.

"What the frig was that?" Jim and me had said in unison, as a crescendo of animal noises punctured the silence. It had sounded like a stampede of wild animals in the African jungle when a lion had been on the prowl looking for a prey for its dinner.

"For Jesus sake!" Peter had shouted, "I may be blind but I'm not deaf... that's just the animals down at Bellevue Zoo at the bottom of Cavehill. Will youse stop scaring the shit out of me?"

"Yes, right," Jim said, "but what's spooking the animals? That's the first time I've ever heard them getting on like that; something may be stalking them.

"Rubbish!" I replied. "What animal could stalk an elephant, a tiger or a lion? Sure they're afraid of nothing—not even Peter without his specks," I laughed.

"Why don't we ask that fella there... that fella coming towards us there?" Jim said, pointing in front of us. "He's probably from around here and he'll probably tell us what's going on."

As I looked intently into the mist I could see a very tall man of around seven feet tall, but I couldn't see his shoes, as if he was floating about a foot above the road's surface. But the man, whose face and head had been covered by a brown or black hood, had been wearing an old monk's cowl, and he had a white rope like a skipping rope tied around his waist. He appeared to be oblivious to our presence, and as he grew nearer to us, just about six feet by now, I was becoming apprehensive.

"I can't see anything," Peter whispered, "Where is he?" Peter strained his little pupils to get a better look.

"Boo!" Jim shouted into Peter's ear, he being fearless and scared of nothing, making Peter almost pull the combat jacket off my back.

"Maybe he's going to a fancy dress ball," I replied, "all dressed up as Rasputin the Mad Monk from Russia."

"Or Padre Pio?" Peter offered. "They say he's omnipresent and can be in ten places all at once. Miss Door our Religion teacher at school said that of that Italian monk who has his hands and ankles pierced like Christ's."

"My father said he must be like Father Christmas," I whispered, as Padre Pio or Rasputin was almost on top of us, "…and my father said Santa Claus is even better than Padre Pio," I added. "Santa can appear in ten million chimneys all at once, and he even knows that all the fires are out! And Santa is even more of a Saint than Padre Pio, what do you two think of that?"

But they hadn't time to reply. I could hear Jim's and my bones rattling with fear and Peter had had his head buried in my back. Suddenly the dark figure was up level with us. I was about to ask him about the restless animals but didn't get a chance when I opened my mouth. "God bless you, my sons," the figure had said, removing his right arm from his wide left sleeve while the other left arm was tucked into his right sleeve, making the sign of the Cross before he disappeared into the mist directly behind us.

All three of us must have been able to read each other's mind when we took off all together, running down the hill facing an old quarry on our left, me being slower because Peter was still holding onto my coat. We stopped at the entrance of the quarry at an old metal gate, breathless and wondering just what we'd encountered earlier. After a five minute rest we'd decided to finally make our way home, straining our eyes and looking over our shoulders in case Padre Pio had returned.

We'd stalled again, as the sound of a chain could be heard being trailed down the hill behind us, and when we'd walked we could hear the chain… and hooves, loud hooves, and when we had stopped, the chain and hooves had stopped. Something unearthly again was following us.

"Wait a minute," Jim said, breathless again, "isn't there a place on the Cavehill called the Devil's Punchbowl? I learned that at school. And

I remember old Annie Brown who lives in our street telling her neighbours their fortunes by looking at their tealeaves in their cups. She told us that about that place, when it was a site for old Celtic farmers who would corral their cattle in at the bottom of the Cavehill. Devil worshippers used that place to call on Satan and to ask him what the draws would be on Littlewoods Pools on a Saturday afternoon. Later, they would mess around with homemade Ouija boards and would sacrifice chickens, rabbits, and even newly-born babies, on a flat rock that had served as a homemade altar at the Devil's Punchbowl. The rock had been surrounded with lit, black candles.

"Then they would chant, while dressed in long black sheets with a hole cut from their necks, 'Arise your dark regal majesty,' and they would drink the blood of the babies and the animals using a wine chalice that they'd stolen from a Catholic church, daubing the church door with the sign of the devil, a five-star, pointed pentangle before they left, with black paint. They tapped the chalice with a small, auctioneer's hammer when the chalice was emptied of all the blood when it would make a '*boing!*' sound so that Satan would come."

The echoing of the chain and the trotting hooves kept on coming when we'd moved and had stopped when we'd stopped, as if the terrible creature was able to see our every move through the heavy mist. There was no doubt about it—something evil was stalking us as we'd now quickened our pace, even running blindly at most times. We didn't want it to manoeuvre to the front of us through the surrounding bracken in the fields to kill us.

We'd watched carefully the rows of blackthorn bushes on both sides of that narrow country road, watching the gaps in them, and suddenly the bushes had started to take on a bright, white, fluorescent colour. We then knew that we'd reached a lime quarry that we'd passed earlier on our way to Carnmoney cemetery. Now we had almost reached the lower regions of the Cavehill, and home, provided that we weren't drained of our blood for sacrifices, now noticing the high, metal quarry machines that had looked like white skyscrapers in the now thinning mist.

"What's that in front of us!? Wha...?" Jim had shouted in panic, as our eyes now stared straight ahead except for Peter, whose eyes were probably, along with his head, halfway up my back-end. Another noise was coming from the front of us now: *"Ding dong! ding dong!"*—the unmistakable sound of a loud bell. At the same time the hooves were still behind us and gaining fast. "We're trapped!" I'd shouted, now waiting for the final collision. What would one of our teachers have been doing up on this mountain with our school bell, sounding exactly like the one that would call us in from our playing in our schoolyard, after our lunch? Now I could hear Peter and Jim sobbing and I wasn't far behind. Now we had our heads buried in our hands as we hurried, only looking around us through the gaps between our fingers. But I'd thought of what my mother had always told me: "If you are ever in trouble son, just pray to your two great uncles, Patrick and Eddie," of whom my mother had, strangely enough, told me: "Both your great uncles used to work in McGladdery's quarry on the Hightown Road, before they'd gone off to war," and now we were outside that very quarry.

Eddie had been eighteen-years-old and Patrick had been twenty-one, and when Eddie had gone to fight in the First World War Patrick had followed him into the army to watch over him because he was so young; but both of them had been killed at the Battle of Messines, in 1916, a place in Belgium not far from the border with France. Eddie had been bayonetted by a German soldier in a trench and Patrick had been blown to pieces by a howitzer shell as he ran across a piece of ground on No-Man's-Land.

This had been one of three quarries around our village, and most of the men had worked in them because there was no other work to be had. "They'd broken the limestone rocks with sledgehammers," my mother would tell us all, "and when it had broken up they'd filled one hundredweight bags to load them onto carts, to be pulled with horses, as there were no lorries in those days, and when they'd returned home they'd looked like snowmen."

According to my mother our grandmother had told her that "Both had joined the 16th Irish division of the British Army and lay buried were they fell."

I'd started to pray, starting with the Our Father... when we'd heard a deep, gruff voice coming from in front of us: "Ramrod! Ramrod! Where are you, Ramrod!"

This was followed by the pealing of the bell again. Then we'd frozen when a giant of a figure with white hair and wearing heavy, hobnailed boots and a heavy, sheepskin overcoat with a thick, brown belt tied around his waist, came right up to us and stared into our, by now, terrified faces. The bell in his giant hand was similar to ours at school, with a wooden handle, and he held a torch in his other hand. "My, my, what are you little fellas doing on this hill at this time of the night?" he said, but we couldn't reply at first because we were speechless with fear, us just staring up at him, open-mouthed, still thinking that he'd been a ghost. The old man could read our shock and distress: "Don't worry boys," he chuckled, "I've seen your looks before when ghosthunters have haunted these hills only to be noticed that they've been haunted themselves."

"But...but...mister," Jim had stammered, "the...the devil is chasing us from the Devil's Punchbowl and... and... the chains... and the devil's club foot!"

The big man laughed out loud: "No, no, son, that's not the real devil, but he is a devil with the women, I can vouch for that... watch. Ramrod! Ramrod!" he said before ringing his bell again, before putting it into a large pocket inside his tattered coat.

All three of us jumped behind the old man and grabbed hold of his coat tails as the chain and hooves were almost on top of us now. Then, before our eyes, a ram had stood there angry, snorting and stamping the ground with a front hoof! It was the biggest ram I had ever seen in my life, with horns the size of a wild stag's antlers. The steam had been streaming out of its snout before the old man grabbed its chain, grabbing hold of the ram's horns, wrestling with it for a while before throwing the chain over his shoulder to quieten it.

"See, I told you boys, Ramrod just escaped from his paddock tonight and was looking for all of his five hundred wives, the horny old goat!" the old sheep farmer laughed. "Goodnight now lads, and safe journey home, I can't watch this old horny fella morning, noon and night, but I'm sorry that we scared you." Then the old farmer and his ram had disappeared for real this time, melting into the mist in the direction of the Upper Crumlin Road, both trying to get the better of each other in their struggle.

Chapter Two

Naois O'Haughan,
the Highwayman

WHEN WE'D REACHED OUR VILLAGE, we'd parted company, and when I reached home I slumped down on the sofa, it being after midnight going by our clock on the mantelpiece. Both my parents were still up and both laughed out loud when I'd told them what had happened, my father remarking, "I believe you, because you are white and look like you've just seen a ghost." But I was glad of the boiled spuds, peas and a big bunch of watercress sitting warmed up again on my plate with a glass of milk.

"Always eat your fruit and vegetables," my mother would always say, "because a sprig of watercress on its own is as good in Vitamin C as a full, Jaffa orange." Our house was very quiet, as my two younger brothers and sisters had been in bed long ago. I'd noticed my father sitting by the fireside in his armchair studying me closely through the puffs of his pipe and tobacco smoke. He had not rebuked me; he probably was doing the same as me when he'd been ten-years-old.

"Anyway, son, that treasure hunt... you're probably looking in the wrong place. The legend is that the highwayman, Naois O'Haughan, buried his loot in hallowed or holy ground, like in a graveyard, where he thought people would be afraid to look... probably a churchyard or a monastery. I'm surprised that more people in this area and Greater Belfast haven't bought themselves metal-detectors to search for it... most of it was gold and that's metal... and where the gold is the jewellery will probably be there too."

"Our church grounds?" I'd asked my father, "Isn't that holy ground?"

"Not really," he replied, "there is no cemetery there, and O'Haughan would have used a Catholic place, seeing that he was a fervent Catholic. Our church is only fifty years old, and, did you know, son, that there was a monastery beside the feeder river to Bodel's Dam just beside Curtain's Avenue that leads to Ewart's linen mill?"

My father had been a great history buff even though he didn't come from our village. He was known as a Townie, like others from downtown Belfast who'd lived in our village. They had called us Mountain Goats while we'd called them Sewer Rats, and he was originally from the Short Strand, a district just off the Newtownards Road in East Belfast, although his father had come from Ardglass, a little fishing village in County Down.

"Some people, and I don't like to see you setting foot on it," my mother had now interrupted, "have said that people have experienced strange vibrations there, and some have fallen off Cavehill while looking for the highwayman's treasure. Some say they have felt an invisible hand on their shoulder as if they've been pushed, to stop them finding the hidden loot."

My father had looked at my mother as if to say "What did you interrupt me for?" before going on: "What was I saying there...? Yes, the old monastery was dilapidated and was falling down and William Ewart senior, a Protestant Presbyterian, gave the Catholic Church all the land where our church is now for one pound note a year... what do you think of that? One pound a year! Could you ever get a better man? And he a different religion to half of his employees!"

But I had always been afraid to go up Curtain's Avenue during the day, never mind at night. It was an eerie place, although once courting couples were always up there playing Doctors and Nurses. My father said it was a new game when I'd asked him what it meant, because an eight-foot-tall man dressed in black robes had watched them all the time, until two teenagers were caught, one standing on the other's shoulder with a black sheet wrapped around them. "Just horny little boys," the local people would say.

"Why don't you get a paper round and buy a metal-detector?" my mother said. "Gold coins are metal and where the gold is the jewellery will be too."

"That's easy," my father laughed, "there is no paper round because nobody in this village can read. Do the shops even sell newspapers up here? I've never seen anybody with a newspaper, just staring at bookie's slips all day, then crumpling them up and throwing them away! Tell you what," my father continued, changing his disliking views of our village, "the next time I'm in town I'll call round to that little shop at Smithfield in the city centre—your mother knows it—called Joseph Cavanagh's 'I Buy And Sell Anything'... if he has a bust of Joseph Stalin he's bound to have an old metal-detector. I bought a long-playing record by the King called 'The King's Greatest Hits' dirt cheap."

"King? Is that Paddy King who lives down the road? I didn't know he could sing!"

"Now you're taking the piss," my father laughed, "I mean Elvis' 'Greatest Hits', the King."

"And don't go running off to the Cavehill too often," my mother started again, getting ready to go up to bed.

My father winked because he had something in his eye. "Those United fellas are thought to haunt that mountain as well, as least five of them, and a UFO, an alien spaceship, was even seen hovering there too."

The stories that my parents were telling me now were getting scarier and scarier, but I was glad he hadn't missed his work shovel that I'd lost on the Hightown tonight. But after what he'd said about him getting me a metal-detector, I was surprised that more people in Belfast and the surrounding areas hadn't bought them for themselves to look for the hidden treasure. At the time that Naois was carrying out his robberies the loot must have been worth thousands of pounds, but would be worth millions now, and as well as their value they would also be antiques. That would raise their value even more.

Ligoniel village had always been full of incidents of hauntings. One night, as usual on a summer's night, a group of men had stood talking at Jack Dickey's corner shop, at the junction of Mill Avenue, where we lived, and the Ligoniel Road, facing Curtain's Avenue. They had stopped talking about the Busby Babes, the Manchester United football players who had been killed in Munich in Germany in a snowstorm the previous year, when something stirring on Curtain's Avenue caught all their eyes together.

A figure had walked out of the entrance to the avenue, had looked up and down the road, but they couldn't see the figure's features. "A monk! A monk!" Barney Toland had screamed, as the spectre moved across the road towards them, as if floating, because they couldn't see his feet. They too had stood frozen to the spot, and the monk had whispered, "God bless you my sons," before walking past them in the direction of one of the other mills in the village, Wolfhill. This had been the first sighting of Abbot John, and local people thought that, as Abbot John had gone to America to teach in Boston, when he had died there he had returned at the end of the nineteenth century to look for his fellow monks.

His spectre had found the old monastery had been demolished and he still wanders the village to this day, looking for his fellow monks and old friends, not knowing that William Ewart had given the Church new land in which to build a new place of worship. And sometimes, according to my grandmother before she died, legends have been taught to the generations of the village about the galloping horses.

At the time of Naois O'Haughan the stagecoaches would detour to our village if one of the horses had lost a shoe, the driver using the blacksmith that had a forge in our village. Sometimes the driver, armed guard and passengers would stay in the smithy's house overnight, if the steep road to Antrim town had been slippery after a light fall of snow, as our village hill to the country was at least two thousand feet above sea level.

Long after that, galloping horses, and the rattle of stagecoach wheels on cobbled roads, could be heard as if they were still galloping through the village. Our village had just fifty people then, but was bolstered to eight hundred when country people would come here to work in the mills because of poverty. The coach, after it had left, had been followed into the village by a neighing of a horse, the thundering trotting of a single horse and the shout of "Stand and hand your valuables over— now!" and he had held an amber-coloured lantern aloft.

But the stagecoach had long gone, and when people, long after the highwayman was operating and had been hanged years before, looked out of their windows to see what the racket was all about, they had to rub their eyes in disbelief when they saw a magnificent, jet-black horse that had been rearing up on its hind legs, its eyes shining with a red flash, and it had a white flash between its eyes in the shape of a Christian cross. A man had sat astride it, wearing a long black cloak that had covered the horse's back and tail. The rider had worn a black, three-cornered hat, shiny silver spurs and a black cloth for a mask over his mouth and chin, and long black hair was hanging around his broad shoulders. Two flintlock pistols were stuck down inside a thick black belt with a silver buckle, and the rider had a lighted lantern in one of his hands, the lantern eerily illuminating, in an amber glow, the horse and rider, and the surrounding area of the village. The rider had worn black boots that ran all the way to the top of his thighs.

The ghost of Naois had been swinging the lamp back and forward at an imaginary stagecoach that hadn't been seen on that road for over a hundred years. He would shout and whoop for nearly ten minutes in a deep, unearthly voice, before galloping off in the direction of Wolfhill Road via Ligoniel Hill, never to be seen until the same time each year. My father had said that Naois had joined the Irish police to escape the intense pressure of the police and yeomen always looking for him, under the alias of John O'Toole.

He'd been captured because of a simple slip that he'd made when he told a prisoner he'd been escorting from a prison cell to the assizes who he'd been and why he'd joined the police after shaving off his beard and cutting his long hair. But the prisoner had contacted a police sergeant to claim the reward of 500 pounds, plus a reduction in his prison sentence for stealing a horse, otherwise the prisoner would have been deported to an Australian penal colony forever, he himself never seeing his wife and two children again.

My mother and father had gone to bed, my father telling me not to be "too long in coming to bed yourself, after you've made sure the doors have been locked and the lights have been turned out." My younger brother, with whom I shared the little box room at the back of the house, had fallen asleep, and my sister, who'd slept in the middle room, hadn't stirred, while my mother and father were asleep in the front room overlooking Ligoniel Hill.

As I was slowly dropping off, now listening for a sound of horse's hooves, I'd thought of the war hero William Ewart Junior, the owner of the mill down the road from us. My friends Jim, Peter and I would often fish at Bodel's Dam that had overlooked Ewart's Mill from a thirty-foot high grassy knoll that had been artificially built by workers over a hundred years ago. It had been surrounded with low reeds and evergreen trees, and a fast-flowing weir had allowed water from the dam to run down into the now, non-existent waterwheel. The waterwheel had been spun around by the fast-flowing water that would allow the spinning and weaving machines to operate, but everything now was run by electricity.

We would always see the tall and impressive figure, wearing a long, white coat, and I had always thought that this man was a hospital doctor, until somebody mentioned that it had been William Ewart Junior. He had lived in a magnificent, Victorian mansion at the top of Curtain's Avenue, surrounded by beautiful beds of roses in the summertime, and a small path away from the avenue had allowed him to walk down to his factory every day, to see how his workers had been getting on.

The left side of his face was badly pockmarked and scarred, and he wore a black patch around his head that had covered his left eye; he looking like Long John Silver that I'd seen in an adventure comic once. "Good afternoon boys," he would say in passing, "make sure you keep me one of those big trout of mine when you catch some"—said with a broad smile on his face.

Local people had liked him, and my headmaster had told us once that "William Ewart Senior had been a great hero during the Second World War." According to Mister Murnaghan, Ewart had been serving on a submarine during the Second World War when his ship was struck with a depth-charge dropped by a German Corvette ship. Ewart and others in the crew had swum to the top and had been captured by the Germans, only to be interned until the end of the War.

Mister Murnaghan had also told us that "The Ewart family were descendants of the Huguenots who'd been expelled from France because they were French Protestants, and after twenty thousand of them had been slaughtered by the French king, Louis the 16th, men, women and children, and that was why the Protestants of Ulster didn't take to us because they were afraid of the same slaughter happening to them, which was understandable." Jim, Peter and I had always liked Ewart, because, despite his riches and bearing, he'd always been very friendly and had never looked down on us or had chased us for trespassing on his property. I still couldn't get it out of my head what my mother said, that "even the United Men had haunted Cavehill", so that week in school I had asked Mister Murnaghan, our headmaster, what she'd meant by the United Men?

"Oh... you mean the United Irishmen," the headmaster had said, rubbing his chin before sitting down on top of his desk. Impressing our class was one of Mister Murnaghan's favourite pastimes. "Yes," he began, "they were Protestant Presbyterians who had made an oath on the Cavehill to, ah, break the link with England. Their leader was called Wolfe Tone, and they signed their declaration of independence on top of that mountain, and..."

"But Sir," I'd interrupted, putting my hand up first or he would have caned me, "I thought the United Men were the Manchester United players who'd been killed in the Munich air crash in Germany."

The teacher looked at me sternly, as if to say 'Have you learned nothing during your five years at this school?' I'd exacerbated my problem when I'd asked him another stupid question: "Did Wolfe Tone come from Wolfhill Road, or was it called after him? And do you think that the highwayman, Naois O'Haughan, could have hidden his treasure up there?"

He appeared to ignore my questions and may have been ready to burst out laughing. "Wolfe Tone came from Dublin," the teacher went on, "and he was a lawyer, and I don't want you to repeat any of this outside this school in case I'm sacked from my job and am charged with sedition, get that?" The entire class of thirty-three had nodded, not wanting their favourite teacher to end up in Crumlin Road Prison. "After the 1798 Rebellion failed, Wolfe Tone—he was captured, and he wrote: 'From my earliest youth, I have regarded the connection between Ireland and England to be the curse of the Irish nation, and feel convinced that while it lasts, Ireland will never be free or happy.'" We had all sat and looked at each other in amazement, that our teacher could say that out without reading from a book.

"Wait, I'm not finished yet," the teacher continued, recognising our restlessness, us thinking that he'd finished. "'In consequence, I was determined to apply all my powers that my individual powers would move, in order to separate both countries.' Yes, a great Protestant Irishman, and after they'd denied Tone a real soldier's death, and because his captors had wanted to hang him, Tone had cut his own throat in his cell because he'd wanted to die by firing-squad, although some said he paid a guard to cut his throat for him. What do you think of that then, lads?" our teacher had shouted, altering his tie and taking his comb out of his back pocket to comb his greasy, black hair back. "A great man, what? He being well-off and all, but just thinking of others... who would do that today?"

"Got one!" Jim's voice had shouted, shaking me out of my day dreaming by the bank of the dam as he reeled in a good, two pounds in weight, brown trout, before unhooking it and smashing its head against the cobblestoned dam wall side, then wrapping it in grass to keep it fresh for the pan at his home. But my mind wasn't on fishing as I'd quickly looked over my shoulders again, like a fox out hunting for food for its young, the fox at the same time raising her head and looking around for the hunting dogs in our village, and there had been plenty.

Even during daylight hours this dam had seemed spooky, it being nine feet deep and muddy coloured, and I'd been waiting for a pair of girl's arms to come up from the depths to pull me under. I'd heard people talking at the corner of our village and the Methodist church talking while we'd played handball until dark. Apparently there had been a tragic incident here during the Second World War in 1939-40.

The story went that a nineteen-year-old girl from another part of Belfast had married her sweetheart before he'd joined the army and had gone off to war in France, like my two great uncles in the Great War. His wife had given birth to a baby girl just six months before he'd left, and the soldier had written to her, saying that "he was looking forward to returning home soon to see her and the baby, while on leave."

The young wife had returned to her own home one day from work, where she'd been employed in a shirt factory in the centre of Belfast. Her mother had been babysitting, and had told her daughter: "An official-looking letter came for you this morning, but I didn't want to be nosey so I didn't open it." It had been a letter from the British War Office, and when the girl had gingerly opened it and read it, she passed out and collapsed onto the floor.

When the girl's mother had summoned some neighbours, she picked up the yellow-coloured telegram and read it: "Dear Mrs Smith, it is with great sadness that I have to inform you that your husband, Corporal John Smith, was tragically killed in action while affecting a withdrawal in Dunkirk, France, yesterday, at 24: 00 hundred hours. Please accept our humblest of condolences, as his remains have yet to be recovered. Very sorry.—Signed, Brigadier Neville Jones Melville."

According to legend, the girl wandered the streets of Belfast clutching her baby, the baby's arms tightly around her neck. She'd last been seen getting onto a tram at Royal Avenue, that had been travelling to Ligoniel, our village, the last stop to anywhere. She and her baby had been missing for a week, until a local villager had reported to the police that they'd last been seen on Curtain's Avenue, and the police immediately dragged Bodel's Dam.

They found the girl in the nine-foot deep part, and after hooking her onto a rope they'd carefully pulled her out of it. Even policemen had wept with some villagers as the sorrowful sight had met their eyes, because the baby's arms had been still firmly clasped around the mother's white neck. Since then, a young, blonde-haired girl and a blonde baby have been spotted all over the place, especially adjacent to Bodel's Dam and the surrounding fields, both wailing and seeming to be in distress, like an old fabled, Irish banshee.

Even my uncle Patrick—everybody called him Paddy for short—was almost frightened to death after the Second World War. He'd been at our house in Finlay Street, just off Mill Avenue, staying at our house until almost 3 a.m. one morning playing cards. He'd decided to return home to his house on the Ligoniel Road, where he'd lived in a row of old, whitewashed houses facing Ewart's Mill.

He'd left after that night and had gone to Birmingham, England, to look for work, and when he'd got there he'd found work on the building sites with some friends from Belfast. He'd been just twenty-three years old then, and when he and his friends had gone round all the boarding houses looking for somewhere to stay, every boarding house had had a cardboard sign in their windows that had read: "No dogs, blacks or Irish here." After that, when he returned home to the village, he fell into bad health. This had been when he had to sleep in public parks, old derelict houses, public conveniences and even graveyards. Patrick died suffering from tuberculosis at the age of just twenty-seven, and I found him that morning. I would call in every morning on my way to school and I was just five years old. He would give me a shilling piece to buy something for my lunch.

But this morning when I entered his house there was no sound, and when I ran upstairs as usual, he had been lying in bed and had drowned in his own blood when his lungs had collapsed during the night. I'd shaken him and shaken him but he lay quite still, and my mother had told me later that "he expected to die soon and he didn't want to worry me by telling me."

When I'd looked at him again his life's blood had covered the front of his pyjamas and the quilt on his bed. Now I knew why he always sat at the fire downstairs with his hand over his face all the time; he didn't want to leave us and couldn't bear to look at us. He was going into the unknown soon, to meet my grandfather and grandmother, and my two great uncles who'd died in Messines in Belgium, and my grandfather on my father's side. He, too, had died young, having been killed in Belfast Shipyard when a steel plate fell on him from above, at just twenty-seven years old.

Chapter Three

The Banshee!

T HIS WAS WHAT IT HAD BEEN LIKE growing up in Belfast and its surrounds in the 1950's, not a single cure for anything or any disease, whether it was TB, all cancers and polio. I remember my mother telling my father about "a curse in the family", and after my uncle Patrick's funeral that day I'd asked her what she'd meant? She'd shifted uneasily in her chair, looking at me as if to say, "No, I can't tell you, you're too young for that sort of thing," but still in two minds to tell me or not.

Nervously, she'd looked around my uncle Patrick's house that had been filled with his friends who had been talking to each other while eating sandwiches, and drinking tea and beer. Finally, as I'd stared at her, she'd relented. "Son," she said, "do you remember the tiny woman who lived just across the road facing this house, beside Ewart's Mill?"

I nodded. I remembered her well, when I would stay with my uncle Patrick every Saturday night, listening to the radio and having our own little party of sweets and lemonade.

The little woman was called Minnie O'Neill, and our parents would threaten us with them handing us over to her if we didn't behave ourselves. She had been tiny, stunted at birth, and had been just three and a half feet tall. She always wore black, painted shoes, a long, black frock and would always wear a black shawl over her black haired head, and her shoulders. We would run away if we even saw her walking down the street towards us.

"Well, son," my mother began, "one night your uncle Patrick was making his way home from our house after playing cards with your father, and as he passed Dickey's shop corner he pulled his coat collar up around his neck as it was a freezing cold January night, and he saw a sight that early morning he would never forget until God called him, which wasn't long after. While after taking you to school that morning, and every morning, I would call into the shop to get his food for the day as nobody had fridges in those days, and food had to be eaten straight away, especially meat and milk. When I walked into his house I could see he was as white as a bed sheet, and I asked him what was wrong?

"'I didn't go to bed last night, Mary,' he'd said, 'and I've sat here since 3 a.m. this morning.'

"He had almost been weeping," my mother said, saying she had to prod him four or five times before he would talk about what had been bothering him. "I made him a cup of tea and finally he opened his mouth, speaking very low at first, as if his tongue had been wrenched out of his mouth. Finally he spoke to me after about fifteen minutes.

"'As... as, you can remember, it was a cold morning this morning,' he continued, 'and light flakes of snow were beginning to fall when I'd left your house. I'd been walking towards Dickey's shop corner and as I looked around me with my head down after pulling my coat collar up around my neck, there wasn't even a cat about, which was unusual, as that is their time for hunting and chasing other cats. As I... as I approached the shop corner, I thought I could see little Minnie O'Neill, who lived facing me, standing there. "What are you doing standing there with terrible weather like this?" I'd asked here, thinking that she was a little eccentric in her middle-age, as she was known for it. But the little woman's head had spun around quicker than the speed of the eye, and I was horrified! Bloody Horrified! The little woman, although she'd worn a black shawl like Minnie, was grotesque! Grotesque! Her hair was long and pure white, unlike Minnie's, and her face was wrinkled and distorted! And her face was covered with bleeding boils and ulcers. She'd looked at least four hundred years old, and she'd stared at me with bulbous, red eyes, like a demon... a bloody demon! And she shouted hoarsely up at my face in the Gaelic, Irish language. I never learned our language at school, but I heard two people having a conversation in it, and it was it. I've never been as scared in all my bloody life so I ran... ran! Oh God, I wouldn't want to see that awful sight ever again! I need to see a priest... a bloody priest!'"

I'd barely remembered my uncle when he was at our house that night, as he said "Goodnight son," when my mother had taken me up to bed. He was tall, fair-haired and well-built, and he had feared nothing, he being a bare-knuckle boxer, and he would travel all over Ireland to fight for money to supplement his meagre income as he wasn't in employment. He and his friends had been poor; all five of them had gone off to England together, shortly after his run-in with the old, ancient woman, who we'd christened Maeve, the Queen of the Leprechauns.

Maeve would have probably been angry, because while widening the road at Mill Avenue, some workmen had knocked down an old, blackthorn tree, a fortnight before, and they'd been warned by some locals not to do it. For years, music, dancing, singing and the sound of musical instruments like Irish bagpipes and tin whistles would be heard coming from the base of that big tree, but when people went to investigate, the music had suddenly stopped, and the musicians had seemed to disappear into thin air.

I'd always wondered, since the death of my father's father in Belfast Shipyard, when a steel plate had fallen on him from a great height, was it the result of a curse or hex on our family? Both he and my uncle had been exactly twenty seven years of age, and both had been called Patrick, like me, and my mother had told me that twins my grandmother had been having, a boy and a girl, who would be called Patrick and Mary, had been stillborn. And another Patrick had died in Belgium, in 1916, with my great uncle Eddie.

As the years went quickly by, I have always asked, is the curse to go on and on? I was called Patrick, so was I next? And there's my grandfather, my mother's father, who was called George—would my mother have another son called George? And indeed she did, two years below me! Now while I was preparing to leave primary school he had taken my place, and was in his third year there now.

It was October and my friends Jim, Peter and I had decided to explore the little willow tree forest at Kennedy's Race, a fast-flowing river whose source was a spring that had risen at the top of the Black and Wolfhill Mountains' junction. The little forest had been overgrown with blackberry bramble plants, and we'd climb up there with four empty jam jars each to fill them with blackberries for our mothers to make homemade jam. October was their best ripening months and the berries would be black and very big and juicy, with us gorging ourselves before we'd filled the jars. We were almost two thousand feet above sea level now, and the river forked off towards a dam adjacent to Wolfhill Mill, and, like Ewart's, the water would flow down a weir to operate a waterwheel for the machinery, but was gone for years now.

The other run of the river ran off towards the Ballygomartin area, of North Belfast, under Belfast city centre and on to High Street and the River Lagan. After gathering the berries, as a bonus, we'd tickle wild, brown trout, before scooping them from below the rocks, throwing them up onto the bank before croaking them. Our fathers had shown us how to whittle down Thornberry bushes to make them into catapults, with penknives, and they themselves would cut thin branches off to make walking sticks, giving them two coats of brown paint and two of clear varnish as protection against the weather, after heating over the fire to straighten them out.

The bracken and ferns had been thick and widespread over the Wolfhill mountain once, and the once numerous oak tree forests had covered everything, until the farmers cleared the land over the years to facilitate the growth of corn and wheat for the bakers in Belfast, and grass to turn into hay fodder for their animals. All along the Wolfhill, Divis and Black Mountains, a necklace of one-hundred foot high electricity pylons ran along the bases of the mountains, shining in the sun like a string of pearls, humming like spinning-tops, if you'd ventured too close to them.

As we'd rested from gathering berries and trying to catch trout, we'd strained our eyes up towards the skyline all along all three mountains, although Peter was going through the motions, not having replaced the spectacles he'd lost in Carnmoney Cemetery on our treasure hunt last month. This had been the very place, according to local legend, where the last grey wolf in Ireland was killed, in 1786. People in other parts of Ireland would claim that terrible record, in Carlow, Tipperary and Clare.

The Irish wolf was demonised and some people had said that it was evil, being blamed for snatching babies from cots and killing household pets like cats and dogs. This hadn't been true, and like everything else, money and greed had been involved in the decision to wipe them out. According to our history teacher, Mister Murnaghan, the British House of Commons had brought in a law in 1662 to exterminate the Irish wolf and also foxes in Ireland. The wolves were just being natural hunters, and they would hunt in packs mainly for Irish deer, and rumours had been spread by some that the wolves had spread rabies, which wasn't true.

Our village legends spoke of a family of wolves, a male, a female, and a juvenile, that had hunted all three mountains, and also the Cavehill. This last adult pair had led a pack of fourteen wolves in our surrounding areas, and these three were the only ones left, the rest being, shot, trapped or poisoned. Soon, after their natural habitat of oak forests had been cleared, they would venture onto the farms and kill cattle, sheep, chickens and goats.

They had originally been vegetarians, and would eat fish, insects, worms and the very berries that we'd been foraging for earlier, and the settlers who'd came to Ulster after the Plantation were mostly farmers. Soon, bounty hunters were brought in from Scotland and England, and the government had paid them £6 for a female wolf because she carried the young, £5 for a male and £2 for a juvenile or young wolf, and ten shillings for a cub. But this had brought bad luck to our villages, and people would say, "If one person dies in the village there would be another two, and this always happened, because the last three wolves had been killed on our mountain at Wolfhill."

The locals would think that if they'd heard the howling of dogs the previous night in our village, somebody would die. Some people would say that "it wasn't dogs howling, but the three wolves that had been exterminated in a cruel way." Howling would also be heard coming from the direction of Cavehill as well, but people put this down to the animals at Bellevue Zoo on the Cavehill slopes, though others, again, had thought differently.

Locals called it the Wolves' Revenge Cry, for there, on the Cavehill, the ancient Celtic Irish farmers had built the Devil's Punchbowl, a rocky and wooded area like a corral, where they would hide their livestock from starving, preying wolves. Some people had praised the brave wolves, in our village, while others had been terrified of them and their howling curse. Even some named streets after the wolves and their lairs—names like Wolfhill Road, Wolfhill View, Wolfhill Drive, Wolfhill Grove, Wolfhill Gardens, Wolfhill Avenue South and Wolfhill Mill, Wolfhill Quarry, so as to be left free from the wolves' curse, and they are still there to this day.

One day a local hunter with a shotgun had decided to look for rabbits and other game on the Wolfhill mountain, and when he reached the summit he'd paused for a while in the chilly air of that February morning and sat down on his hunkers for a while, steadying himself with his weapon that he'd held upright while it had rested on the three-inch snow that covered the ground. He'd jumped when at least three targets had come into view, as they'd crossed the skyline of the mountain. To him, they appeared to be three foxes, two adults and one cub, and all three were walking in a line, and they were howling like devils out of hell.

As he'd stared at them, the three foxes had frozen, putting down their heads in unison and staring at him, but, according to him, "what was most unusual about them was they didn't run off, as foxes would, as if they weren't afraid of him at all. They were much larger than foxes, even bigger than Labrador dogs. Then when they thought that I wasn't going to fire on them—I thought that they could read my mind—they just put their heads down, walking off towards the brow of the hill and disappeared down the other side, and they were gone, as quickly as they'd appeared."

The hunter ran up the hill in pursuit of them, "keeping back a distance, afraid that if they'd attacked him they would overwhelm him." When he'd reached the top of the hill and looked down the other side he'd said, "I was astounded! There were no tracks in the snow, and what was worse, the foxes had completely disappeared into thin air! There were no paw prints, absolutely nothing! And there hadn't been any grassy patches where the beasts could step on, the snow being uniformly spread over the entire mountain!"

I recall another unholy sight that was all too prevalent in our village and its surrounds. As we'd scanned the mountain-top where the beasts had been first seen, I was wondering why Peter had his hands over his eyes as well. He'd been just going through the motions in that weakening sun, as he'd yet to replace the spectacles he'd lost the previous month when he'd fallen down that grave in Carnmoney Cemetery, when we'd been looking for Naois O'Haughan's resting place.

"I wonder if those big Irish wolfhounds were bred to track and kill the wolves?" Jim asked.

"Probably," I replied. "According to Mister Murnaghan, the bounty hunters would use four dogs and two musketeers to shoot them when the dogs had cornered them. Then they would cut the wolves' heads off for the payment, and to show evidence, for their bounty."

"Didn't they do that with white men in America?" Peter said, changing the subject completely. "The American Indians, I mean?"

"But now you're on that subject," Jim countered, "You're half-right. The white men scalped the red men first, and their women and kids. The whites were paid fifty dollars a head, and that's where the phrase 'a head' came from. And I'm not talking about Tottenham Hotspur supporters scalping Manchester United supporters because United are always beating them!"

"Does that mean then," Peter had replied, "that if my mummy bought me a pair of jeans she would have to pay for them by the leg?"

This had been getting ridiculous now! What had started off as a debate about wolves had ended up as a farce about clothes.

"No!" I'd shouted in frustration, "You are saying that if my mummy bought me a pair of shoes she would have to pay for them by a single foot on each shoe!"

"Unless they were two odd shoes, how would you get them on?" Jim had said, and that's when I gave up.

In the canyon where we were walking I could imagine the wolves before they became extinct, nearly two hundred years ago. They were probably doing just what we'd been doing, picking blackberries from the vines and trying to catch fish while searching for them with their paws under the same age-old rocks.

I'd remembered a poem from my grandfather on my father's side about the wolves, before he'd died:

"Only those who have heard
the howling of the wolves,
like the screaming of the devil,
that had every person fearful,
of the vent of growling evil."

But even he had said that "The wolves had been demonised for the money," and that "they were only trying to exist in the only way that they'd known."

It was almost dark now as we'd made our way along Kennedy's Race and the narrow path beside the river, towards Wolfhill mill. The mist had fallen without us noticing in our fierce debate about nothing important in particular, drifting slowly, like grey ghosts, off the grassy knolls of the three mountains towards Belfast city centre and the outlying housing estates. The city had looked as if it had been submerged by a giant tidal wave that had sped up the River Lagan, from Belfast Lough and the Irish Sea. Only some of the city lights had been visible, they seeming to flicker out by a street at a time as the rear of the mist had caught up with the head of it.

But we could still see the lights of our village ahead, and the three, red-lighted BBC transmission tower that had risen a hundred feet into the air from the top of Divis mountain. This mountain, too, according to my mother, had had a tragic history of its own. "On June, 1937, a Royal Air Force plane had slammed into that mountain in heavy mist. Flying Officer Archie McGrath had been killed instantly, just like the American airmen, five short years before them."

"Archie," she'd said, "had just been 23-years-old, and had been on his way back from Yorkshire to Aldergrove RAF Base. He was to have a holiday with his extended family that'd lived in Coleraine when his plane had crashed. He'd been stationed in Iraq where he'd been serving in Baghdad. The Curse of the Belfast Mountains had claimed another unwitting victim."

As our village grew closer I'd just realised something. "Do you know, lads," I'd said, "there were at least nineteen ghosts that had been spotted in our area…"

"Is that all?" Jim had replied, as Peter was counting them on his fingers.

"Yes," I'd replied, "let me see now... the ten American pilots... the RAF pilot, Naois O'Haughan... up to five United Irishmen, and the mother and her baby who were pulled out of Bodel's Dam. That's right—nineteen?"

"And the banshee," Peter had counted, "and Abbot John the monk, and the three wolves and frig knows how many leprechauns! That makes nearly thirty!"

"And the Eight-Foot Man?" Jim had volunteered, but I'd smiled because that had been two boys from our next class up wearing a black sheet, one sitting on the other's shoulders, spying on courting couples. "Let's get home," I said, "before another three are included on that list and before some of us die of fright! That would bring the number up to thirty-three!"

We parted on Mill Avenue, dividing up our spoils of the day's safari, three small trout each and four jam jars filled with blackberries, the tops of them wrapped around with a piece of brown paper and fastened and wrapped around with fishing line.

It was after midnight when I entered by our inside hall door, and my father was sitting reading an American detective magazine while at the same time listening to Radio Eireann, my siblings already in bed.

"Where's mother?" I said, my father replying without lifting his head out of the magazine.

"She's round at your cousin Eva Copeland's house in Wolfhill Lane, probably nattering away as usual. Could you do me a favour, son? Could you watch the kids until I go round to get her? It's late, and she may not like walking around those dark streets on her own. She has the only key to the door and I've to get to bed early because I got a few days' work over on the new construction site at the new Wolfhill estate."

"No, I'll go," I volunteered, as my father nodded his head, taking the trout and blackberries off me.

"Thanks, son, I'll have one of these little fellas for my breakfast in the morning."

It had started to drizzle earlier but now it had gotten heavier, my father handing his big black umbrella from behind the scullery door over to me. I had to go, because my father had been a bit wary because of what had happened to my uncle Patrick eight years earlier at Dickey's corner, which was on the way to Wolfhill Lane.

On the street the rain was starting to run down fast now, but the street had been deathly quiet, save for a solitary, large rat that had ran up our street from the little river at the bottom of the street that ran from beneath Wolfhill mill sewer pipes. There were thirty-two houses in our street, two down and two and a half rooms up, sixteen on each side, and all seemed to be in complete darkness. The people were probably be in bed for work in a few hours, that is, those who could get work.

I'd been still wary, though, for it had been quiet—too quiet—as I realised I was the only one out on the street, or probably the entire village. After walking along Mill Avenue and past Wolfhill primary school I still smiled, although I was afraid. We once took a steel railing from the fence at the back of the school one Sunday, and the teachers turned a blind eye to our thirty-a-side football on Sunday and on bright, summer nights. Although the teachers at Wolfhill were as puritanical as our own, the Wolfhill teachers had made us promise not to play cards for money in the playground, and not to bring any girls in there for any "hanky-panky". This had been particularly funny, because Wolfhill school, unlike ours, had mixed boy and girl classes, and if the pupils had wanted to get up to "hanky-panky" they could have done so in the classroom where they sat close beside each other.

I'd reached the top of the steps at Dickey's shop corner, and a row of twelve steps had led down and into the top of Wolfhill Lane. Silently I'd walked down the steps, my heart racing, and I could feel the goosebumps on my skin rise and also the hair on the back of my neck. I'd reached the top of Wolfhill Lane, my eyes darting down the narrow street where there were almost forty houses, mostly small, two-up and two-down, and it was bucketing down now.

I loved these houses, because they had small plots of land at the rear of them where people would grow their own vegetables, and one or two even had chickens and goats, for the fresh eggs and milk.

Facing these houses were the rears of the garden houses, were the better-off people had lived, and they had the first bathroom extensions in our village and also had pigeon sheds, with high walls; the front of these houses faced the main road to Nutt's Corner Airport.

Suddenly, I thought I heard a cat: "*Meow... meow...*" As I listened carefully, afraid to lift my head, I froze! "Hello...? Hello..." It seemed to be a young girl's voice directly behind me, but I put my head down further and ran down the street, not looking back for love nor money...

Chapter Four

Walking the Watery Sewers

I REACHED MY COUSIN'S HOUSE that was halfway down the street. When I entered the inside door without knocking, around nine women had been there. They were gathered around an old woman in her seventies who had been swirling a cup that had been half-filled with tea. The old woman entered the small scullery at the back of the sitting-room, emptied the tea out and returned to the floor.

"Where's Joan?" the old woman said, until a dark-haired woman put her hand up. "I can see money here," the old woman said, "and it's not your family allowance, because I can see a horse's head here and it is in front."

The women around here would often back horses on all the main races, like the Grand National at Aintree, and the Derby at Epsom, both in England. I was alarmed at this old woman's attitude, and I thought the only thing missing here was an Ouija board, to call dead spirits. This had been against the teaching of our Church, and if our parish priest had been here, Father Thomas Lynch, he would have beaten them out of that house with the heavy cane that he'd always carried.

He'd caught five of us while we were on our school, lunch break, and we had been playing cards behind our chapel for money. He'd slapped us a few times before, ordering the masters to keep us in for an hour after school.

"I'm coming now son," my mother said, without looking up at me. "I'm next and I might win the football pools this week... I won't be long." While I stood over them, the old woman had stopped what she was doing and stared up at me, a knowing look that had scared me. My legs had felt like jelly and I was still shaking all over, and I felt like one of the guys on that TV programme, 'The Twilight Zone', where he had been abducted and left somewhere else in his town. While I had been running down the street I had looked down at my legs, and although they had been moving, I couldn't feel my feet touching the ground. "So, this is your eldest?" she'd said to my mother while nodding in my direction. "A tall fella for his age, what—ten?" the old woman had enquired, while my mother didn't even look at me and just nodded. "Have you seen a ghost, young fella?" the old woman had asked again, her face now more wrinkled and again giving me that knowing smile.

That comment had made all the other women look up at me, but I couldn't reply but wanted to say, "I'm not sure, but I thought I could feel some kind of presence on my way down here. And I thought I could hear somebody calling me."

"Why son," my mother had chirped in, "you are as white as that cup in the fortune teller's hand there! Are you sure you weren't imagining things?" But I had been staring at the old woman; she had reminded of the witch in a photograph once about Hallo'ween, that I'd seen in a comic once.

"We have to go home now anyway," my mother had said. "Your father's got a few days' work over in the new building site across the river there, in the new Wolfhill estate. I have to get round to make your father up a packed lunch anyway." Soon we were saying "Cheerio!" to the company while my mother had put a coin into the old woman's hand. "See you all in the morning!" my mother had said again, but every time we were through the door somebody called her back to tell her something, but eventually we went out into the street.

My mother took the umbrella and put it over both our heads, before we stooped down and walked up the street. The rain had become much heavier now, and drops had bounced all over the street in big splats. We neared the top of the street and reached the bottom of the steps beside Dickey's shop when my mother froze and shook my shoulder.

"Look, son, look," she whispered, but I didn't want to look. My mother was edging back slowly, which eventually caused me to raise my head gradually from beneath the umbrella.

"My God son!" my mother had almost screamed, "What is that little girl doing standing in the pouring rain at this time of the morning?"

When my mother had walked towards the steps I ran after her, because I was afraid of being left on my own.

And then I saw it, a young girl who was aged around eight or nine years old. She was leaning against the back, double gates of Dickey's enclosed yard where he would bring in his deliveries for his confectionery shop. The girl was humming a pretty tune but I couldn't make it out. She sang like an angel from Heaven, but without the harp. This had been just yards from where my uncle Paddy had seen the ghoulish old woman, eight years ago.

Time seemed to stand still again as we looked at this beautiful girl. She had worn a brilliant white dress with blue frills all around the cuffs, and neck. She had beautiful blonde hair, all the way down to her waist, and had worn a golden ribbon through it. On her feet were black-painted shoes with silver buckles, and she had white bobby socks right up to her knees.

"Maybe it's the Virgin Mary!" my mother had whispered, but I knew if other unscrupulous people had seen this they would have made a fortune showing people around this area, and could even resort to selling religious icons.

Suddenly the girl turned, chuckling again, before running up towards the steps facing Curtain's Avenue, my mother following her and me following my mother. "Who are you?" my mother had shouted after her, "And what are you doing out here at 1 a.m. in the morning and in the heavy rain?"

The girl had suddenly stopped at the top step, before waving at us before running onto the main road.

And although my mother and I had been soaked right through, the girl had appeared not to be wet at all. Her hair and dress had been bone dry. We had been just six yards behind her, but when we'd reached the top of the steps the girl had gone—vanished. Both of us looked down the main road, up the Ligoniel hill towards the country and along Mill Avenue, but there wasn't even the sign of a single cat, never mind a young girl. We looked towards Curtain's Avenue, directly across the road from us, but we couldn't see up there.

The avenue had been totally dark as there was no street lighting up along there, only two rows of thick, oak trees that ran up both sides of the avenue towards Bodel's Dam, that had led up to the Ewart's mansion at the top. Now my mother had looked as if she'd seen a ghost, but I knew the feeling, for now I knew that I'd heard it first.

"That was strange," my mother finally said, for like me, I knew she was in shock and was almost speechless.

As we hurried past Wolfhill School she would keep staring back over her shoulder, as if half expecting to see the girl running up behind us and going "Boo!" But the girl had gone, and I had a theory she'd been sent by my uncle Paddy to tell us that after his horrifying experience at that corner, just eight years ago, he was all right and was in Heaven, and we would see him again someday.

When we reached home my father emerged from the scullery with a gutted trout in his hand, but my mother and I had agreed to tell nobody about our experience, for who would believe us anyway? "Did you two get lost on the way home?" my father said. "You look as if you've seen a ghost. That's what you get when you listen to that old hag of a fortune-teller with the long, white hair... going to win the Pools again, are we?"

"Well, near enough," my mother replied. "She said she seen a horse's head in front of others. Maybe that's the Grand National?"

"No," my father said, "more like that old hag herself running after you all for your money... there's one born every day!"

The autumn nights were closing in now, and my friends' and my usual custom was to do the Sewer Run, before the heavy rain came and sent torrents of water cascading down Kennedy's Race, from the Black mountain river, towards our village. The floods would then pour into the Top Dam, an artificial dam, one of four in the village, before entering a storm drain beneath Wolfhill mill, where another old waterwheel turned the machines. This too, like Ewart's, had been replaced with electricity many years ago.

The concrete pipe storm drain, still there to this day, was around five feet in circumference, and my friends and I would have to stoop down before entering it. The entrance, leading from the river at the bottom of our street, was hard to see in the summertime, because of tall reeds and evergreen trees, and we would hop over stones in the river to reach the entrance as soon as the colder weather had started to clear the reeds and long grass. There would usually be seven of us, Tony Brown and his sister Jean; Robert and David Dickson; and Peter, Jim and me. I would usually take the lead, while Peter would take up the rear and with the rest in between. But after this rat run we would refuse to enter the storm ever again. I had bent over to enter the drain first, that was seventy feet below a steep bank up near the middle at one point, my voice echoing all along the full three-hundred foot length of the drain when I'd shouted out, "Are you all ready! Let's go!"

We were now inside the drain after we'd all bent over in unison, and the *thump! thump! thump!* of our collective feet had been deafening in that confined space. Jean Brown had been holding onto the belt of my jeans at the rear of me; the Dickson brothers had been behind her, and Tony Brown, Jim and Peter had been at the end of the human train, with Peter at the rear. Ahead of me I could see the exit of the drain in the distance, around three hundred yards away, and it had looked like the size of a Ping-Pong ball. This exit would bring us up to an opening where once the waterwheel had been, and beside that was a nine-foot high waterfall with a deep pool below it.

The water flowing through the drain was just at a trickle as we'd manoeuvred along it, and now and again Jean would scream out in terror every time we'd disturbed a rat, the rat scurrying along the sewer and out of the exit, their territory invaded by crazy humans. "For frig' sake!" Peter would shout up from the rear, "Are we even halfway there yet? I can't see a friggin' thing!" Although Peter couldn't see a thing even in the sunlight. But we'd been only just halfway along as another rat scampered along in front of us, squeaking in terror. But the little ball of sunshine had been getting bigger, about the size of a tennis ball now.

"Will you stop pushing me from behind, Tony?!" Peter's voice had echoed all along the sewer. "Slow down! Slow down! And you at the front are going too fast! My friggin' back is breaking here! This idiot Tony is tearing lumps out of my back!" Perhaps Peter was imagining things, I'd thought, as I was sure that there was nobody behind *him*, not unless another of our friends had joined the train and we hadn't seen him?

Even Jean had whispered to me: "What's Peter shouting about, sure he's the last one at the end? And Tony is behind me, I can hear him whimpering."

We were halfway up the drain, and soon we'd reached another storm drain that had cut off to our left. This had been used as a rescue drain and it had stepped up two feet. Years ago, the workers would use it to reach the blocked main sewer when it had backed up with old tree branches and other flotsam during winter floods. It had been blocked with concrete years ago, at the other end, and when I squinted my eye and looked along it, it was pitch black. We would never bring a torch, because with no torch it had added to the excitement of the run.

Then suddenly I sprang back, as a flapping of scores of wings had swooped around me, and one of the bats had been caught entangled in Jean's long, black hair, like a trapped fish in a net. When she screamed I stretched my hand over my shoulder, being appalled when I came into contact with a bat's leathery wings against my skin. "Don't bat an eyelid!" I shouted, as I was able to pull it from her hair and push it inside the second sewer again. But the rest of Dracula's little followers had made a dash for the opening in front of us, this time failing to get a blood sample from Jean, squeaking to the outside one at a time.

"Will you stop! You're holding me too tight! Ah, that was *sore!*" Peter had squealed again, but with more urgency this time. By now, the exit to the sewer looked about the size of a basketball, and I could feel the cold draught running up my jean's trouser legs and against my face. The rushing air was now feeling and sounding like a speeding locomotive. Another rat had appeared from between my legs, running on in front of me, as I quickly followed it out of the sewer. While we emerged Peter had half-fallen, half-scrambled out behind us.

Everybody had lain down on the small patch of rough lawn beside the waterfall, as a brown trout dashed for a large rock in the middle of the waterfall pool. We'd disturbed it as it was leaping for a swarm of gnats. This would be the last feeding frenzy by all the fish until their breeding, winter season, and the fish was stocking up for her strength to be built up.

Just to be sure, I'd counted our company: "One, two, three, four, five, six and seven... but there was no-one holding onto you, Peter—are you sure you weren't imagining things in there? Are you definitely sure? Seven went in and seven emerged, and none of us could have doubled back to trick you, because there was no room for us to turn. It was impossible to trick you. Maybe it was the bats?"

Peter was putting his hands up his back while the rest of us had been laughing. "It wasn't the bats! It wasn't the bats!" Peter had cried. "This was long before the bats showed up! If it was the bats, how do you comedians explain this then?" Peter had pulled his shirt up and we all jumped back in horror. Ten scrapes ran down his back, like somebody with sharp and long fingernails had dug into his back, and small spots of blood had started to seep from the scratches.

It had looked as if an invisible force had grabbed hold of him, and indeed those rats weren't three feet tall and weren't riding on his back.

"Maybe it's Dracula's lair?" Jean laughed. "And you know he only comes out in the dark!"

But Peter wasn't to be convinced. He'd thought that something unnatural had latched onto him inside there. "That's it!" Peter had shouted, "No way am I going back in there again!"

Jean had gotten a handkerchief out of her jeans pocket and cleaned Peter's scratches up, and his whimpering didn't help the situation.

But what if he had been right that something was in there? Hitching a ride on his back? Maybe over the years, somebody had been murdered in the village, and the murderer had hidden the body down that sewer? Funny that my mother did not mention that, as she was born and reared there.

"Fancy a return trip?" I joked, and Peter ran up a narrow path beside the waterfall, making his way along the fields and towards Milk Avenue.

We never entered that drain ever again, and when we'd pass its entrance, as often we did, we would wonder... was it just bats or rats, or was it something more sinister?

Chapter Five

Getting my First Metal-Detector

T RUE TO FORM, my father had kept to his word when he bought me a second-hand metal-detector. He had bought it in the 'I Buy and Sell Anything' in Smithfield Market in Belfast. "It was just five pounds," he'd said. It looked more like a vacuum cleaner, with a dial sat on top of a rounded part that would scan the ground. It was American made and was called a Kellyco.

The Kellyco had a high-powered transmitter, a control box with earphones. It also had a 40-watt rechargeable battery and the battery charger had come as a free bonus from the shop. A little yellow box was fixed to the shaft, up near the handle, that had an On/Off button, and a face dial with instructions and a one-to-ten console, and a little, red hand that would shoot up to maximum if any sort of metal had been discovered, and the noise from it was so great with the droning when he tried it on a spanner that I had to remove the earphones! It made me think of those Geiger-counters that soldiers had used when testing for radiation after an atomic bomb explosion in the Nevada Desert, in the USA.

"You and your friends should first check out the old monastery ruins just off Curtain's Avenue," my father suggested. "The graves of all fourteen monks have long been exhumed," he said, "and although that hallowed ground would be still blessed, the monks would have left a sort of an impression on the old ruins in there—but where possibly the treasure of the highwayman, Naois O'Haughan, may well be buried.

"I'll also check out the local libraries," my father said, "and depending on what I discover it may be possible to pick up an old map of this area, going back to the eighteenth century. I will sketch you out a map myself, while in the libraries... but don't forget, fifty-fifty, for me and the rest for you three."

I didn't know if my father was joking or not, or maybe he just wanted me to take up some sort of a hobby to keep me out of trouble. But I wanted to hang around the area of the old monastery, if just to catch another glimpse of that beautiful girl we'd seen at the corner. I couldn't wait, and at school the next day Peter, Jim and me had decided to try out my new metal-detector that night, although Peter had reservations as he didn't like to be in the dark after his experience in The Barrels, also known as the sewer run...

After school the next day all three of us had met up at Dickey's corner, Jim bringing his bicycle torch. Peter had managed to persuade the local scout leader to lend us a small, short-handled spade with a diamond-shaped scoop. The nights had been growing chillier and all three of us wore our fleece, denim jackets, monkey-hats, gloves and thick boots. My machine was tightly wrapped around my right shoulder as we set off, not having far to walk to the monastery, just about fifty yards away.

But I'd switched on my machine prematurely. "Do you hear a humming sound?" Peter said, as we walked up Curtain's Avenue. "Do you think that's a UFO? An unidentified space ship?" Peter had strained his eyes, looking up at the perfect cloudless sky, although darkening.

"No, it sounds like the humming of a metal-detector," Jim replied. "Are you stupid all the time, Peter, or just after six o'clock at night?" Jim had also carried a small Hessian sack in case we'd strike it lucky on our first run out, but had felt like covering Peter's head with it.

We'd turned into a small dirt track just fifty yards up the avenue, before crossing a vegetable patch that Jack Dickey had carefully laid out, red labels for cabbages, green for beetroot, black for rhubarb, and all were hanging from lines of white twine. Behind the plot sat a little greenhouse where he'd cultivated his tomatoes, all to sell fresh in his shop, and behind that sat the ugliest, scariest, Georgian house that I'd ever seen, that had been shaped like that house out of that movie, called Phycho, about that guy who'd dressed up as his mother and had killed people. Luckily for us, old Jack had never kept a dog, unlike most in our village, so we would work away undisturbed.

A solitary light bulb had shone in the house's kitchen as we'd made our way around to the rear of the house, us having to negotiate a gap in a thick, blackthorn row of bushes before we could reach the monastery ruins. A breeze was building up, swaying the bushes and trees all over the place. I'd spotted old Jack the shopkeeper cleaning his home-grown produce, to sell in his shop while I passed, and at least we could work away undisturbed to at least 11 p.m.

When we punched a hole in the bushes with difficulty we slowly crawled down a steep embankment. At the bottom we could see the remains of the monastery, as four rows of grey, square, granite stones had protruded from the ground, almost covered by clinging ivy and moss, looking like rows of rotten teeth that had been eaten away over the years, almost near the gums.

I could see, in the semi-darkness, why the monks had built their monastery there, beside a small river that had run under the main village road under a viaduct. This little river had run all the way from the summit of Black mountain and the monks had seen the viability of handy, fresh water, as in those days piped water into any building had been unheard of. Judging by the markings on the inside walls, the monastery had had eight or nine different chambers, clear to us as Jim had lit his torch, shining it all around the inside of the ruins.

After warning Peter "not to fall into any hidden graves like the one in Carnmoney" we inched forward, as Peter had let out a loud scream because he'd fallen over one of the outer walls. I lowered my metal-detector close to the ground and pushed the On button, as I pulled my earphones from around my neck and onto my ears. There was a light buzz from it as it revved up, and as I looked around with the glare of Jim's torch I thought of what it may have been like here two hundred years ago.

The massive, creepy, Georgian house that had now been inhabited by old Jack Dickey, and the garden house behind the hedge, had probably been established by Abbot John and his fellow monks, and I wondered, were they at peace while seeing what changes there had been? "Prise your spade between the marble slabs, Jim," I'd suggested, "and hand Peter the torch to shine on you."

Jim had dug the spade deep between the first two slabs, straining and puffing until it eventually began to rise. "Don't move! Don't move!" Peter shouted, straining his dim eyes towards the small forest of willow trees. "Jesus! I can see a big pair of yellow, fluorescent eyes staring straight at us!" Peter yelled. "Do you think it could be Abbot John?"

Jim took his torch off Peter and held it under his chin, lighting up his face. "Boo!" he shouted in Peter's ear.

Peter backed away with fright, only to fall into the old ruins backwards.

"See? See?" Peter yelled. "Look! Look! The yellow eyes have swivelled right round to behind its back, and back again!"

I stopped what I was doing, asking Jim to shine his torch in the tree's direction to allay Peter's nervousness.

But it had made us just as worried, as sure enough, the biggest pair of burning, yellow eyes that I'd ever seen were staring right back at us. The head of the thing was swirling around like a toy spinning top, but with no sound.

"Maybe it's a distant lighthouse?" Jim had suggested, trying to edge closer to the thing with his torch.

"No," I replied, "the nearest lighthouse from here is at Saint John's Point, and that's forty miles away on the County Down coast, down the road a mile or two from Ardglass... I stood outside it once. My grandfather came from there, and I used to go there for my school holidays."

Peter had found a small rock and had thrown it in the direction of the yellow lights, but that had just made the thing swell out and get bigger, and now the entire form was a brilliant white colour. The thing was on the move and when it stirred, the branches of the trees were shaking furiously. Now it was almost upon us, and it was flying, as we dived to the ground just as my metal-detector grew louder, like a loud, crackling sound when my father couldn't find the station he was trying to locate on his old radio.

I'd found something in the disturbed ground and was being attacked at the same time, but couldn't move my detector in fear of losing it. We'd all covered our eyes, fearing we were about to be torn from limb to limb, and I couldn't move or do anything about it. Suddenly the white blob was hovering there in front of us. *"Hoot! Hoot! Hoot!"* and the biggest White Owl I'd ever seen just barely lifted over our heads, its massive wings flapping furiously and almost blowing us off our feet, its orange talons dragging along limply. Close up, its massive white and yellow eyes had looked like two fried eggs, sunny side up, before flying off towards Curtain's Avenue like a giant, escaped parrot.

Meanwhile, I'd relieved Jim of the torch, all the while the buzz in my headphones becoming unbearable. I shone the torch down to where the crackling had been coming from, at the same time yelling at Jim: "Dig deeper at that spot, where you upended that piece of white marble—there!" As Jim dug furiously we had forgotten our frightening experience with the giant owl, all three of us now down on our knees digging with our bare hands.

"Ah frig'!" Jim had shouted. "Look, it's only a little baby's bootee, but what would a little baby be doing all the way up here?"

I'd held it up to my face to examine it more closely while Jim, at the same time, shone the torch onto it. "A baby's bootee my foot!" I'd yelled, "This thing is some sort of an ornament and it's made from a coppery metal, and there's a green, velvety material covering the inside of it. And a lace, a sort of golden lace and golden eyes for the lace, and the lace is still there! Look!"

Jim and Peter had taken it off me, excitedly examining it and turning it every way to get a good look at it.

"I'll drop it into my bag," Jim said, "and we'll see it better in the light in the house."

When Jim dropped the little shoe into the sack a sort of *ping* noise had come from it, while a beam of light had lit up the inside of the sack. "Did you see that?!" I exclaimed, "Did you shine your torch into the sack Jim, while you were dropping the shoe in there?"

"Not me," Jim replied, "but it was like a light bulb being switched on... did you, Peter, strike a match, you know, the matches you bought with your five cigarettes tonight?"

"Definitely not!" Peter protested, "And I'm not responsible for that music either, coming from the sack... listen!"

But Jim had thrown the sack to the ground, as if he'd lifted a dinner plate that had been kept in the oven too long. We all prodded the sack with our boots, and soon the most beautiful Irish music I'd ever heard wafted all over the area of the old monastery and Curtain's Avenue.

"Are you sure we're not hearing things?" Jim wondered. "That could be coming from the village below there, because it sounds distant."

The music had been as clear as a bell, and various musical instruments could be recognised, like harps, fiddles, flutes, tin whistles and even the old, hand-held Bowran drums. The most beautiful voices of singers filled the air, beautiful sounding, the singing lilting up high, then the tempo would drop again, until a mighty crescendo of voices and music would be the finale, then silence... deathly silence.

"I'm terrified," Peter said, his voice shaking, "and although I'm terrified most of the time, I'm terrified more than you two know now. These singers were even better than our church choir, much, much better."

"Yes," Jim said, "and I get the feeling here that we heard something that we were not supposed to hear... we trespassed onto something that we weren't meant to. Shall we go? Run? Get back to your house,

Patrick, and have a look inside the sack? Maybe we were just imagining all this and somebody is having a house party down in the village?"

"I'm terrified too, Jim, but we have to admit that that music was very beautiful, out of this world, not from the earth?" I agreed. "Shall we get the frig' out of here, to our house? Maybe my father can work out what all this means?"

"We can come back on Sunday morning early when our imaginations aren't playing tricks on us," Jim ventured. "Maybe we'll find the rest of what's here, if anything... those white, marble slabs must hold far more than we found."

"And that thing lit up by itself... do you think it has a battery?" Peter suggested, "Or maybe it's an ancient jukebox that plays when you lift it?"

Maybe Peter and Jim had had something there, I thought, but from where did that beautiful Irish music come from? Surely a dead thing like an old kid's bootee couldn't make such beautiful noises like that?

That music had sounded even better than when the girls' Irish dancing class was in session, in our church hall, Saint Vincent's, and we would often hear them from our Nissan hut classrooms beside the hall every Wednesday afternoon. Or perhaps somebody in the village had had their radios turned up to full blast, as these Irish music programmes would be on all the time on the Irish radio channel, Radio Eireann.

My father would laugh and call it "Irish nationalist fairy music" because he was a socialist, and he said that "the parish priests had us all brainwashed, and had taken the side of the Free Staters during the Irish civil war. They had caused our poverty and foreign wars," he said.

"Yes, you're half right," my father said when we'd arrived at my home in Finlay Street, breathless, and showed him our booty. "It looks like a child's shoe, or it's as small as a little baby's shoe, but it's not that." My two-year-old sister Mary had been lounging around the floor in front of our fire and I could see that it was too small, even for her. George, my four-year-old brother, stared at the bootie as if in a deep trance, looking at the relic and then down at his feet, as if to say, "Now that is the smallest baby foot I've ever seen."

"I can't see that this is a baby's shoe," my mother interrupted. "If you look at this little shoe you can see that the toe area tapers right down to a fine, sharp point, like those winklepickers that the Teddy Boys wear... and the little eyes for the lace, they are almost as small as the eye of a needle. The eyes look like gold to me, and comparing them to my wedding ring, they are gold, but *pure* gold." My mother gave my father a dirty look as if to say, "Miser!"

"And yes," my father interrupted, "you're right Mary, no, not about the Miser part—the lace looks like gold as well, like it was spun from a gold spider's web. I've never seen anything like this before... remarkable!"

While my mother, father, Jim, Peter and my brother and sister were occupied with the little shoe on the table at the parlour window, I removed the metal-detector's battery from the console. It had looked like a yellow block of my mother's butter, as I put it into the charger before putting the plug into the wall socket, having the strange feeling that this metal-detector would be working overtime from now on.

"And you say the little boot lit up when you dropped it into your sack, Jim?" my father asked, "and you thought it played music as well?" He blew a ring of smoke up towards the ceiling from his tobacco pipe. Both Jim and Peter nodded, but I hadn't seen it, thinking that that owl was about to snatch my head off.

"Maybe it was a party in Lavery's house?" my father suggested. "They have parties down there morning, noon and night, although we heard nothing earlier. But it's strange, very strange." But looking again at my little sister I'd thought, maybe Peter had been right and little space aliens were landing on our hills, as some strange ships have been seen hovering over the top of them. Whatever they were, if they'd existed in the first place, must have been very small creatures. "It's logical to assume," my father went on, blowing another smoke ring towards our ceiling, "going by the shoe the little person who once wore that had pointed ears as well... that's my interpretation of this anyway."

Jim, Peter and me all looked at each other. Inter... int...? What does that mean?" Jim asked, reading Peter's and my minds.

"Never mind Patrick's father," my mother laughed, "he's just read his new Oxford English dictionary last night... He means *his* understanding of it."

"Under...? ...un?" Peter asked, "What were you standing under?"

"And it lit up all by itself?" my mother asked. "Are you absolutely sure?"

"Well, we think it did," Jim replied. "We can't be sure, though. We were frightened at the same time by the biggest white owl we've ever seen in our lives, or the first white owl we've ever seen in our lives, except in a comic; gigantic and monstrous it was, too."

"Maybe the owl owned the shoe and it fell off when the owl attacked us?" Peter surmised, as we all broke into a hysterical laugh. "Well, it is possible," Peter added with an injured look, "and the other one is still on its other foot with its socks."

After Peter and Jim told me to keep the little shoe safe and both had gone home, my father told me to fetch a neighbour called Matt Collins. Matt knew everything about contraptions, was a watch repairer by trade, and usually fixed watches and clocks for all his neighbours. He would free up jammed watch springs and workings by taking their backs off and putting them over a darning thimble that he'd filled with lighter fluid petrol, leaving them to sit for a day or two.

Matt was both renowned and infamous in our street, and the police had arrested him early one morning... after a neighbour had told the police that Matt was in the IRA and was making timing devices for bombs. They had released him again after our parish priest, Father Thomas Lynch, had told them he was a watch repairer, and some of the neighbours had vouched for him as well, showing them the watches and clocks that he'd repaired, and the scratches on their backs where he'd opened them.

My father had told me to tell Matt to bring a nail file and a small shaving brush to clean the shoe up.

"Interesting, very interesting," Matt said, after he'd scraped some hardened soil off the object. He'd also brought a small, magnifying glass.

He was very interested in Egyptian mummies and the Aztecs of Mexico. He would also have books on the lost island of Atlantis, that he thought had existed thousands of years ago, in the Atlantic Ocean. The locals had christened Matt the Grand Master of the Ancient Order of Atlanteans, because Matt had thought that Ireland had been Atlantis and that it hadn't sank beneath the waves of the Atlantic after all. He was very intelligent looking, and wore little grandfather spectacles and had a little, white goatee beard, always wore a smoking jacket, and his long hair was as white as snow.

"Your son there may have discovered a very important piece of ancient Irish art," Matt said, scraping the underneath of the little bootee with the little nail file, then brushing the dust off with his shaving brush. "Alternatively," he went on, "this could be a relic since the time of the ancient, Irish fairies... yes, important, very important, the little people of the underworld."

But I was puzzled: the only fairy that I knew was pointed out to me by my father one day, and it lived in Lesley Street. It had been a man who'd dressed in women's clothes, a ballet tutu and knee-high white socks. He, or she, would do a comedy show in the pubs in Belfast, and would sing a tune to the music of that well-known song, 'They Tried To Tell Us We're Too Young,' but changing the words to 'They tried To Tell Me I'm A Man.' He called himself Paddy Perspire because he'd always been sweating a lot.

"How old do you think the piece is?" my father had asked Matt.

"Well, let me see now," Matt studied the item closely, "this little lace here... looks like gold webbing sewn together, like from a spider's web, yes, gold, finely spun gold, and the little eyes for the lace to go through, gold as well, made by hands that couldn't make that today unless using special machinery, and that special machine doesn't exist today either. The inside is made of a fine velvet, very fine, ancient leather I would say, and the tongue is a mixture of a gold and silver material... how much do you want for it?"

"Not for sale at any price, Matt," my father replied. "Anyway, it's not mine to sell, it's the lad's and his mates—it's up to them, they discovered it... and anyway, I think I'll take it along to the Ulster Museum in Cultra, North, County Down. If any organisation would know for sure just what this relic was it would have to be them—they know everything. They even have Egyptian mummies there and even dinosaur bones, that are very ancient."

While listening to my father and Matt, I remembered the legends of our village, how locals would hear beautiful Irish music being sung and played by angels, mostly under the old, blackthorn tree in Mill Avenue—singing and dancing in Gaelic, the ancient Irish language and music.

Locals would call them leprechauns, and when people had gone to investigate, the song and dancer had suddenly stopped, as if by an invisible, secret, silent, signal by an invisible guard or lookout. I lifted the little bootee again to look over it, when old Matt had gone, after my father had made him promise to say nothing to anyone, and he agreed.

While talking to my mother and father, my little sister had pointed at the bootee, as if to say, "That is the same as mine." But it wasn't; this was unlike anything that me or my family had ever seen before.

I ran my hand along it, and a little bell seemed to ring, and my parents suddenly looked around. My little baby sister had been playing with her rattle, but the rattle hadn't got a bell attached to it. I'd put the relic under my side of the bed, in an old shoebox, while little George had slept soundly. This was one toy that I couldn't let out of my sight, and it wasn't for sale.

When I switched the bedside lamp off, I could hear that someone in our street had decided to play Irish music on their record player.

It *had* to be a record player, because all the radio stations had closed down at 2 a.m., and it was now 3 a.m., when our cuckoo clock downstairs went *cuckoo! cuckoo! cuckoo!*

Then I dropped off to sleep, exhausted.

Chapter Six

My Leprechaun Visitor

THE NEXT FRIDAY, Jim's father, who'd been working in Dublin as a carpenter, had driven home to our village for the weekend, as usual. Jim's father, also called Jim, drove a little two-door Morris Minor car, although I wondered how he could get behind the steering wheel as he was over six-feet tall, like my father, but heavily built. After my father and Jim's had gone for a pint of Guinness as usual in the local, Terminus Bar, and he had explained to Jim's father about the relic, they had agreed to take all three of us to the Ulster Museum in Cultra, and the next morning we had driven into the centre of Belfast from our village.

We crossed the Albert Bridge into East Belfast and drove along the new Sydenman motorway. I remember coming this way, the scenic route, when I would go to the little fishing village of Ardglass where my father's father had been born and raised, but had settled in Ballymacarrett in East Belfast when he met my grandmother who came from Belfast.

We would arrive at Portaferry village, then would catch the ferry across Strangford Lough, arriving in Strangford village after a short, ten minute sailing. We would then travel the eight miles to Ardglass. As me, Jim and Peter had muttered to ourselves in the back seats of the car, this was our first time at the Ulster Museum, and we were very excited.

The journey of around twelve miles to Cultra was soon over, and before long we reached the Museum. "We need to go to the Folk rather than the Transport section of the museum," my father suggested, as we were in awe of our surroundings.

We could see that the Museum staff had travelled far, all over Ireland, and had demolished old Irish houses, according to the instructions on their walls, then had carefully and meticulously built them up to their original state. There were farms, cottages, crops being grown and even live farm animals. There were also churches, shops, and terraced and detached houses from all periods in Ireland. There was also on show an old, Irish poteen still, an illegal whiskey-making brewery, and even the first bicycles in Ireland, plus a section on Irish, traditional music.

The curator was a plump, dark-blue uniformed, jovial man, who showed us around the film, photographic, BBC TV and radio broadcast material with thousands of hours of radio and sound broadcast material. "Ask him father, ask him," I said excitedly, nudging my father while Jim held the little sack tightly. But my and Jim's father had been otherwise occupied, an exhibition catching their eyes about the history of the Irish Famine that had started in 1845, over a hundred years ago.

"This was a terrible time in the history of Ireland," the curator said, following me, Jim and Peter, after we'd followed them to see what all the fuss was about. "The staple diet of the Irish then," the curator went on, "was the humble spud, that had failed because of a disease called Potato Blight. When the Irish had nothing else to eat, over a million of them starved to death and another two million emigrated mostly to the Americas, Britain, Australia and New Zealand... a lot of the Irish perishing from diseases such as cholera, dysentery and typhoid fever, and lots of people died on the so-called coffin ships when emigrating."

"That's funny," Jim said, "we weren't taught about that at our school... just the War of the Roses, between Lancashire and Yorkshire, and the Battle of Hastings in 1066."

"That's because you kids are being brainwashed," Jim's father said. "There had been plenty of food in Ireland like pigs, cattle and poultry, but that was exported to feed the English. They could afford to pay for it while our ancestors couldn't. The free market system, no money, no food—it was a bloody disgrace!"

The curator appeared to be embarrassed, holding a hand over his mouth and pretending to clear his throat. "You were saying, young man? Show me what?" the curator said. "Did you find a dinosaur bone or something that you have in that sack?" My father nodded to Jim to open the sack, and he produced the little shoe.

The curator donned a little pair of grandfather spectacles, after rubbing them with a handkerchief. He gestured for us to follow him into a little, musty smelling office, where he switched on a table lamp. He held the shoe almost up against the light bulb. He must have stared at it for at least five minutes, and had even bitten on the little lace hard with his teeth. He then pulled a thick, ancient book from a place underneath his desk, quickly fingering through it as if his life depended on it, as if wanting to find something quickly.

He then turned and stared at us as if in shock. "Pray, tell me," he said, "just where did you get this little boot? And most importantly, are you ceding it to the museum? How much do you want for it? Have you had it valued?"

"Valued?" my father said. "You think it's worth getting valued? Is it very valuable to you?"

"Well, let me see now," the curator said, removing his little glasses, "there's an article in this catalogue here that says that a relic was found similar to this in County Cork, in the far south of Ireland in 1366, a long, long time ago, but it was lost again, some say stolen. Like this boot—the little boot then was made of an unknown material, like leather, a material not seen then, and yours is something similar. The lace and the eyes are gold, a fine gold, the finest gold I've ever seen, not the most valuable gold at twenty-four carats, but I would say, if this was possible, fifty carat gold, the best. And how the laces were spun? No machine on God's earth today could make an article such as this— remarkable!"

He continued: "And this little tongue on the boot here, pure silver and gold mixed, but again, no machine on earth today could even come near to manufacturing this... not even near! How did you come across this fine piece of wondrous artistry?"

"Well mister..." I was about to explain, but my father tapped me on the shoulder.

"Actually," my father interrupted, "it's a family heirloom, and it was passed down to me for generations and generations."

"Generations?" the curator said. "Your family must have been circus midgets in those days—you didn't call her Bridget the Midget by any chance? But it's the oldest piece than even anything that's in here... and I can see my boss to get a valuation, if you want to leave the piece with me and call back sometime next week. How much did you say you'd sell it for again? I can probably get you a very good price for it."

My father had liberated the little shoe from the curator's hand, then carefully putting it back into the sack again, tying the top with one of the laces from his shoe this time, nodded to us to leave immediately.

When we were almost out the door, I looked back, to see the curator wiping his forehead with a handkerchief while holding his peaked cap in his other hand. "Do you think there's more where this came from?" Jim's father asked. "Is that why you cut the little, fat guy short?"

"You heard what he said, Jim," my father replied, "and we mustn't tell anybody where the lads got this one from... who knows, there may be another boot there, maybe an entire suit of golden clothes, or even a hidden treasure trove. It's possible that the highwayman liberated this one from a rich merchant, and this could have been some kind of gift, or birthday present, who knows...?"

"This guy, Naois O'Haughan, probably buried his loot all over the village and the surrounding hills, and there could be more, lots and lots more! And the Cavehill, especially the Cavehill..."

"Keep your talking up," Jim's father said, "and I may have to leave my job if this pays us. Let's go back to the village and plan a strategy for what to do next... and listen, lads, tell nobody, we could all be on to a good thing here. Not even your friends at school. The less who know about it the better."

"Yes," my father interrupted, "and we should stay away from the old monastery grounds for a while, in case Matt, the Grand Master of the Ancient Order of the Atlanteans, mentions it. The entire village will be hunting the bloody place then! We could come out into the open when we've found the rest. Then we can call ourselves The Society for the Discovery of Ancient Artefacts... right?" We all nodded in unison, hoping that we'd have a great adventure in front of us, and we would all become very, very rich.

That Saturday night, my father, mother and Jim's father and mother would go out for their usual drink in the usual, Terminus Bar, in the main street of our village, and our neighbour, the little snotty Teresa Collins, a sixteen-year-old from next door, would be babysitting us as usual, although I could have done it but my mother had said that "somebody older would be better doing it."

Teresa had long, blonde ponytails, and she always wore a big, round, tin badge of her idol Elvis Presley, on her chest. We'd all settled down to watch the Black and White Minstrel show on BBC1. This show showed white men dressed up as black singers with their faces covered in shoe polish, and they wore straw hats and bright clothes, and always sang the song, 'Mammy', by Al Jolson. I often wondered while watching this show... could black men not be better singing black-type songs, instead of white men dressing up and making fun of them? And the religious hymns from Alabama, in the American Deep South, where black people were expert at it?

"Patrick?" my younger brother said to me while sitting on the floor playing with his spinning top.

"Do you want the TV turned up?" I said to him when the Black and White singers were trying to sing that old Irish song, 'Danny Boy'.

"Music, music," he said excitedly, "music last night... last night!"

"What music last night?" I replied. "There was no music on the TV last night. Are you sure?"

"After you got into bed last night, Patrick, I wanted to go to the toilet, but I forgot to bring the milk bottle up, and I had to come downstairs to the scullery and pee in the kitchen sink. I was afraid to go out to the toilet in the yard because of the rats, and the loud music... there was a party out the back last night!"

"What time was that at?" I asked. "I heard nothing when I was going upstairs."

"Three cuckoos," George replied. "When our cuckoo clock up on the wall there went *cuckoo! cuckoo! cuckoo!* Our mother and father were sleeping, the baby was sleeping, and so were you."

"And what was the music like, George? Like on the TV now?"

"No," George replied, "it was like the music that we went to see last month when it was on in the Parochial Hall... ceili music, but there were people singing along too, in the entry. Flutes, drums, tin whistles, fiddles and singing, beautiful singing, but in voices that weren't in our language. It was like a funny language that older people learn, like they're chewing a sweet, like a big, gobstopper. They went on and on chanting for hours and hours. And clip-clop, like horses' hooves, as if they'd been running up and down our back yard."

"I think they were probably singing in Gaelic then," I replied. "I think we heard that too, the other night on Curtain's Avenue. And George, what...?"

I was about to ask, "Are you sure?" when the inside door of our front room opened and in walked Teresa, still wearing the large, round, tin badge with Elvis on it, her pigtails gone this time, her hair hanging down like rat's tails. She'd got stuff wrapped up in a brown paper bag.

"Are you little fellas and girl all right?" she asked. "I've got lemonade, crisps and sweets here for you three little blondies, but if you give me any trouble like you did last week, you'll get nothing!" She sat down in my father's armchair by the fire, then got up every five minutes to turn over the stations of the TV. "Were you all up all night last night?" she asked.

"We were... my mother, father, my two sisters and two brothers and me."

"My father thought the music was coming in from here, but it was after three o' clock in the morning, so he thought it couldn't be from here. Then he thought the music was coming from the rear of one of the houses facing us, in Lesley Street, or it was Lavery's again... they're always having parties morning, noon and night."

"Music?" I asked. "What, rock n' roll music, that you like, and are always playing loudly, so loud that we can hear you through our walls?"

"No," she replied, "real loud Irish music, like the kind my father listens to on Radio Eireann—you know, Irish ceili music? With beautiful singing and chanting, and musical instruments like fiddles, whistles, drums, harps and bagpipes. Although while it was beautiful it had still been far too loud for that time of the morning. And it had been in some foreign language too—we couldn't make out the words."

I'd sat there on the floor, cross-legged and stunned, while Teresa had reached up and brought down a Snakes and Ladders game from our sideboard. Had this anything to do with our little ancient shoe, I wondered? The shoe that I'd had hidden upstairs in my and George's room?

Meanwhile, a little circus clown had appeared on the TV, all dressed up in funny, black and white clothes, with its face blackened, like the black babies we'd collected for in our school, for the starving black babies in Africa. The clown also wore little bells on its heels, a little funny hat, a wig, and baggy, pointed shoes and a one-piece suit. My attention was drawn to our baby Mary; she had been giggling loudly and clapping her tiny hands, trying to say, "Little man! Little man!" but had been facing the scullery door and pointing to the entrance with her finger. "Little man! Little man! Out! Out!" But Teresa was too engrossed with George trying to teach him how to play the game.

Now I was beginning to worry: George had heard the music, the baby had heard it; Teresa and her family had heard it, and Jim, Peter and me had heard similar music the night we'd found the little, ancient boot, and apparently something strange had been going on. What next? I thought, would they all see Peter's UFO next? I had thought of Peter, and how all the pupils in our school had always made fun of him, not only because he was so short-sighted, but because of his father as well...

His father had also been called Peter, and he also wore thick-lensed spectacles, and had a shock of red hair as well. They had christened Peter's father the Birdman of Crumlin Road Prison in Belfast, after he'd been caught stealing exotic birds like parrots and budgerigars while working at Belfast Docks. But Jim and I would never make fun of Peter junior because all three of us had been best friends since we were five-years-old. Some of the fathers of the other kids had read a book by an American writer called Thomas E. Gaddis, and he'd called the book *The Birdman of Alcatraz*.

One of the fathers had cruelly remarked that Peter's father was like Robert Stroud, the prisoner in the book, and it had spread from that, and Stroud had murdered a fellow prisoner while in Leavenworth Prison in Kansas, USA. He was then transferred to the high-security prison in San Francisco Bay, called Alcatraz. Peter's father was sentenced to six months in prison after the exotic birds that he would steal dried up because the demand for them in the pet shops in Ireland had fallen away.

He was caught red-handed when he couldn't get any more birds and would go around the trees and hedgerows of our village and put glue onto the branches where birds like Sparrows, starlings, blackbirds and magpies would roost for the night. He would then bring the birds home in nets and paint them, red, white and blue, representing the British Union Jack flag, when selling the birds in unionist, Protestant areas of the North, and green, white and orange if selling them in nationalist, Catholic areas. He'd been caught when he'd sold a painted bird to a judge, without realising that the judge's wife would wash her birds every weekend.

He would always tell his customers that he had a special supplier in Thailand, in the Far East, who would give the birds a special feeding recipe. That would make their birds lay a special egg that would produce birds of these great colours, especially for the Irish market. This had gone on for a while, until the judge's wife washed her bird one morning, and the paint had run off the bird, turning it entirely a one colour of mauve, when the red had mixed in with the blue paint.

The judge had phoned the police, and Peter's father had then confessed to the exotic bird thieving in the docks, and had asked the judge to take that into consideration to receive a lighter prison sentence. Peter's father had always been a joker, some said the village idiot, but Peter junior had never lived that down.

Peter senior had said to me one day: "Hey young fella, what do you call a Jewish gentleman who lives in Scotland?"

"I don't know," I replied, "what do you call a Jewish gentleman who lives in Scotland?"

"He, he," Peter senior had laughed, "Rabbi Burns, kid... get it?"

I was wondering about Rabbi Burns, because I'd read once that he'd been a famous poet, but I didn't understand the joke until my father told me. "Rabbie Burns was indeed a poet, but a Rabbi is a Jewish clergyman. Pay no attention to Peter's father... he tries to be funny but it doesn't work."

Peter's father would always attend political meetings in our house every Friday night, along with my father and Jim's. They'd all belonged to the Republican Clubs, a radical, political group that had been established by the Presbyterian, United Irishmen, on top of the Cavehill Mountain in 1795. I'd heard them talking about a fella called Marx, and when the meeting was over I'd asked my father, "Is there anybody in your Party called Marx? Is that Harpo, Chico, Groucho or Zippo? A famous person? A well-known comedian or people called the Marx Brothers, the comedians?"

My father was drinking tea, and when I asked him that, the tea must have gone down the wrong way, which had caused him to curse, followed by his doubling up with loud laughter. "Well, you could be right there son," he gasped as he caught his breath, "as some people, mostly the Churches, would call Marx a comedian, but not one of the brothers, but Karl Marx the socialist." He continued: "Marx wanted to confiscate all the lands belonging to the Churches and the rich landowners, to divide them out to the poor people, or to the people of no property at all. Karl Marx died at the beginning of this century before he could see his dream realised, and is buried in Highgate Cemetery in London. He was a German Jew, that's why socialists of all shades are not anti-Semitic, meaning not anti-Jewish, like the fascists and Nazis."

Chapter Seven

The Disappeared Horses!

O N SUNDAY MORNING my mother had gotten us all out of bed early for Mass at Saint Vincent De Paul church, at 10 a.m. I'd felt too tired to attend and I'd had a splitting headache anyway. My father had excused me, but he wanted to "show a good example because he never, ever went himself." He'd had words once, with our parish priest, Thomas Lynch, about politics. Despite this, my father had liked the priest, because, like my father's father, the old priest had come from the seaside village of Ardglass.

When my mother and siblings had gone out the door I confided in my father about an eerie dream I'd thought I had last night. "I'd dropped off," I told him, "and had been barely asleep for ten minutes when I'd decided to go to the toilet down in our back yard. Although not remembering getting up and going downstairs, I pictured myself opening the yard door and going outside. I'd lit a candle that had been kept on the scullery sideboard that would always be kept there, because the electric flex in the toilet had been chewed through, by rats, and the light bulb would never work.

"I remember," I went on, "of vaguely pulling the toilet chain, then walking out to the yard again. As I neared the scullery outer door, I heard a little voice, me thinking that little George wanted to go to the toilet as well, as he didn't like coming out there on his own."

"Then what happened?" my father had enquired. "Did little George fall and hurt himself?"

"It wasn't George," I replied, "not when I heard the voice coming from the top of the yard wall, as if somebody had been sitting on top of it looking down at me. *Padraig, a Chara...? Padraig, a Chara...* what did these words mean, father? Were they in some kind of foreign language?"

"Not really foreign, son—that was Irish Gaelic that everybody used to speak years ago, not anymore. *Padraig* is the Gaelic version of your name, Patrick, and the *a Chara* means My Friend... so the voice was really saying, really calling you, 'Patrick, my friend?' What did you do then?"

"I looked up at the window of our bedroom, thinking that George had opened it and was calling down at me, but there was no-one there. Then again, I heard the words, *Padraig, a Chara...* Then I quickly turned around to my right and looked up at the wall... and I nearly died! My heart was going like the clappers, *bump, bump, bump.* Honest to God, I nearly collapsed when I saw a little man, sitting astride our wall, looking down and smiling at me, and he had a little fiddle and a bow in his hands.

"He had a little, green uniform on him, the same that Robin Hood would wear, and with a Robin Hood hat on his head and a little, white feather attached to it. He wore green stockings, like my mother's, up to his waist, and his eyes, his staring eyes... were as red as coal embers. I froze to the spot! Then he spoke again, or rather he sang: 'My shoe, my shoe, or I will steal your little baby sister! *a Chara, a Chara*, my shoe, my shoe!'"

Suddenly, my father jumped up from his chair, running through the scullery and out into the yard, with me following him. He quickly jumped onto the yard wall, via the little shed that he used to keep his little, brown, black and white-patched Jack Russell dog for hunting rabbits, but it had died from distemper that the dog Toby had caught from a rabbit last year. "No son, nothing here at all; whatever it was, is now long gone... Are you sure you saw a little man and not a rat? The entry is crawling with them at night, and they like to climb walls and drainpipes."

"Well, I told you father, I can't be sure, but it looked as real to me as you standing there." I didn't want to tell my father about last night, because I'd promised my mother that if I had strange experiences, like seeing that beautiful girl ghost at Dickey's Corner, I wouldn't breathe a word about it to anybody. But the little man had been different, menacing even, and I was afraid, very afraid, even more scared when the little ghost girl had called me. "Try to think back, son—did the little man say anything else, and what size was he really?"

I concentrated for a while, trying to recollect about last night, because I thought it was as if I'd been hypnotised for a while, and it had seemed like an hour or more.

"Yes! Yes!" I shouted, as three starlings took off from the TV aerial in fright. "He said: *'Padraig... Padraig*, my boy, the old monastery... the old place where you and your friends were searching for the highwayman's goods, you were searching in the wrong place.' And in between his raving he would play little tunes that I didn't know. He said: 'That owl that you disturbed, my boy, that owl stole my shoe from another place, not where you found it. I spoke to the owl, and he said you disturbed him and he dropped it into your lap... he also stole my cap but I got that back, and now... I want my shoe back, now! This very day, or your sister will go to the underworld, where we reside, and have resided for thousands of years!'"

"Did he tell you his name, son, anything? Did he even give you a clue? Was he violent towards you?"

"No father, not violent, only in his tone of voice, real nasty! He even mentioned that the old, wise owl had flown off because Peter's father was capturing the birds of the air and was selling them for money, exploiting them, but he paid for it, and that he will do so again. The owl had thought that Peter's father was trying to catch him and that's why he dropped the shoe.

"And his name, father? I think he said Cuculliane... yes Cuculliane. The old ancient king of Ireland, and he kept on saying, 'I want my boot back, now!'"

My father appeared to be distracted now, walking up and down the yard, scratching his head and rubbing the stubble on his face.

"Now I remember what else he said, father. He said that the villages had chopped down their christening tree, the blackthorn on Mill Avenue, but that our village suffered for it and it will suffer again! The little guy was raving and ranting."

"Listen son, I think there's something fishy going on here," my father said thoughtfully. But I had gone into the scullery to fetch a cup of water, then gulped it down thirstily when I'd realised the implications of all that the little man had said last night. "Listen again, son... I think there's something funny going on here, and I think it's possible that old Matt Collins, the Grand Master, could be playing tricks on us to get us to take the little boot back; then he can grab it for himself! Do you remember when you went up to fetch him the other night, how his face lit up when he saw the little boot? I knew that look—it's called the Green Eye, meaning greed... and remember, he's the only one outside our little group who knows about it. He could have sat a little, dressed-up puppet up on the yard wall, you know; like those little Chinese mannequins that the operator works with bamboo sticks?"

"But father, how did the little man speak like that? And his eyes, the irises of his eyes, were a bright red, like burning embers, and he was very, very angry!"

"That's easy, son! Old Matt is a ventriloquist and he can throw his voice a long way. He has demonstrated this time and time again, in front of Jim's, Peter's father and me. To say that old Matt was a bit strange would be an understatement, and that's the truth."

I wasn't too sure about my father's explanation; he was just trying to reassure me, I thought, and maybe my father was in denial about what happened to me because *he* was the one with the Green eye?

"Well, how come, father, that when the little man disappeared he *really* disappeared! Right in front of my eyes up there? And where did all the Irish music come from? Not only from his fiddle but all around our house? The drums, harps, pipes and whistles? Old Matt couldn't have done all that, could he? And all the neighing and galloping of horses in the back entry? Like there'd been dozens of people out there? And what did the words *Padraig* and *a Chara* mean when he called me?"

"Son, *Padraig* is the Gaelic version of your Christian name and *Chara* means 'my friend'. If the little man called you friend that is all right then, but it wasn't a little man as such, it was probably Matt the faker."

But I'd felt that I couldn't convince my father; and what about the loud noises of the music? Just where did all that come from, the loud music and the many singing voices?

"Matt could only throw one voice at a time, not fifty, father, and he should be on the world's stage if he could really do that!"

"I'll give you another theory, son: remember that Matt not only repairs watches but radios and record players and tape-recorders as well. What you heard may have been tape recording that Matt had taped from one of those Irish ceili music shows on Radio Eireann—you know, the ones you've heard me listening to on a Sunday night? And another thing, son, don't tell anybody, nobody, what you heard last night. Your teachers would only inform the School Authority, and they would make us make an appointment with a psychiatrist for you. You don't want that, now, do you?"

Now I became really confused; my mother had told me not to tell anybody about the little girl ghost at Dickey's corner the other week, and now my father wanted me to tell nobody about that horrible little man last night. My father's perception of him was that either he didn't believe me, if the devil himself had appeared on our yard wall himself, or that nasty little midget was him in person, in all his evil glory. But it had been understandable that my mother and father were loath to talk about things like this, and I was aware of the treatment that Peter had gotten when he's father had been jailed for painting and selling wild birds.

It would be far worse if my mother and I were to end up in a hospital for the mentally insane, if after all we'd just been imagining these two spooky ghosts. The stigma of that would never go away, and we would never live that down. Perhaps all these magical creatures had just been our imaginations working overtime, because of the old, wives' tales in our village?

"Listen son," my father said, "let's just leave things for a week or two, just to see what happens, and if we can catch old Matt Collins at his work, then I'll be proved right, okay? And we can all relax then.

"I'll stay up every night until daybreak... lying on top of our shed to catch him in the act, for a week or two. Believe me, son, there's more to this than meets the eye. Hand me over the little boot and I will lock it inside the sideboard wrapped up in a brown paper bag. That way, you'll be able to sleep soundly at night, with it locked up and me outside on top of our shed."

My father's explanation had sounded plausible, and if indeed old Matt had been messing around he would be spotted by my father, Matt just living two yard-walls away from us. When I thought more deeply about it, it was very possible that he could have done all those things, but I still had doubts in my mind. Matt had indeed lived on his own, and he used an empty bedroom as a workshop. I'd seen it a few times when he was repairing my father's watch. He had everything in there, all sorts of tools, including an electric welder that had looked like a fountain pen with heat coming out of it, and he could have, as my father had mentioned, rigged up some sort of device that shone in the darkness and emitted fluorescent light. He'd lots of spools of electric flex, and dozens and dozens of dismantled radios and record players lying around, with their speakers and receivers lying all over the floor. It would have been quite easy for Matt to rig up some sort of sound system that could run from his back bedroom cum workshop, to the outside of our yard wall.

I'd ran upstairs to retrieve the little boot, unwrapping it from the tangled mass of an old, window cleaner shammy that my father would use for putting brown polish onto his shoes to shine them. When I brought the boot downstairs, before Mass got out, I was astonished. The little boot was spotless, as if it had shined itself clean during the last couple of nights.

My father was surprised too when I showed it to him. "You did a great job, son, you gave the boot a good going over then? It seems to sparkle even more now, and there's some sort of engraving and signs on it that I never noticed before. Look! Those little shiny things on each side of the boot there, shaped like little shamrocks... are they little, green emeralds? And the little figures, human figures beside them... done in white diamonds!

"They look like two Druids of old Ireland, thousands of years before Christianity came to this country... before Christ was even born... and each with a crook or shepherd's stick in their hand, and both are wearing garments of that period, white vestments... bloody marvellous! No wonder the little King of the Leprechauns Cuchulliane... I mean, Old Matt, wanted it so badly!"

The King of *who*, I wondered? What did my father know that I didn't, and what made him say that? But he acted as if I wasn't even there, shining and shining over again the little diamond-studded boot.

"In the meantime, son," he went on, "Jim's father is returning to Dublin this afternoon to get ready for his work in the morning. Tell you what, son... when he returns next Friday I'll ask him to get his lurcher dog out and we'll go up to the old monastery ourselves... in case Matt follows and takes it upon himself to follow you all up there again. We can dig up the old grounds thoroughly, and if anything else of value is there, then we will find it. When we're seen with the hunting dog, son, a spade and a sack, the nosey rumour mill will not think any differently. As far as they will be concerned we will be hunting for rabbits and badgers. And starting tonight, son, I'll keep an eye from the roof of our shed on the entry below and old Matt's back door. If the old fella shows his face with his dirty tricks and contraptions then I'll catch him out this time!

"Cuchalainn indeed! He was talking to the old, wise owl, and the owl told him that you and your friends were digging at the old ruins! Does he think we were born yesterday?"

"But father, old Matt didn't know we were digging up at the old ruins. He may have seen us carrying the metal-detector, but he didn't know where we were going to!"

But perhaps my father had a good point, I thought. Matt *could* have followed us without us seeing him, and then had followed us home again. And it was possible that Matt could have been sitting listening on our yard wall although he was old, and had heard where we'd found the old relic. Our front room window at the back of our house backed onto the yard, and my mother may have left the window open slightly that night.

Monday morning had come too quick for me, as I was very tired after our intense escapades over the weekend. I didn't look forward to going to school in case old Matt had mentioned what had allegedly happened on Friday and Saturday night; but when I'd arrived there after calling for Jim and Peter, I was relieved that none of the others in our class had mentioned anything, although nine of the pupils in our class had lived in our and the adjoining Lesley Street.

But, unexpectedly, we had an unwelcome visitor to our school in the middle of the day. A farmer called Frazer had arrived, along with his sixteen-year-old daughter Samantha. The farmer had around fifty acres of land that had straddled both sides of the Wolfhill Road, and he farmed mostly cattle and a herd of thoroughbred stallions that he would race at Down Royal racecourse just outside the town of Downpatrick, just eight miles from my father's ancestral home of Ardglass. This wasn't the first time that Frazer had been at our school. Last year, Jim, Peter and me had mitched school one day, and we pinched one of the farmer's horses to take it for a gallop on the Wolfhill Road. It had been one of his finest and fastest black stallions with a white blaze between its eyes, but we'd been caught when Frazer had blocked the narrow road with his tractor, and we couldn't turn the horse because it had had no reins. He had come to the school because he had identified our green badges on our mauve blazers, and he'd picked us out in a line-up.

The horse had reared on his hind legs, throwing us backwards. All three of us had been astride the horse, and when we slid off we'd landed in a mess of horse pat that the horse did when he'd reared up on us. We received six of the best from our headmaster, and our backsides had been sore for a week afterwards. We received another six lashes for mitching school as well, and the farmer had promised not to inform the police as long as we promised not to do the same again. And we had to pay the laundry bill for our uniforms.

"Our school's good name and reputation has to be preserved," the headmaster said then, "and if this rustling is repeated I will have no alternative but to expel all three of you—period! You same three are always making trouble for this school, and only the other day Father Lynch caught all three of you smoking and playing cards, five stud poker, behind the church during Mass! Where do you three think you are, in a saloon in the Wild West?!"

Then, we had to apologise to the same farmer, and now it had looked like we would be held responsible for every bad deed that had happened in our village. Now Frazer was standing in the parochial hall with his snotty daughter, and Mr Murray the maths teacher, looking all around them. Frazer's daughter Samantha was wearing her usual riding britches and her tubby face was a mass of freckles, and she'd looked like a coconut, her head covered with a little, black riding hat, that had hidden long, blonde hair that had been tied up in a bun.

Then both of them, accompanied by Mr Murray, had begun to walk up and down the hall, between our tables, while fifty pairs of eyes had followed their every faltering step. Frazer was a big, ugly man, nearly as ugly as his daughter, and all three were staring at Peter, Jim and me intently, with Mr Murray especially, narrowing his eyes and looking over his spectacles. Mr Murray then smacked one of the tables with his hooked cane, making the boys there jump and spill their custard. "Pay attention, boys!" Mr Murray started, his voice echoing around the hall. "It has come to my notice that five of farmer Frazer's stallions were stolen... stolen on Saturday night, and his daughter Samantha here is able to identify the culprits as she was just leaving the stables when she had bedded-down for the night.

"I want all of you boys to sit where you are, and when miss Samantha comes abreast of your table I want you sitting there to stand up immediately. She will have a good look at you and if she can point out any of you to me, then woe betide you! You won't be able to sit down for a week!"

Samantha the coconut then walked down between the tables, with her father, looking us up and down as if they'd been at a cattle auction, and I was waiting on them making an offer for us.

They slithered past our table, Samantha then pausing before she back-stepped to our table again, seeming to know us because they already did, from last year, when they pointed us out then. But I wasn't worried... I knew that on Saturday night I was at home helping to mind my siblings with our next door neighbour, and gladly I could prove that. Finally, after her grand tour of the hall, the coconut had relented—she didn't recognise any of the boys in the hall as having been the rustlers who'd rode off on her father's horses to fight the 7th Cavalry.

She shook her head. "No, none of these boys look even vaguely like the thieves on Saturday night, to be honest, sir," she'd said to Mr Murray, probably thinking she'd been at her own school. "The ones that I'd seen were much smaller than the boys here, and the boys that I'd seen looked as if they'd been dressed as little clowns in a circus, or had worn hallo'ween costumes, and all of them had been wearing wigs, I think, as a disguise, red wigs, the colour of that boy's hair there." She pointed at Peter and another boy in the hall. "They looked more like six or seven year olds, and..."

But Mr Murray had cut her short, becoming angrier now. "Don't tell me you want to see the pupils in grades five and six?" he said, ignorantly, "Just how can kids that age, late on a Saturday night, jump onto five horses and ride off on them? Do you not think you've wasted enough time of this school, and these boys who would like to finish their lunch? They usually take it outside, but not with today's rain. Perhaps both of you could go up to Wolfhill Primary and ask them there if any of their pupils saw anything on Saturday night?" Mr Murray sounded angrier by the minute. We knew that Mr Murray didn't mean to insult Wolfhill school, as relations had always been good with them.

Even during the Coronation of Queen Elizabeth the 2nd, in 1952, Wolfhill had invited our pupils to a party of celebration in Ligoniel Park, and our pupils had waited outside the gates of our school while the Wolfhill pupils had walked down the road and joined up with us, all of us then walking down to Ligoniel Park, two hundred yards further down the road, when Wolfhill had presented all of our pupils with sweets in a china cup, with Elizabeth's head painted on the cups wearing her crown and jewels.

But all this got me thinking again. Stolen horses? Little midgets wearing clothes like hallo'ween costumes? Saturday night when I'd had the nightmare and had heard horses in our back entry? The more I thought about all this the more I was thinking that something strange was going on in our village, and centred around me, and that little, ancient shoe.

Should I take the little shoe back to where I'd found it, and not tell my father and the others?

Chapter Eight

Calling on the Priest for Advice

T HE REST OF THE WEEK WAS UNEVENTFUL, except for the fact that the farmer's horses had still not been found: Frazer had even posted a reward of £500 for the return of his horses, and £1000 for the capture of the rustlers, in the local papers. The villagers had searched everywhere, including on top of the surrounding mountains, but without success. All they'd been able to find were five old, wild donkeys that nobody had ever seen before. Incidents such as this had happened before, but had only concerned a few cattle, pigs, goats and chickens.

Everybody had wanted the reward as things were tight economically, and on that next Saturday night when my parents had gone out for their usual drink, I searched the sideboard where my father had hidden the little, diamond-encrusted shoe, but to no avail, for it had gone. I'd breathed a deep sigh of relief: perhaps, I thought, my father had taken the little shoe back to where I'd first discovered it. He would have some explaining to do to Jim's father though, him thinking that he'd retire from work early soon and make a new career in treasure hunting.

This would enable Jim's father "to remain with his family in the village instead of running all over Ireland and England looking for employment," he said.

"I see, father," I said after he and my mother had returned from the bar, "that you've returned the little boot to where we first found it?"

"Not really, son," he'd whispered to me, in case my mother would find out about the visit from the little, evil midget last week. My mother had been in the scullery making her and my father a sandwich.

"I left it in a safety deposit box in a bank where it would be quite safe... even old Matt wouldn't be able to fake his false voices and music down there."

But I was horrified... no matter what excuse my father made, he was in denial that something strange had happened at the rear of our house last week.

I hadn't been imagining what had happened, and now I feared for my little sister. If he returned and hypnotised me again I'd be powerless if, not being able to get into our house, he would climb down our chimney and whisk her away—that little evil dwarf had been small enough. My father didn't appear to comprehend that, and I think that he actually had thought that I'd been telling lies, that that little creature had only existed in my imagination.

I hurriedly locked our back scullery door from early on that night, making the excuse to Teresa that our toilet chain had snapped and "could we use her's all night?" and she'd fallen for it. After my parents had come home I went straight to bed, this time bringing an empty milk bottle upstairs for me and little George to use as a toilet. Not for all the gold shoes in the entire world was I going back out into that yard tonight.

I couldn't sleep when I put my head down on the pillow, always jumping up and looking through our little box-room window at the yard wall below, now and again looking in on my baby sister in the middle room. I'd brought my catapult to bed with me, and a dozen marbles, but what could they do against a creature that could appear and disappear at will? And could stop people in their tracks by just looking at them?

I'd spent most of the early Sunday morning standing behind the bedroom curtain, listening intently for the sounds of Celtic, Irish, ceili music, for the tin whistles, drums, harps and especially for the clatter of horse's hooves, since I thought our little demon had arrived last Saturday, and wondered how he was able to jump up onto the yard wall from the height of the horse's back.

Then I'd made my mind up: tomorrow I would go to Mass, and when it was over would visit the parish priest, Father Lynch, to get some advice from him about what to do. He had been into things like space aliens and the Little People, and he'd know what to do, if my father didn't. I would ring the bell on the front door of the massive, Victorian house that the priest and his housekeeper, Mrs O'Rourke, had lived in. He would keep a secret, I thought, just like when he hears people's confessions every Saturday night, for Holy Communion during Sunday morning Mass. He would never repeat something that somebody had told him, no matter how implausible or fantastic. The priest was tough but fair, and although he wouldn't take any prisoners if he'd caught us doing what was against the school's or church's rules, he wouldn't suffer fools gladly and would be sympathetic if he'd thought you were not trying to make a fool out of him.

"I'm going to wait a while, mother," I said when the Mass was over, and when the tail-ends of the people were disappearing both down and up the road, I said, "I'm going to call for Jim and Peter to see if they're going round to Wolfhill school playground for a game of football." But the more I'd studied it, the more I was becoming reluctant after I'd made my first Holy Confirmation at our church. Our bishop had slapped me on the face, and didn't know that he had to do that, for that was part of the ritual, and at the time Father Lynch had stood there beside him smiling, letting him off with it.

I'd remembered that day well. It was the day I'd worn a nice, new brown suit and a tie for the first time. Not only that, but when the bishop had confirmed us, we'd all returned to our pews again, with our sponsors. I'd spent at least an hour on my knees, and they'd felt as numb as my hands at the time when Mr Murray had caned us for stealing farmer Frazer's horse the first time. When the Confirmation service was over I'd seen other adults in the church looking over at me and pointing. One had said, "No, he was praying for me, not YOU," while another had said, "Yes... looks like it, he's going to be a priest or the next pope."

People outside the church were coming up to me and giving me money, most in coins but some in paper, and I couldn't work out why I was the centre of all the attention while the other twenty boys were receiving hardly any money at all. Finally, I could stand it no longer, asking Jim and Peter: "Why is everybody giving me lots of money while you get almost nothing?"

"Because," Jim replied, "after we'd said an Our Father, three Hail Marys, and a Glory Be to the Father, Amen, our sponsors had to tap us on the right shoulder to let us know we could sit back on the pew again for the rest of the Mass, but your uncle John had fallen asleep and had forgotten to tap you on the shoulder. Wish I had thought of that—I would have been weighed down with money instead of you!" My uncle John had then approached me. "Sorry son," he said sheepishly, "I was out having a drink and I had too much last night. Here's five pounds for your sore knees; hope the money eases them a little bit?"

After I'd hung around the chapel steps for fifteen or so minutes, I plucked up the courage to approach the priest's house. "Hello, can I speak to Father Lynch?" I asked the housekeeper, Mrs O'Rourke, who was in her fifties and who'd also worked in the school canteen at lunchtime serving the food.

"Why of course, Patrick," she said, probably thinking I was very religious and had missed Confession on Saturday and had wanted another appointment with God. "The Father is just finishing up in the vestry where he's changing into his black uniform. Come into his study and have a seat, he shouldn't be long."

She then left the room, going back to getting the priest's breakfast ready, as I could smell the delicious, eggs, bacon and sausages wafting from the kitchen at the back of the house. It had seemed at least half an hour went by while I sat and waited in front of the priest's large, oak desk. I could see he was well-read, having at least six hundred books in his collection behind his desk on three shelves. And he had his own telephone, something that most of us in our village couldn't afford, having to make do with the bright red telephone box outside the post office that was, more often than not, out of order because some locals had liberated its money box.

I jumped when the massive kitchen door of the large house had slammed shut, followed by a low, murmuring of voices. Then the study door eventually opened, and in strode the old priest, who'd reminded me of Ward Bond, the fella who'd acted the part of the priest in the film *The Quiet Man*, that had also starred John Wayne and Maureen O'Hara,

The priest was a big man, and sometimes he would set up a boxing ring in the parochial hall, to get the boys in our school to learn how to box; if any of the boys would fight in the school playground, or in the village after school, he would hear about it and make the offending for boys to settle their problems in the ring, with him doing referee. Now, he was to act as a referee, hopefully, on a completely different issue.

The big priest stood in the door frame, almost blocking the entire area where the door was. He was well over six-feet tall and broad shouldered, and carried a linen bag that had resembled a pillow case. Then, sinking into the dark-brown, swivelling leather chair behind his desk, and without lifting his head, he began, "Well son, what can I do you for? You wanted to speak to me, yes?" He emptied the white bag out all over the table, where coins, a few money notes and a single cheque lay.

After a moment of silence, he spoke again: "Well? I'm waiting, don't be backward at coming forward. Talk away, son; I'll just be counting the money collected from the collection plate—I have to get my wages too." He lifted his arm and waved his hand, wanting me to start.

"Well... well father, "I... I...," but I'd felt strange because he was calling me son and I was calling him father, while my real father was at home, and he, the priest, wasn't allowed to be married and have sons. "Well... father, I think, I think I've seen a fairy father, a real, live fairy!"

The priest lifted his head slightly, looking strangely at me this time. "Really?" he said in disbelief. "Oh!" he exclaimed, "Do you mean that you've seen your fairy father or just a fairy on his own? Anybody that I know?"

When I laughed out loud, the priest kept a straight face. I'd been told that he was a great joker but even his remarks had surprised me.

"Twenty-four, twenty-five, twenty-six..." he counted, and I took those to be pounds. "Believe me son," he said, "I've heard and seen everything, and have seen much, much more than what you've seen, believe me again, son!"

"Father, no, no, you don't understand, not that kind—I really *did* see a fairy, a little midget fairy!" After half an hour I'd managed to tell the priest everything, and to my surprise the priest hadn't even been a little bit surprised.

He rang a little button on top of his desk and Mrs O'Rourke entered the room quickly. "Mrs O'Rourke, I'll have my breakfast now, and bring the young fella there a glass of lemonade, thank you... and the usual, no sugar for my coffee." After a minute or two, the priest ran his hand over his desk, sending the money clattering into a large opened, money box. "I know your father son, don't I? When he was your age growing up in Ardglass where he'd come every year during the school holidays—he doesn't come to church, does he? Yes, yes, I knew you straight away when I walked in, and I thought you were him and had shrunk... you are very alike, very alike."

I waited on the priest's backlash.

"Your father is a Marxist, son, but I won't hold that against you; you're not your father's keeper... we can't convert them all, and that Karl Marx fella, son? If he had his way he'd be sitting behind my desk there counting the money instead of me. He said that people like me smoked opium, and I don't smoke."

After Mrs O'Rurke had left the priest his breakfast and me my lemonade, the priest finished it quickly, and after wiping his mouth, stood and paced up and down the room. "Now, your little problem of that nasty fairy, son—let us see how we can see it off... and..."

"Then you believe me, father, you actually believe me?"

"Of course I believe you, son. If we are expected to believe in God then we have to believe in Satan and his acolytes, right? There are more strange things in God's heaven and his earth, son, that we can't even begin to imagine, and believe it or not, but I saw an alien spaceship once... through my telescope upstairs in my bedroom. They landed on top of Divis Mountain, and four of them got out and collected plants, lots of plants! A magnificent sight, really magnificent!"

"And the four little green men, father, did...?"

"Sorry to cut you off short, son, but they weren't green, they weren't green at all. And what did this little fairy rogue say his name was, son? What else did he say, and was he solid? Like you and me, I mean? Or was he transparent enough that you could see right through him?"

I'd explained to the priest further what the little man had said about "kidnapping my sister if the boot wasn't returned," and about the five missing horses.

"These little creatures are very devious, son, and there are more angry ones than there are happy ones. They strongly dislike human people if they think humans have stolen something on them, and if you were to decide to chase them for their treasure you will end up with so much more trouble than it's worth."

After the priest had paused, I told him about my uncle Patrick, and how he had encountered an old, evil woman eight years before, and that was why he'd died so young.

"Yes, son, the proper name for them is Faeire Women. Others call them banshees, and some say it's a terrible sight to behold. I remember your uncle's experience well, and it was me who'd suggested that he go to England for a while; unfortunately he got sick over there and came home to die. Tragic... very tragic."

Now the priest had drawn a thick, green-covered book from his collection, hurriedly fingering through it until he came to the page he was looking for. "She could be the ghost of a young woman who was killed violently, and her tortured spirit is left to wander the earth. She watches the remainder of her family and loved ones, and will warn them that violent death will be visited on them too. She will appear as an old woman with long, white hair, with long, sharp fingernails, and would have rotten, pointed teeth. Her eyes would be blood red, and when you look into them it will mean death, either immediate or later."

As I sat there trembling I didn't want to hear any more, and was now sorry that I'd came here, thinking that my little sister was now doomed as the little midget had promised to return for her. I jumped when the priest spoke again. "And what's more, son, these little people can be smartly dressed in small suits and waistcoats, the suits being either a red or green colour, little hats and buckled, very expensive shoes because they are cobblers by trade. They also play tricks on farmers, like turning their horses into useless donkeys, and other people in the villages.

"They're also keen musicians, son, and will play tin whistles, harps and other traditional Irish instruments. They love wild music sessions, and they dance and drink until dawn, poteen, and moonshine, the drink we know as whiskey. They are also called Leprechauns, and their name in Irish is Loacharma'n, or pygmy in Anglo Saxon. They think that humans are greedy, and maybe son, just maybe, Karl Marx the socialist was a leprechaun, because he always thought the same about us Clergymen."

The priest saw that I was now terrified, and he appeared to take great pity on me, resting his big arm on my little, puny shoulder. "I'll tell you

what to do, son. Put a glass of milk and some slices of bread in your
back yard every night, and maybe, just maybe he will leave you alone."
But I couldn't see how so little could placate old Cuchuliann. And
anyway, maybe Karl Marx had been right when he'd said that the clergy
were out of touch with the ordinary people, that read the paper my father
would read, the United Irishman newspaper. Because every night the
rats would be scrambling all over our back entry, and a glass of milk and
bread would last just two minutes.

I had to get the little diamond boot back, and return it to the place
where we'd found it, and quick. Nothing else would satisfy the little
pygmy.

"In the meantime, son, tell Mrs O'Rourke nothing... you have my
confidence in this. And if things grow worse, well, you know where you
can find me. This was a proper Confession from you, and I'll treat it as
such. And don't thank me son, nobody would believe me never mind
you, and I'm a priest."

The priest ushered me off the chair, making the sign of the Cross on
my forehead after sprinkling Holy Water all over me, the best bath that
I'd had in months.

"Don't forget!" he shouted after me at his front door, "And pray,
don't forget to pray... prayer moves mountains, and hopefully it will
move these evil, little creatures," and the priest handed me a little plastic
bottle filled with more Holy Water.

When I arrived home, I asked my mother where my father was.

"You just missed him, son. Jim's father called here, with his lurcher
hunting dog and his polecat ferret... they said they were going hunting
for rabbits today. At least we'll have rabbit stew for supper tomorrow
night—they always bring something back."

But I was delighted that our fathers had gone to the old, monastery,
as long as old Jack Dickey wouldn't spot them. Old Jack was very
puritanical, especially on a Sunday, and he would never open his shop
on this day. He would go to his church service at the village's Methodist
church, and they would return home to patter about in his garden all day.
Hopefully, my father had changed his mind and had gotten the little,
diamond encrusted shoe out of the bank, and would leave it back at the
old ruins.

Chapter Nine

The Old Monastery Ruins

I N ORDER TO REACH THE OLD MONASTERY RUINS, if Jack had been pottering about in his vegetable patch, was to enter the area of the ruins through a bull field that had belonged to another farmer, Andy McBride. Jim, Peter and me had often been in that field, when us and a group of Protestant friends from Wolfhill school had made a verbal pact that we would help each other to chop down trees and gather them for both of our bonfires, the first on the 12th of July for their Celebration of the Battle of the Boyne, and ours for the Feast of our Lady on the 15th of August.

We'd prided ourselves in the fact that we'd been the first group in the north of Ireland, of mixed religion, who'd made such an agreement, and our first targets for our lumber-jacking operation would be that field. There'd been a tiny, wooden mission hall that had belonged to the Pentecostalists, beside the field, facing the village bus station, and we'd all go along on a Friday night to make up the numbers. We hadn't gone just because we'd been religious, but we'd gone for the free bags of sweets that the pastor would supply us with.

We'd sit and sing from a Protestant hymn sheet while eating our sweets and we'd start off with the hymn, Onward Christian Soldiers, Marching off to War, while the parson's wife would play her little organ in the corner of the tiny room. The field had been lying desolate for three years now, but we never found out what happened to the parson and his wife—they were probably playing their little organ in Heaven now. When we would enter that field, Atilla, the big massive bull, would be waiting for us, but I would give it a swift wallop up its back-end with my catapult and it would run off.

Jim, Peter and me had scoured that field, not looking for old Atilla, because he had long gone to the abattoir, but for my and Jim's father and the lurcher hunting dog. They were at a field that contained nearly two hundred blackthorn trees, save for the few dozen stumps that had remained after we'd chopped them down and burned for our two bonfires. This was also the field where Peter's father had sprayed glue onto the tree branches, and was still in prison for his bird-baiting activities. We'd climbed over the steel entrance gate, and sure enough we could see our fathers coming towards us, but running, the lurcher hunting dog trying to keep up with them instead of the other way around, with all three fighting for breath.

"We searched for more treasure at the old ruins, lads," my father gasped, "and guess what, we found an old, ancient leather bag and it contained dozens of Spanish doubloons and they must surely be worth thousands of pounds! But old Jack spotted us and fired into the air with his shotgun, so we lit out of there in case he thought we were breaking into his house for his shop takings and he would call the police!" But my heart sank again—all that trouble I'd gone to, to seek out Father Lynch for his help, and now this!

My father and Jim's father had probably hatched a plan to hold on to the little, diamond-studded shoe, and I doubt if even my father had told Jim's father about the trouble that I'd had with the little pygmy. "Did you not leave the little shoe back there, father?" I asked.

"No son, me and Jim senior and I think that we are on to a good thing here, and we should consider holding on to it for a while to see if we can work something out. Don't worry, it's still in the safety deposit box, and it's safe."

But I wasn't worried about the shoe. The shoe was in a strong box, but we weren't, not me, my sister, my mother and my little brother. And my father could look after himself. What would my mother do if my brother and sister were kidnapped, and never seen again? "Where's the bag of Spanish coins then, father?" Jim asked, now having his doubts as well when he saw no little, leather bag. "At least you got something out of your forage at the ruins?"

"Afraid not, lads," my father interrupted, "we had to bury them underneath one of the trees in the field there, in case old Jack had called the police and they'd searched us on the way to the village... the monastery ruins are protected by law, and if you're caught stealing from it that's even worse than painting and selling wild birds." Then Peter took a fit of blushing, he knowing what my father was talking about.

"But, but father!" I protested, "there are nearly two hundred trees in that field... how are you going to find that place again? And it was nearly dark when we were coming up the hill!"

"That's easy son," Jim's father interrupted, "we wrapped one of our rabbit nets around the base of the tree; we'll find it again tomorrow, no problem. And when old Jack is back in his shop in the morning we'll return here and dig it up again. Wait until you all see, those coins are beautiful! Words are stamped in Spanish on them, and when you examine them tomorrow you'll all have to wear dark glasses to look at them, they are so shiny! And they're probably worth hundreds if not thousands of pounds—we'll be set for life!"

But I was doubly worried now, for no-one here but me had known about the terrible warning that I'd gotten from the creature. I hadn't told my closest friends and I don't think my father had told his closest friend, Jim, either.

Now I'd felt even worse than the time when our headmaster had caught us smoking behind the Nissan huts of our classrooms. We'd been beaten so hard that we couldn't sit down for nearly a fortnight, on both our hands and backsides. What was worse, the teachers had told all the shops in the village to bar us; but the shopkeepers had been innocent because Peter's father, while working in the docks, had stolen cartons of cigarettes as well as exotic birds. He'd given them to Peter to bring to school, and we'd not known then that Father Lynch was a keen astronomer, and it was he who'd spotted us with his telescope behind the huts smoking.

Unknown to us, the priest had tipped off our headmaster, and as we'd not been allowed to fraternise with the girls in our school, they had their own classrooms up behind the chapel; but Peter had taken it upon himself to invite two of them down to join him behind our huts. They had their own rules and regulations, and we were warned "never to climb the steps to their classrooms, under pain of death!"

Peter had slipped his sister and her friend cigarettes, to sell in their class, but the school had always favoured the girls because they would collect more money than us and sell more ballots around the doors of our village for the starving black babies in Africa. When I'd returned home from school at 4 p.m. the next day, my mother had been in the scullery making rabbit stew for our dinner after my father had skinned and gutted the rabbit he'd caught yesterday, before they'd gone to the old ruins, to keep the pretence up and in case "old Matt was watching them."

My little brother George had already been collected from nursery school at 2 p.m. by my mother, and my father had been sitting in his chair staring at the *Irish News* newspaper, but he wasn't reading it. I sat down beside him after I'd grabbed an apple from the fruit bowl in the kitchen.

"Did you dig up the Spanish coins?" I asked my father excitedly. Had he got them in the house? How many were there, and could I see them?

My father didn't reply at first, just staring at me blankly instead for a few minutes before he spoke. He poked the fire again before pouring on another four big, wooden blocks. He was in a deep daze, and he sat there, playing with my little sister's long, blonde ringlets. "The Spanish coins, son," he finally said, "lost, gone, kaput!" he moaned, and I'd noticed that for the first time, his once red, ruddy face was as white as our wallpaper.

"Why, what happened, father? Did old Jack phone the cops after all and recover them?"

"Worse than that, son, and forgive me for not believing you before, but I sure as heck do now! We returned to that field this morning after you all went to school, again with the dog, rabbit nets and spades as cover, and guess what?"

I shook my head as if to say, sorry father, but I'm not a mind reader.

But if he was going to tell me something fantastic, then I would believe him, although I think he never believed me about the horror on the yard wall last week. "It happened like this, son, honest, we counted one hundred and ninety-nine trees, and one hundred and ninety-nine green, rabbit sett nets, instead of the one we'd tied to the tree last night!

Somebody had played a prank on us, and now we don't know which tree under which the coins were buried! Every friggin' tree had a rabbit net tied to its base! And not in a million years could we recognise the tree where we'd buried the little, leather bag! Old Jack Dickey must have followed and watched us, then had tied all those rabbit nets to all those trees! Now we'll never recognise the tree under which we buried those coins, unless we dig all of them up!"

But what my father was saying just didn't add up. Perhaps old Jack had found the treasure first, and had not wanted anybody anywhere near the monastery, because, after all, it had been on his land and he could do what he liked with it. Old Jack had been seventy-five years-old, and no way could he have ran around that field tying rabbit nets to the bases of all those almost, two hundred trees. And anyway, it had been almost dark when we came across them.

I'd read in the *Ireland's Own Magazine* that my father bought monthly about one of the tricks of the little pygmies; if somebody had buried stolen gold somewhere in a field, the leprechauns would do just what happened to my father and Jim junior, in the bull field; the leprechauns would fool you into wasting your time looking for their treasure, then would steal it back when you were suitably occupied. "Another thing, son, and you may not believe me, there was two other things, or was it three?" I nodded, feeling like the time when I was in the Confessional on a Saturday night while Father Lynch was hearing my confession.

Father Lynch would nod his head like I just did while I looked at him through that little perforated, wooden screen that had separated us. After I'd confess, the priest would say: "Go to the Holy altar, kneel down, and say an Our Father, three Hail Marys and a Glory Be To The Father, and if I see you back here again with a tall story like that I will come across your little, lying face!"

"We'd seen some strange things earlier, son, very, very strange, but Jim's father there swore that he saw nothing! As we stood in that deep canyon in the middle of the bull field, I just happened to look up to my right, and you know what I seen? A massive, Irish wolfhound! It was just staring down at us, and even worse, much worse," my father continued, looking around in the direction of our scullery in case my mother had walked in and had heard him, "on its back was a little horseman, or should I say, a dog man? It had sat on a little, green saddle, and it had resembled the little man that you'd described that you'd seen on our yard wall last week, and his garb was green as well. The big dog howled and galloped off when the tiny jockey heeled it in its flanks, and his roar of laughter echoed all through the canyon!"

At last my father was now open to what I'd seen, and hopefully he would recover the little diamond encrusted shoe from the bank vault where he'd hidden it. It wasn't ours in the first place.

"And before I forget son," he continued, "when Jim's father nudged me and I looked up, on the skyline, to the left of me, I thought I'd seen three foxes, two adults and a cub, and they were staring down at us too. They had their heads down, as if they were going to attack us; then Jim's father remarked that they were too large to be foxes and had been the wrong colour. Foxes were red, and these animals were grey, like wolves, and were the same size as wolves. The only wolves in Ireland, son, are in Ireland's zoos, and when I checked with Bellevue zoo in Belfast they'd said that none had escaped. And funnily enough, when the little man and the Irish wolfhound had galloped off, the wolves went too, as if by a signal!" He shook his head. "For God's sake, son, don't tell your mother what I just told you. Old Fearless, Jim's father's lurcher, is afraid of nothing, but when these things had appeared he dashed off in the opposite direction! He was even more terrified than we were."

Things were getting much worse now, and although I didn't like Jim senior's mangy old hunting dog, if the little, evil creatures could steal five fully-grown horses from Frazer, what would they turn the lurcher into—a rabbit?

And Jim's father had also kept a goat in his back vegetable plot in an enclosure for its supply of fresh milk, and he had chickens for fresh eggs every day; they might all now be rode away by the creatures! It had been obvious to me all week that far worse trouble would be coming our way, and these little people were making their presence felt, and stronger by the day.

At the risk of being laughed at by the rest of the class, I made up my mind to find out more about these little people. Perhaps Father Lynch had left something out last Sunday and I was determined to find out more about them. The history class had come round, and I said to Miss Dore, our teacher: "Miss, do you know what leprechauns and other little people are? Are they harmful to humans?"

Miss Dore was level-headed and sensible, and I liked her a lot, and she didn't flinch or laugh when I'd asked her that silly question, in our classes eyes. "I don't want most of you to laugh, boys," Miss Dore said, rebuking most of the boys who were laughing, and her rebuke was followed by complete silence. "Patrick is asking a very pertinent question. These little people exist, and they are never known to age. They are hard-working shoemakers, and can manufacture by hand beautiful little shoes for kings, queens and their subjects. They are exquisite makers of diamond and gold footwear of all kinds, and if you happen to be having a walk along a path in the woods and hear, *tap, tap, tap*, softly, of a little hammer, keep your eyes open—it may be one of the little leprechaun shoemakers at work."

By now the entire class were enthralled, most of them sitting at their desks with their mouths wide open, their chins resting on their hands. It may have been a fantasy fairy-tale to our class, but Jim, Peter and I had known much better. "The little fellas are very fond of a smoke," Miss Dore said, "like some members of our class here who I won't mention," she said looking at us through clear blue, narrowed eyes. "These ancient people use a tobacco that is foul smelling, with a little, clay pipe, which each one always carry about him, and if you smell smoke that reeks of an old, unwashed sock, you will know that one or more of these people are nearby. Furthermore, they were the first bankers in Ireland, and they guard the many treasures that came from the sunken, Spanish galleons, and also the treasure that the Vikings left behind when they raided our churches and robbed our noblemen, many, many years ago." Miss Dore went on: "This treasure was buried by the little people all over Ireland, and sometimes they will spend weeks, months and even years moving it about, in case we humans have seen them burying it. The little people are two different races, one is the leprechauns, the others the cluricaun, and the cluricaun are the most dangerous of the two. They will steal anything, but woe betide you or yours if you steal anything from him or a member of his race, because he will return to where you live and kidnap somebody in revenge, usually a female member of your family, during the hours of darkness. And they will clean out the larder in your kitchen or scullery, and after they eat all that, after the kidnapping you will never see your female relatives ever again; but if you're brave enough, you can catch the little devils before they do any of that, by using strong rat or badger steel-wire traps."

But Miss Dore didn't know what I knew. If these deceivers can tie nearly two hundred rabbit nets around trees in the blink of an eye, then they will know that a trap is being set for them. They confused two grown men when my and Jim's father had tried to take away Spanish doubloons that hadn't belonged to them in the first place.

"When you buy the trap or borrow one," Miss Dore went on, "buy gold and green paint, green if you're trying to trap the little creatures in the countryside, or red paint if in the towns or cities, or the colour of building bricks. Gather some coins, and if they're copper or silver, the gold paint is to make the creatures think that they're gold coins when you paint them. Then get a baby's little shoe or bootee and paint it gold as well; then you put the coins and the shoe inside the steel trap. Don't forget, make sure you paint the steel trap the same colour as its surroundings, and you must have patience, rather like an angler, a fisherman. You may have to hide for days, even weeks or months, and hopefully, when the little devils see the so-called gold coins or boot they will crawl inside the steel trap and spring it, trapping it." She gave us a stern look. "But a serious word of warning, boys, never allow the little captive catch your eye, for if you do, he will hold you in a deep trance, and force you to free him again. Nobody has ever caught a leprechaun or a cluricaun yet, but there's always a first time, but you must be very strong willed to do it."

Again, when I'd returned home from school I could see that my father had been covered in mud and Jim's father was there too. Both had been drying themselves at the fire because it had been pouring with rain, and they must have been out hunting again.

Both of them had looked absolutely exhausted, and my father had been scolded by my mother because both of them had walked thick mud all over her brand new oil-cloth floor covering. She'd bought it the day before from two Sikh gentlemen who'd called around the doors of the village while they also sold knives, spoons, shoe-polish and other odds and ends.

Mother had said to my father the other night, "Why has Jim's father decided to give up his job in Dublin when he was making very good money?" She may have suspected that Jim's father may have been up to something, and she'd worried even more when Peter's father had ended up in prison, as all three were very close friends ever since I'd been brought by a big, stork.

Chapter Ten

The Saddled Hare and the Leprechaun

"HOW DID YOU AND JIM GET COVERED SO MUCH IN MUD?"** I asked my father, and, as usual, he'd waited until my mother had gone into the scullery to make our dinner. It had been rabbit stew again, and although they'd just used hunting as a cover they'd still been successful because they had brought three rabbits home the other day.

"This country is getting worse, son," he finally spoke. "You remember old Jack firing his shotgun into the air the other day? Well, when we went into that bull field today, to try to dig up the Spanish Doubloons, Andy McBride spotted us digging up his field and he, too, threatened us with a shotgun! We'd already dug around nearly fifty trees, and when McBride saw us at first he burst out laughing. When we asked him why he was laughing, he bent over double, laughing again.

"Is this you fella's first time hunting?" he asked. "Don't you know rabbits don't hide up trees after they run up them? Why have you got nets around all the trees for? Are you waiting for the rabbits to run back down again?"

"This little nasty midget is making us out to be laughing stocks, son."

"And guess what?" Jim senior had interrupted, also looking round to make sure that my mother wouldn't come out of the scullery and hear him. "Just before McBride arrived, and after we'd dug around the second-last tree, a large hare ran up to us... and it had a little green

89

saddle and a little rider on its back! Imagine that, a little, midget jockey!"

"Are you sure?" I asked. "You sure you saw a saddled hare and a little jockey on its back?"

"Well, this one did," my father interrupted, the expressions on both their faces a look of shock and disbelief.

But I believed them, although my father and Jim's father didn't at first, but they probably did now. "Did the little jockey say anything, father? Did he speak in English or Gaelic Irish?"

Both of our fathers looked horrified by now, and my little brother and sister had even sensed that something was wrong, sitting on the sofa staring at them. "The little rider, son, the little rider laughed out loud and repeated 'If Pieces of eight! Pieces of eight!' and as you know, son, if you'd seen the film Treasure Island, you will remember the pirate, Long John Silver, saying that... it means Spanish gold coins! And that tiny jockey looked very odd, too. It was similar to the little man that you say you'd seen sitting on our yard wall.

"He wore a little, red cap, like a human's nightcap, and he had silver buckles on his black-painted shoes. The shoes had fine, gold laces, and above them he wore blue drawers up to his knees. He also wore a little, green coat, like a laird's, and had a little red nose, and he was obviously drunk, very drunk! He had a little, clay-pipe in his mouth, and then he pointed an accusing little finger at us, then heeled the hare on its flanks before the hare dashed off! It sped through the bull field in a flash, before disappearing down into the area of the old, monastery ruins. Even Jim's lurcher, Fearless, was anything but, running in the opposite direction... terrified, completely terrified!"

As I looked at my and Jim's father, they had been completely spooked. Once, they had been afraid of absolutely nothing, and their once, well-groomed hair was now dishevelled, and their eyes were black underneath them, as if they hadn't slept for a month. But I felt sorry for them: they hadn't believed me at first, but now they had known what it was like to be terrified. But although I'd felt sorry for them, I'd remembered an old Irish proverb that my mother had told me once: "What goes around comes around," and now it was their turn.

After I'd told my and Jim's father what Miss Dore had said today, about "trapping the little, mischievous cluricaun in an animal trap, using gold-painted coins or shoes to draw him in," both of their eyes appeared to light up. "Now there's a thought," Jim's father said. "If we catch the little guy we could sell him to a circus as the first leprechaun ever in captivity!"

"But, we don't need gold paint or gold-painted coins," my father remarked. "Let's use the real thing and play the little monsters at their own game!"

"Yes!" Jim's father enthused. "I've got a Havalaput badger trap in my shed at home, and we could wait until Friday night. We could then leave the badger trap among the ruins of the monastery. For good measure, seeing that the little fiends are fond of a drink, we can buy a bottle of whiskey and leave it inside the trap along with the little shoe."

"That may work!" my father said, "Old Jack is down in his shop until 10 or 11 p.m. every night except Sunday; that will give us the hours of darkness to try and trap the little pest, and if the midget doesn't turn up on Friday night we can return on Monday night... Saturday is for our relaxing and drinking, Jim."

That night my father and me called at Jim's house on the main road. Their house was the same size as ours, although they had what we hadn't, a large vegetable and shed space out their back. When we went through the house and through the back door we came to a large, enclosure area. A nanny goat stood staring at us when Jim's father had switched the outside light on, and beside its chicken-wire enclosure another smaller area had held a rooster and around a dozen chickens.

The nanny goat was almost the same brindle colours as the lurcher, with black, brown and white patches, but the dog had returned to its shed when it saw us. I suppose it didn't want to be chased by a hare, instead of the other way around. When he emerged from the dog's shed, Jim had been carrying a silver-coloured, green-painted eighteen-inch long cage box, and it was around two feet high. "This guy will trap and hold badgers, rats and even small dogs," Jim senior said, "and hopefully little, mischievous, angry men, who like a drink of whiskey.

"And it can't do any harm to children, but watch your cats though, if you have one, and it opens at one end only, the front or the way in, and when it springs the trap the victim can't turn around to escape because it would have to use its head to get out again. If something goes through that little trap door there, it will trigger a little, trip-bar, and this in turn slides the door down, trapping the animal, or little humans.

"This is so complex that it works like a dream... although, in our case, I hope it won't be a bloody nightmare! Even Peter's father couldn't escape from this one!"

This week this could be the end of our supernatural troubles, I thought. My father had said "that he and Jim's father would go down the Belfast City Bank to get the key off the bank manager and recover the little, golden boot from the safety deposit box."

Peter was disappointed because he said he couldn't make it with us on Friday because his father had sent him and his mother out at visiting time at Crumlin Road prison. His father had found a little, sparrow with a broken wing, and he'd brought it back to his cell to cure it, after he'd read the book *The Birdman Of Alcatraz* that he'd gotten out of the prison library. But we thought that Peter had been too frightened, after the unseen hand, or fingernails, had scratched his back while we'd walked up the old sewer pipe weeks ago.

On Friday evening, at seven o' clock, my father, Jim and his father, had gone on up Curtain's Avenue by another route so that Jack couldn't notice them while he sent me into the shop to get him a pouch of Golden Virginia pipe tobacco. When I'd seen that old Jack had had his hands full, trying to serve customers and stock-take all at once, I walked up towards the old ruins and told our team.

Then we'd made our way along the little, pebble-stoned path behind old Jack's house from the avenue, entering through the rear of Jack's land and towards the little willow-tree forest. Jim senior had carried the badger trap and my father had a bottle of Irish whiskey and the little shoe that had been tightly wrapped with thick, catgut fishing line tied around it. We stopped at exactly the same place where we'd first dug up the shoe, after I'd pointed out the place to my and Jim's father. The large sheet of marble tile that we'd pulled up at first was still sitting in the place where we'd left it, leaning against the top row of the wall of the derelict building.

Another slab beside ours had also propped up the old wall, where my father and Jim senior had found the little leather bag that had been full of Spanish doubloons, and a large crater was still unfilled where they'd dug for hours...

Jim's father had walked across to where the large crater was, poking around it with his blackthorn, walking-stick that he'd fashioned himself with a hacksaw and penknife. Suddenly, the walking stick that Jim's father had been poking around the ground with disappeared, as if it had been snatched from him by an unseen hand. It had fallen between the joints of where the marble slabs had once been, and it had hit something metallic below the ground with a resounding twang. Jim fell to his knees, shining his bicycle torch that he had brought with him between the cracks. He had brought the torch for when it would get dark later on. Then all four of us fell to our knees, each of us taking it in turns with the torch to look under the ground between the cracks.

It had looked like an old, underground wine cellar or a grave vault, and it looked like there were some old bottles and kegs that still remained there. "By any chance, do you think this is an old burial site?" my father asked Jim. "It looks like it's definitely a wine cellar."

"More than likely," Jim senior replied, "because Clonard Monastery in West Belfast still have their burial vault, with dead bodies still interred there, but I don't know about a wine cellar in Clonard, although they would need wine to serve as the blood of Christ at the Masses. Didn't all monasteries?"

"I remember the stories of the village," my father replied, "and somebody said that all the monk's bodies were re-interred, but to where I just don't know. But probably not the old monk called Abbot John. Didn't he go to the USA, and didn't he die over there?"

"Maybe," Jim senior replied. "Isn't that Abbot John who's been seen in the village more times than enough?"

Now I'd worried just what the heck what we were in for here... first it was a banshee; then that little girl at Dickey's shop corner; then the monk was seen three or four times; then the nasty little midget on our yard wall; saddled hares; phantom wolves and now an underground cellar. This cellar could lead to Hell for all we had known.

Intermittently, Jim junior and me would take turns apiece to go back down the little lane to Curtain's Avenue, under our father's advice. "You can see Jack's shop from the avenue," my father said, "and as long as Jack doesn't see any of you, you will see him coming from a mile away." This was just in case Jack may have forgotten something and would come up to the house for it, and he was only one of a few people in our village who had a telephone in his home; and if he'd spotted us, he would have phoned the police, thinking we were breaking into his house.

My father had unwrapped the little shoe that he had hidden in his window shammy, tying it all around with some of his catgut, fishing line. He carefully placed the shoe into the badger trap, leaving it lying down flat beside a bottle of Bushmill's Irish whiskey.

A trap had operated opposite to a trapdoor where a condemned man would be hanged in Crumlin Road prison. While a prisoner would drop down through a trapdoor, a badger, or hopefully, a nasty little midget man, would enter the trap head-first on all fours, trapping the prey inside. The little upright bar would be pushed, and that would spring to life a little trapdoor, that would slide down and clamp shut tightly. Like our foray into the sewers under Wolfhill mill, the captured creature wouldn't be able to turn around. When the trap had been set, Jim's father strategically placed the trap where the little trench had been, where our fathers had dug it up during the week.

If the little cluricaun had watched our fathers digging up his bag of coins he would probably be watching us coming back to the scene of the theft again. We then settled down behind some bushes at the foot of the first line of willow trees at the front of the little forest, my father telling us "to keep quite still, and no loud talking, just whispering and making hand signals." Jim senior had decided to leave their lurcher cross between a sheepdog and a greyhound at home "because although he was called Fearless, the old dog had been anything but," and said that although his blackthorn walking stick had gone, he will retrieve it again tomorrow.

"Old Jack is back in his shop again," he said, Saturday being "his busiest day of the week, when he calls in all the credit he gave out during the week to his best customers." It had been almost pitch dark now, save for the light from my and Jim's father's matches, for my father's pipe and Jim's father's Gallagher's cigarettes. Jim junior would point his bicycle torch close to the ground, switching it on and off occasionally to ensure that it would work in an emergency.

Jim and I jumped when we'd heard an eerie sound coming from behind us. "*Who-O-O...*" and then a clicking sound, like a grasshopper, followed by "*Whee-tuh, whee-tuc, whee...*"

"Relax lads," Jim senior whispered, "that's just your owl friend... he's probably angry because his date has probably jilted him and has run off with his brother." While sitting there on my hunkers, my legs were beginning to numb up, and all four of us now were straining our eyes even more after hearing the owl. Perhaps the owl had been the guard, and the noises he was making were a warning to his little pigmy friend... "Come and get your other shoe, the idiots are here..."

"It's now nine-thirty," my father said, looking at his watch. "We'll give it to eleven, that will give old Jack at least an hour to clear up after he's closed. If we find nothing here tonight, we'll return here tomorrow night, and I'll take a Saturday night off from the pub for a change."

It had grown much colder all of a sudden, although it was still October. A heavy, thick mist was coming down off the Wolfhill Mountain and slowly enveloping our village, reaching up to the old, monastery ruins in quick time. It was as if a low cloud had floated over the village and decided to drop down and rest for the night.

Now we were barely able to see the row of blackthorn bushes and old Jack's house directly behind it, fifty yards away. The mist had steadily crept towards us, and now it had been swirling around the ruins, and the area where our fathers had placed the badger trap. We would imagine all shapes of things forming in the mist, a cow, a horse, a dog and other shapes, the mist rising, then falling, but still no little, angry man turning up for his shoe and his consolation present, the whiskey.

"It sounds like somebody down in the village is having a Friday night party," my father said, "and it sounds like old Eric Mawwhinney playing his banjo too. Would you listen to that great music there... Eric was always a great player... just what is that beautiful tune he's playing?"

"It sounds like the old Irish air, Roisin Dubh... isn't it beautiful?" Jim's father said, jumping back down behind the bushes again.

"Roisin who?" Jim junior asked. "Is she a local? Is she in the top twenty?"

"No son," Jim senior replied, "Roisin Dubh is an old Irish tune and song, about Red Hugh O'Donnell, a great, Irish chieftain, and the song was written hundreds of years ago... and I could listen to that music all night, very, very beautiful."

But I was worried, and wasn't so sure: those familiar goose-bumps and the hair had stood up on the back of my neck again, exactly similar to the night the wee man was sat on top of our yard wall, and the violin... and harp music, and this music, just like the last time, was getting closer and closer.

"What the Hell!" my father shouted out, pointing towards the ruins through the thick bushes, as a mist was now forming into a human shape, a female, human shape.

It was appearing to happen in slow motion, very slow motion, as the form changed into a female, a young female aged about twenty years. Now she was humming beautifully while plucking a golden harp. The harp had beautiful, golden strings, and carvings of Irish animals—hares, rabbits, salmon fish, and beautiful lakes. The young, beautiful girl had worn a long, white dress that had reminded me of an old framed photograph in our house.

It was of my mother's mother when she was married, and she'd worn a white veil, but through the veil, that had half-covered this girl's face, I could see that she'd bright red lips, long red hair down to her very slim waist, and wore a claddagh broach on her right breast. She was floating along the ground as if her legs had been amputated at her knees, and her face, as white as snow, was looking all around her.

"The torch! The torch! Quick... the torch!" Jim's father shouted at him, but Jim had fumbled and the torch had fallen to the ground.

"No! Not yet!" my father countermanded, "Don't switch on the torch yet... not yet! We have to find out if she was sent by the little leprechaun." While he spoke the beautiful apparition had floated to where our fathers had planted the badger trap. We lay down flat on our stomachs now, afraid that the girl would come over to us to harm us.

"Jesus, Mary and Joseph!" our fathers had chanted, "Saint Bernadette, please keep this thing away from us and keep us safe!"

But at least, I thought, although the little leprechaun had terrified me, I was hardened to anything now, after I'd gotten strength from the parish priest after my enjoyable visit. I was still terrified of the girl in front of me, but not as much afraid as I'd been of the little demon. The music she had been playing had gotten louder now, and it would have put to shame the best opera singers in Ireland, even our organist and choir at Mass on Sunday in our chapel. We lay there and watched, frozen and terrified, slowly creeping backwards in case the apparition came towards us and gave us the evil eye.

Then I thought of the poem that I'd glanced at in Father Lynch's study, trying to remember from his opened book that he'd left on his desk:

"Hast thou heard the ancient Banshee at night,
passing by the silent lake,
Or walking in the fields of orchards,
Alas! that I do not rather behold,
White garlands in the hills of my fathers.
The Banshee's mournful wails,
In the mists of the silent, lonely night,
Plainly, she plays the song of death."

Her fluorescent, white dress had reminded me of an old, black and white photograph that hung on the wall of our house above the fire. It was my grandmother, my mother's mother, and the dress of hers, her wedding dress, and this beautiful apparition's, had been very similar, only the ghost's white veil had been dancing like gentle waves on a lake. But there wasn't even a breeze here. This lost girl's voice in front of us was more like a child's, and the soft language came out in words that I'd heard lately, the Gaelic words spoken by the evil little man on top of our yard wall.

"She's singing and playing the ancient Irish song called Roisin Dubh," Jim senior said, "or in English, Dark Rosaleen—isn't it truly like an angel singing? I just wish I had a tape-recorder; we should have borrowed one off Matt Collin's, but then again, we didn't want the Grand Master to know our business, did we?"

"And a movie camera?" my father suggested. "She's the most beautiful girl I've ever seen, bar Patrick's mother, even better looking than those pampered film stars in Hollywood." He paused as he listened. "That harp there alone," my father said, the mercenary showing in him again, "that harp must be worth millions... other people would murder to get their hands on something as beautiful and priceless as that." But I could excuse my father's greedy outlook, for he would often tell me of his poverty—his stricken upbringing when he'd been my age, and things hadn't changed that much for us in our village.

Then the ghostly girl sat down on a wall beside the ruins, her voice and the harp rising to a crescendo now. "I can translate that if you all want," Jim senior said when the girl was singing again in Gaelic. Jim senior had been educated in the Christian Brothers school on the Antrim Road in North Belfast, and one might wonder why he'd become a tradesman because he had the qualifications for something better. On this occasion now the girl had appeared to float over to the place where our fathers had hidden the badger-trap, and the girl had appeared to contort her slim neck, her head seeming to stretch like elastic from her shoulders, as her face pressed up against the trap. She was having a good look while playing and singing, but if she'd seen the little shoe and the whiskey, she'd made no attempt at opening the trap.

Then she rose again, only to sink back again for a second, look, like a trout rising to look at a Mayfly, but rejecting it because it had been a man-made, artificial one, and had appeared to hover over the trap, singing and playing, for at least five minutes, before rising and reverting back to her misty, human shape again. Still, her beautiful voice was punctuating the mist again, growing louder and louder by the second.

"I wonder?" my father said, "Surely this couldn't be a messenger for the little King Cuchullainn, the King of the Clurchain—would he have such power over something as beautiful as that?"

But I would dispute what my father had just said, although I would never answer him back, at the risk of a slap or being kept inside our house for a week for being disrespectful. How can a misty figure, that wasn't solid, spring a solid trap made of steel, I wondered? How could a gust of wind grab something solid, twist a little bar, then open the door?

Chapter Eleven

Rosaleen the Singing Spectre

AGAIN, HOW COULD HER WAIST-LENGTH HAIR and the white, flowing veil be meandering around her, if there wasn't as much as a slight breeze? We knelt up on our knees now, slowly creeping forward to get a closer look at this magnificent, luminous exhibition. We had to be careful because the little, King Cuchullainn, of the Churthain, could change shape, and maybe he, or she, was trying to draw us in to kill us.

Now the girl was dancing and we could see that she'd been in her bare feet. Still, we didn't know if she'd came from Heaven or Hell. This could go on all night, and what if the evil little King was using the girl as a decoy, knowing that me or my father wouldn't be at home? He'd had a clear run to our house, where my little sister would be in bed in her cot this time of the night. He might carry out his threat to "kidnap her, and take her to Hell, and we wouldn't see her again."

"Shall we retreat and back off?" my father had whispered.

"No!" Jim senior yelled, the yell stopping the girl from her dancing and singing, and she looked all around to see where the shouting was coming from.

The apparition turned in our direction, but we'd dropped down to our stomachs again. Gently plucking at her harp, she continued singing.

"I'm not leaving here without our badger trap, whiskey and the little shoe," Jim senior whispered this time. But we would be here until morning if this apparition decided to sing to the bats and the owl for the rest of the night.

"Let's give it another ten or fifteen minutes," my father said. "We can't move anyway."

"Yes, I agree," Jim senior whispered, "and to keep us occupied I'll translate what she's singing from Gaelic into English. Now shoosh... be quiet!"

"*A Roisin, na blodh bron ort na ch as aroilis,*" the girl's voices sung beautifully, "*ta do phardun O'n Roimif agus o, n bPapa agat...*" As hard as I and Jim junior had tried, we couldn't make out a single word of the girl's song, probably because we never learned Gaelic before... but would be learning when we were to go to Saint Gabriel's Secondary Intermediate School on The Crumlin Road in north Belfast after next summer when we'd turned eleven-years-old. The girl's ghostly voice was rising in tone now: "*...ta na braithre ag teacht thar...*"

"What's she singing about! What does it mean?" my father asked impatiently of Jim's father.

"Oh my dark Rosaleen," Jim senior started, "do not sigh, do not weep, The priests are on the ocean green. They march among the ocean deep, and there's wine from the noble Pope, upon the ocean green. And Spanish ale shall give you hope, my Dark Rosaleen! My own Rosaleen! Beautiful," Jim's father said, "truly, truly beautiful!"

But my father didn't seem to be impressed: "Trust a bloody apparition to bring the Pope into this!" my father moaned, "as if the Pope would give a toss about the poverty-stricken people of Ireland! I'll bet if the Pope was here tonight, he'd run over to that beautiful girl and hit her over the head with his mitre! Then he would try to strangle her, before grabbing that gold harp off her hands.

"He would then export it to the Vatican, along with all the great arts and treasures there that the Crusaders and the Knights Templar looted from Jerusalem, when they sacked and burned the city to the ground a thousand years ago! And his Swiss Guard would probably come and murder us too, and steal our little shoe as well, if they knew we had that!"

But the apparition, when Jim senior persisted in translating the Irish song's words, seemed to contradict my father's comments... and Rosaleen seemed to prefer a throne of her own. "Oh my Rosaleen! 'Tis you who will have the golden throne, 'Tis is that shall reign, and reign alone..."

"Do any of you, like Peter," I'd asked the company, "believe in spacemen and UFO's?"

"Well... possibly," my father quietly replied, "I know that Peter's father is a spaceman, why?"

"Well, I do too now," I replied, pointing in the direction of the little gravel path beside old Jack's Psycho house. A brilliant beam of light was illuminating the entire area around the monastery ruins, and as quickly as the light had appeared, the last sounds came from the female apparition... *"Beidh an Eirneina tuiltu dearga 's an speir 'na fuil beidh an saol ina choghadh craorach is readfar chnoic..."*

"Woe and pain, pain in woe, are my lot, night and noon. To see your proud face clouded so, like to the mournful moon," Jim senior had translated, then pointed: "I think she's going, now, look." Jim senior pointed, and as we watched the beautiful girl intently, her beautiful music had ceased suddenly. "Now where is she going?" my father asked, as the girl stirred... then just drained away slowly, like fine sand running through somebody's fingers at the beach.

At the place where Jim senior had lost his walking stick earlier, the girl's legs sunk down through the crevice; then her torso, arms, her harp, then finally her head and hair. How could something that had looked as solid as that and had sounded as heavenly could just drain away into that little, narrow crevice? Why did all beautiful beings like that just disappear from this world?

"Hey! Who are you? Are you all having a bloody drinkin' orgy in there? Turn that bloody transistor radio off... who the Hell invented them anyway!? I'm phoning for the police! Get out of here... now! I have a rifle and revolver here with me and I will use them!"

As we strained our eyes in the lifting mist, I could make out old Jack Dickey. He was wearing his trademark, cloth cap, and a long, beige working coat that had ran almost down to his ankles. "Sure enough," my father had remarked, "he was indeed cradling a long stick-like thing under his left arm, and he was waving the strong torch around with his other hand." I believed that the old man could be armed: he was once a policeman, and during A State of Emergency, which was all the time in the north of Ireland, the police could bring their working tools home with them... their arms and ammunition, because they usually had to buy them themselves—while Jim senior would bring his tools home with him, a hammer, a saw, and a set of screwdrivers. The comparison said a lot about the mentality of our little country, and my father had met Jack for the first time while he and Jim's and Peters fathers, were hunting for rabbits at the base of the Black mountain, when my father had married my mother and had just moved to the village. While all three of them were digging into rabbit warrens, after their Polecat ferret had killed a rabbit and had refused to come out while feasting on it, they'd been tapped on the shoulder by a black-uniformed group of men.

The police, all carrying .303 Lee Enfield rifles and Webley revolvers belted to their right hips, including Jack, had been patrolling the Divis and Black Mountains, guarding the line of electricity pylons that had ran into West Belfast, in case they were blown up. Nobody would have dared to break into these policemen's houses in the village, because they were allowed to bring their weapons home with them for safe-keeping. So when Jack had shouted "I have a rifle here!" we believed him!

"What the frig' do we do now?" my father had said. "We've a chance of being scared to death by that apparition, or if she fails Jack will shoot us!"

"We can't leave," Jim senior replied. "We can't leave the shoe and the badger trap behind, and most importantly of all, the bottle of whiskey! Better to lie here and wait the old boy out."

Then we'd heard a welcoming noise, for the second time, not for the first and second "*Who-o-o...*" followed by the same clicking sound, like a grasshopper.

Then "*Whee-tuh, whee tuh,*" old Jack now taking his cap off and scratching his balding head, looking towards the little, willow-tree forest that we'd been hiding at the base of. Again, with a loud rustling of the tree branches, the white owl, our old tormentor, made a break for it, flying over Jack's head. He ducked down low and it only just missed him.

Old Jack appeared to relax, seeing the great, white bird, which appeared to ease his anger and curiosity. The old man took a quick glance towards the forest and then the ruins before climbing through the gap in his hedge with difficulty, effing' and blinding when a low prickly branch almost took his head clean off. Then Jim and me crept after him, as we'd watched him disappear into the door of his kitchen in his big Phycho house, then switching off the kitchen lights and retiring to his front room. When we'd returned to the ruins, our fathers had collected the badger trap, and as old Jack had retired for the night, so would we.

My mother, Jim's and Peter's would be going out tonight on their own, as we'd all intended to return to the ruins. But this time we would be more prepared, intending to bring our heavy Duffle coats with hoods and Wellington boots, and some sandwiches.

Our mothers would go to a concert in our parochial hall, where usually a showband or a local comedian would play, although Jim's father once said that "Most people in our village were comedians anyway!" although some others would say that our village was full of idiots, just like us, out chasing spectres.

Again, it was Saturday, and Jack would be kept in his shop later tonight, because he would call in all the credit that he'd given out to the shoppers all week. We would be bringing an extra torch, two shovels and a pick this time, plus a larger, hessian sack in case we'd gotten closer to the rest of the treasure.

Our mothers still hadn't cottoned on to what we'd been doing, they just thinking that we'd decided to do a lot of hunting before the winter had set in, which meant that in our village, once the snows started, we'd been marooned into the village for months, because we'd been so high up in the Belfast hills. But Jim senior and my father couldn't get Rosaleen's harp out of their minds, they thinking that it might have been solid gold, or have magical powers.

But despite that, we'd all seen with our own eyes last night how the harp had just evaporated into thin air, or into the crevice in the ground. "We'll bring old Fearless with us tonight," Jim senior had mentioned. "He can run around the monastery ruins while, hopefully, we'll be underground filling our sack, and if any apparitions, devils or old Jack want to kill or abduct anybody, they can take old Fearless… he's a useless brute of a dog anyway! He couldn't chase his own tail! He will definitely make a great decoy."

"If his bark warns of something or someone in the vicinity, we can lie still, down below, and old Jack will think it's just a stray animal, like the owl; better the dog being shot than us."

"Catch any rabbits last night, son?" the voice said behind me, while I was putting the rubbish bin out in the entry to be collected at twelve noon. What a coincidence, I thought, Matt Collins putting his bin out at exactly 9:30 a.m. ... Was he waiting for me to emerge? "You had to be lamping last night? You all got home very late last night, son, or there's no sense in going out, what? You can't see in the dark unless you've the eyesight of an owl, what?" Matt the Grand Master was watching us going up the street last night. I saw him looking out the side of his window blinds, and when we'd returned he'd still been there. "Is your father's friend Jim not working down in Dublin anymore, son? Did he get a more lucrative employment? Win the Littlewood's football pools, did he?"

"Sorry, Matt," I replied, "I've just heard my mother there calling me for my breakfast. Talk to you later." I'd been fibbing to Matt, for I'd already gotten my breakfast, and when I'd told my father what he'd said, when my mother had been out of earshot, my father leaned into the fire, lighting his pipe with a bit of newspaper "We need to change tack, son... and we have to be careful. Matt and his loony-bin friends will be watching us now, especially after I was stupid enough to show him that little diamond boot that I've hidden upstairs."

"And the museum curator, father... we showed it to him."

"That's different, son. He doesn't know who we are or where we live, while Matt lives practically next door to us, just one house away. I would have kept on saying that Matt had tried to frighten you into leaving that little boot back, so he could grab it for himself, but I know you were telling the truth now. But even he couldn't have put on that fantastic apparition exhibition last night; even movies couldn't use special effects like that today—they just haven't got the technology.

"Wasn't that something else, son? Yes, I hope we see more of Rosaleen again tonight son; still not as good-looking as your mother though, and Rosaleen was hauntingly beautiful! Hauntingly beautiful..." He shook his head. "But we need to find another secret way into the underground section of the old ruins, son... think, you and your friends are up around hills and dales all the time—have you noticed any wide sewer pipes or tunnels up there?"

"Nothing that I know of in the bull field father... but there is something strange up beside Curtain's Avenue. We call it the 'ancient mound' in school, and our teachers brought us up there once. It runs from a small field, between Jack's gravel path and Ewart's big mansion, and it's possible that it was an underground tunnel that ran from the monastery when the monastery was occupied by the monks, and the teacher said that the tunnel, around three hundred feet long, was "an escape tunnel in case the monastery was attacked hundreds of years ago."

"Yes, son, the monasteries had them all over Ireland in ancient times, in case the Vikings or savages had attacked. The attackers would steal holy, gold crucifixes, silver and gold cups and even the cooking utensils belonging to the monks; then they would slay them."

"Yes, father, and the mound has a thick, steel door and an old, rusted padlock, the first industrial one, I think. To get inside, we would need a hacksaw and some spare blades in case they break all the time; but what if the tunnel, when it's going in the direction of the ruins, goes through old Jack's cellar? He will definitely have the right to shoot us then if he catches us inside his property?"

"That's the chance we'll have to take, son. Either we clean out these evil little creatures or we'll be cleaned out, proper; anyway, Jack's house wasn't built until hundreds of years after the monastery, so they are bound to have built over or around the tunnel. Anyway, son, we won't be long in finding out, will we?"

But when I'd thought twice about it, I was sorry that I'd mentioned that old, possible tunnel, because it had lain between Jack's house and the Ewart's mansion, in a field near the top of Curtain's Avenue; this could cause double-trouble if we were to be disturbed.

Old Jack, our parish priest, Ewart's house, Doctor Rolsten's and the police station were the only five places that had private telephones in the entire village, and while we would be trying to break into the tunnel we would be within ear and eye shot of all of them. And Matt Collins and his bunch of crackpots, The Society of the Atlanteans, would probably be watching us too, after Matt had been shown the little, diamond-encrusted fairy shoe, although my father hadn't been thinking straight about his evil little organisation when he'd sent for him.

Matt would have known about the legends of the treasure belonging to the highwayman being buried somewhere in our village, but our own little crackpot group hadn't been dealing with a dead highwayman, and didn't consider whether a map may have existed about the whereabouts of his treasure. It was possible that we didn't need a map if we could get into the vault at the monastery, and that may have been the final place of the treasure. But something was wrong—the little pygmy fella never returned to our back yard since that first, terrifying night. Perhaps the little man had been a psychic or a mind-reader, and he could read us from a great distance. He would then know that we would come looking for him, or the highwayman's treasure sooner rather than later, and it was possible that he would be lying in wait for us.

What if he'd returned last night while we were up at the old monastery? What would have happened to my mother, or my little brother and sister, if they'd ventured out to the back yard to use the toilet? My father had decided to hide the little shoe up in his bedroom for tonight.

He had to hide it carefully, he said, and well out of sight, because Teresa "would be looking after the youngsters, as she would any other Saturday night." But, for the first time, I would miss my Saturday night snacks as Teresa had minded us for the last three or four years.

My friend Jim and his father had called for Peter earlier that evening. Peter had lived just across the main village road from them, in Lever Street, a little street with just twelve houses in it. The little terraced houses had been paid to be constructed by William Ewart for his workers, with the mill just a stone's throw from them. They would make their way through a small, vegetable garden from there, then would go along the bank of the little river that had kept the mill going for over a hundred years. Then they would cross the narrow but deep river, walk across Curtain's Avenue, before joining us beside the ancient earth mound.

The mound had looked like a large, soup dish turned upside down, it being ten feet high. A little grassy knoll ran down to the locked steel door in front of the mound. The padlock had looked like it had been there for two hundred years, and would take the strongest of efforts from both my and Jim's father to get this door opened, even if they'd had fifty hacksaw blades.

We'd all sat down, with our backs to a thick, oak tree. As we looked over the village the thick clouds that had threatened rain had been dispersed by a gathering breeze, blowing the clouds away towards the Divis and Black Mountains and on into West Belfast. It was around 7:30 p.m. when Jim junior began to unpack the jumbo-sized, hessian sack that had once been a coal bag. "Two torches," Jim junior started to count as he implied the bag's contents, "two spare batteries, one pick, two spades, five packets of biscuits and five bottles of lemonade, and an extra-strength pair of binoculars that my father bought me for my birthday last year."

"And I have," Peter began, "…and before I forget... my father told me to tell you all he was asking about you, and don't be trapping any of his birds in the bull field... a spanking new pair of spectacles, and one cricket bat in case we're attacked later tonight!"

"And I have," Jim junior said, "five Mars bars, and five packets of Tayto potato crisps."

"And I have," I said, "two packets of sandwiches, five Craft cheese and five of corned-beef."

"And I have," my father said, putting his hand inside the right pocket of his combat jacket, "myself, and a packet of fizzy Love Hearts, in case our Sweet Rosaleen shows up again tonight, and you will all have me as well. I will grace your presence with my good manners and handsomeness, and Patrick's mother doesn't call me Elvis Presley, Mark Two for nothing! I am here to guide and protect you all, to keep you all safe, and out of harm's way."

My father said "Shoosh! Somebody might hear YOU," when we'd applauded him enthusiastically; then he pulled the hood of his coat up around his head in case somebody came along and recognised him. "*Woof! Woof! Woof!*" old Fearless went, his ears shooting up, as if to say, I'm here, don't forget about me, probably just scenting the beef sandwiches in my denim, schoolbag.

"You ain't nuthin' but a hound dog, a cryin' all the time!" my father sung, mimicking Elvis Presley, because the Elvis song of that name had just gone to the top of the record charts.

We all headed down to the front of the mound and the heavy, steel door, and we could see, when we shone the torches, that a thick, iron arm ran along the length of the four-foot wide door, vertically, from left to right, and at the end of that was the biggest padlock that we'd ever seen. The bar of the padlock ran through a holed bracket that jutted out, while our fathers got the hacksaw and blades ready. Jim senior picked a spot on the padlock and sawed furiously. Now and again, my father dripped WD40 onto the hot metal, the sound of the still rasping, squealing of steel on steel piercing the fields and little forests all around. Jim's old mutt had run off when he must have heard a rabbit, badger or a fox around somewhere, like Peter's eyes, although the mutt hadn't been a great hunter; he had just been a nuisance, just like Peter. Jim senior had stopped sawing, when we'd all heard the mutt screaming and whimpering, and thought he may have broken his leg in the darkness while chasing something; it sounded like it was coming from around four hundred yards away, from the direction of the bull field where we'd buried the old Spanish doubloons.

I looked all around me for anybody who could hear the dog, noticing that the village was quiet, as some people went about their business, to the shops or the five pubs and one parochial hall in the area, while a solitary London-type red bus had sat at the bus terminus, facing the now derelict Pentecostalist hall. Jim senior began again, then pausing now and again to listen for the dog, while the stench of the burning steel had become overpowering. An echo was coming from the other side of the door as he sawed, letting us know that the tunnel hadn't caved in.

"It's going! It's going!" Jim senior shouted, while my father changed over from him, now sawing more frantically, Jim senior raising his tired arm up and down to get the blood flowing into it again. But we could not tolerate the dog's squealing anymore, all of us more worried now.

"Let's all go and see what's wrong with the mutt," my father suggested. "We can't work with all that howling going on!"

All five of us ran up a little, narrow dirt track in the direction of the bull field. Old Jack's house below was in total darkness, and there was no sign of life coming from the direction of the Ewart's house, although they were known to have two German Shepherd, watchdogs. The yelping from Jim's dog was getting louder and louder now, but for much longer, us now thinking that he'd stumbled onto a fox or badger, metal trap, a nasty trap that was fitted with great ugly steel teeth.

We'd left our working tools behind us lying on the ground except for the torches, running straight through a thick, evergreen, row of bushes, arriving at the top of the seventy-foot high canyon where the dog's yelping was coming from, and where my father and Jim had lost the gold, now disappeared, coins.

"We're at the exact spot," my father remarked, "where we saw that little man sitting on a little saddle, on the back of that big hare... right here on the skyline seen from down below there."

We'd all dropped flat on our stomachs, as Jim's father had dived down and said, "Kill the torches! For Christ's sake, kill the torches quickly!" I had a bad feeling about this—this may have been the trap I was worried about, and my feeling was that this little treasure hunt was to swing the other way around, us being the hunted.

Then we slowly crept towards the canyon's edge, carefully looking over. That music again... the same music that I'd heard in our back entry last week, was getting louder by the second! My father could hardly breathe, the pipe smoke catching up with him as he wheezed and coughed, putting his hand over his mouth so as not to give away our position to whoever was below there. Again, another terrifying yelp, and when we crawled closer to the edge and looked over, we gasped because we couldn't believe our eyes.

Two old-fashioned metal beacons were ablaze, lighting up the entire canyon—it looked like a party of some kind was about to start, us thinking it was the travelling people who would sometimes rest up in a field for the night. But these were no travellers—they were too small, much too small. Shadows of various kinds of animals and tiny people were dancing around the canyon walls, and along with the trees there, everything seemed to move. Little people were playing, and were dancing themselves, with the sounds of Irish bagpipes, fiddles, harps and tin whistles. A little old woman, tiny with long white hair and wearing a red dress almost covered by a blue cloak around her shoulders, was handing out something to the little men.

"We have to get closer," my father suggested. "Nothing can be seen from this far up."

"No!" Jim senior said, almost shouting, "We were almost shot the other night. If we go down there they'll throw us on top of those beacon fires... let's watch from here, it's safer! Safer because I've my binoculars around my shoulders here. I thought they would come in handy!"

Chapter Twelve

The Leprechaun's
Furious Gathering

"**W**HAT CAN YOU SEE? What can you see!?**" the rest of us asked in unison as we could make out movement down below in the canyon, which looked as if it had been a massive bomb crater that had been gouged out of the ground by a misdirected strike from a German aircraft when they'd bombed Belfast during the Second World War.

"I'll let you all have a turn in a minute, but this is madness, utter madness! Listen, that's our dog Fearless down there, and it's saddled up... friggin' saddled up! Complete with a little, green saddle with a stirrup and reins to match. Animals of all types are lined up, and at least fifty, maybe more, little people are putting saddles onto at least thirty different animals! This is friggin' madness!"

"There's a little, white-haired woman down there," my father said when Jim senior had passed him the binoculars. "The woman is running up and down, stopping now and again to milk the cows and a tan, black and brown nanny goat... *your* goat, Jim, and I see five sheep, and the biggest four-horned ram I've ever seen in my life, with four reindeer-like horns! Some of the little men are putting saddles onto all the animals, and then mounting, and the woman again is pouring a white liquid into little gold and silver cups, from a larger, golden jug... Wow! And I can also see five old broken-down donkeys, like the ones we found up the hill when farmer Frazer had his thoroughbred horses stolen the other week."

"And there's old Ramrod!" I shouted to Peter and Jim junior, "You remember, the horny ram that followed us all along the Hightown Road, when we searched Cammoney Cemetery for Naois O'Haughan's treasure last month?"

"Get down... quick! Your dog's staring up to us, Jim—he must know we're here, he must have heard or scented us!" my father whispered, and my father had sounded like Michael O'Hehir, the racing, sports commentator who was on every Saturday afternoon, on Rte Sports, the Republic of Ireland radio station.

O'Hehir had prided himself on being the fastest talking commentator on radio or TV, but after hearing Jim senior and my father, I wasn't so sure that O'Hehir didn't have any equals. "There's our racing hare and the little man who laughed into our faces!"

"Pieces of eight! Pieces of eight! Up here the other day," my father said. "He's just rode into town on the hare's back again. He's dressed like his little friends, red suits, little green waistcoats, little, red nightcaps and black, buckled shoes. And that little, old woman again— she's pouring clear liquid into the gold and silver cups again, that the rest are drinking from... looks like clear alcohol to me."

The priest had been right, I thought—these little people enjoyed their parties and their illicit drink, if that's what it really was. Probably the same kind of alcohol that Jim senior would bring from my father when he returned from Dublin, every Friday night, called poteen here, or moonshine in the USA, and I heard my father saying that it was ninety per cent proof. As we watched we could see that a little man was marking out a racing track with sawdust or lime around a large, hawthorn tree that had sat in the middle of the grassy canyon.

I pitied Peter, because he was hugging the ground, while trying to put his hands over his ears, trying to drown out the Irish and Gaelic music that was now building to a very loud crescendo, that was echoing around the canyon sides and floor, driving this bunch of unusual little people into an out-of-control frenzy.

"Have they gone yet? Have they gone yet?" Peter would moan, and I'd wondered why he'd brought his cricket bat with him. Peter must have been the human equivalent of old Fearless, pretending to brave but when something happened would run in the opposite direction.

But this was Peter's father's fault, because his father had spent more time in prison than he did at home, and Peter, our friend, was timid, too timid for his own good. I looked down to the foot of the canyon when it was my turn with the binoculars. "That little woman down there," I said when I adjusted the binoculars, "she looks like the little woman spook that our uncle Paddy described to our mother when he'd been scared stiff, eight years ago," and as I zoomed in there I could see that she had the same long, white hair; she was swearing all the time, and had long, painted fingernails and rotted, pointed teeth when she opened her mouth to shriek! She sounded awful, terrible! Her red, bloodshot eyes were rolling in her head, and she looked at least a thousand years old! She was screaming at the terrified animals, as if she was telling them and the little men what to do or else! Carefully, I edged down the side of the canyon, resting on a thick, bent branch that was jutting out of a hawthorn tree, twelve or fifteen feet from my father and friends, while they urged me to "watch out, and go no further!"

But I was mesmerised, and couldn't take my eyes away from the frenetic, unbelievable scene below. Before long even the white owl was saddled, while a tiny jockey sat on a silver saddle on its back. Jim's rooster and chickens all wore saddles as well, and they too, wore little saddles and bridles, being mounted by what now looked like drunken little men.

They'd all been flapping their wings furiously, chomping at the saddle's bits, rearing to go, some of them taking off and landing again like miniature, silent helicopters. Now even the full, bright moon, appeared to be looking down at the scene intently, while I could have sworn that I'd seen a little flash of light on the inside of the moon's right eye, like a twinkle. The little King Cuculainne, who was on our yard wall last week, appeared to be throwing little stones at his mounted friends, until I adjusted the binoculars to see that the stones were gold coins.

They probably were the Spanish doubloons that he'd stolen back from my and Jim's father, and green, emerald jewels, that he'd taken from a little saddlebag on the side of his saddle. Another little man had appeared to be taking bets from the rest, writing numbers down on an ancient, parchment-like scroll with a feather quill after dipping it into a little, inkwell, or a gold cup that had appeared to contain ink or some other liquid. Now other riders had ridden into the camp, mounted on five fat pigs that were snorting every time the five little men smacked them with horsewhips, these animals also rearing up on their hind legs.

These little jockeys had been wearing a different dress from the rest, each with black, swallow-tail coats, green waistcoats, red breeches and white stockings that ran up to their tiny knees, and wearing little, black-painted shoes with buckles. The leader of these new arrivals carried a little, golden sword, and he wore seven rows of gold buttons at the front of his coat, with seven buttons to each row.

Some of the little women were cradling what looked like tiny babies in their arms, little long red-haired children, while the mothers were milking the cows to feed their babies with, out of what had looked like animal skin water bottles. These tiny children were dressed in jet-black baby clothes, and appeared to be very ugly and horribly deformed. While their mothers were feeding them, other little women who hadn't any children had been dancing wildly around the beacon fires while holding hands to form a ring. *"He-haw, he-haw!"* the five donkeys bellowed, *"He-ha, he-ha!"*—setting off the rest of the animals while Jim's lurcher howled like the last wolves in our village, knowing that their time might be running out. At the same time his rooster went *"Cock-doodle-do!"*—perhaps thinking it was early in the morning instead of in the evening.

The little people had been dancing and singing in the Gaelic language, not that I'd understand. *"Aynia! Aynia!"* they'd screamed, *"Aynia!"*—all bending down in homage to the ancient woman who'd been giving drinks to the rest.

"That was Aynia... the queen," Jim senior had said when I returned to the skyline at the top of the canyon wall. "One ugly woman, isn't she?"

"I wonder what happened to Rosaleen tonight?" my father had asked.

"Rosaleen was probably a good apparition," Jim senior had replied, "but those ones below there appear to be the evil ones... and their children! I thought I was ugly when I was growing up! They are probably from two zones in the stratosphere. Rosaleen is from Heaven and the ones below are really from below—Hell!"

But I'd wondered how we'd get out of this one, and we couldn't lie there all night either. It had been scary enough when we'd seen Rosaleen, and it was certainly as terrifying as this when we'd seen old Jack cradling his rifle threatening to shoot us with it.

"Listen lads," Jim senior whispered, "I have a plan... but we have to be like lightning here." We'd all crawled around Jim senior in anticipation. "Old Fearless, my dog, knows a secret Signal whistle that I use when we're out hunting for rabbits. It's a high-pitched signal that farmers use to give their sheepdogs, signals to round up their sheep, and Fearless is a half-sheepdog, and before I bought him from a farmer on the Seven Mile Straight Road, the farmer had already taught him this signal while he was still a puppy. Hopefully when I whistle it, the dog will hear and they won't. That will give him a chance to throw his little rider and run up that steep bank there, in the canyon. But we have to be fast on our feet, because when the dog escapes these little monsters will be on his tail, and ours! Now, get up and get ready to run, back the way we came. Patrick's father and me will take the torches, one at the front, the other at the rear. Come out into Curtain's Avenue and head straight for the village where there will be other people about, but never breathe a word about what we saw here tonight—they'll only lock us up and throw away the key!"

"But...but... what about our tools, sweets and sandwiches?" Jim asked his father.

"Don't worry about them," Jim senior replied. "They'll keep until we return on Sunday night. We still have some unfinished business when we get into that tunnel—that's if we all get out of here tonight, all in one piece, and with none of us missing! If we don't hurry up we'll end up on top of those beacon fires, or will be turned into one of those ugly little kids! And the King's spouse, my God! If your mother had looked like that, son, I wouldn't have married her!"

Then Jim senior put his fingers up to his mouth, as if he was about to play a flute, and although he blew on his fingers, the rest of us heard absolutely nothing. But the dog had, as we watched, and so did the rest of the animals. They all reared up on their hind legs before upending all the little jockeys, and while the animals ran mad around the beacon fires Fearless had taken off in our direction, running and panting up the side of the canyon. "Ready lads? Then let's go! Now!" But we didn't need to hear a second prompting from Jim senior—we were all off and we had already left him behind!

As we looked into the canyon as we ran, we could see that most of the little men had lifted themselves up again, running around to catch their strange riding mounts, as the ugly old Queen jumped on the owl's back and kicked him in the flanks to get him to fly off after us. Suddenly there was the sound of a hunting horn, similar to the ones that the Landed Gentry would use when they guided their foxhounds onto the scent of the poor old fox, us knowing now what the fox had felt while being pursued by us.

We'd reached the gap in the hedge at the end of the bull field, and the three of us had gotten through first, Peter, Jim junior and me, but were horrified when our fathers shone both torches behind us. The thunderous thump was like a stampede of bison from a Western film. Fearless had already ran past us, but others, the owl, the chickens and the pigs, were almost up to us, the owl now swooping low, its talons tearing into Peter's hair as he was the last of us at the rear. "My spectacles! My spectacles!" Peter had yelled, and when our fathers stalled and shone the torches at him, he was falling down to his knees, feeling around the field for his glasses. The old, cackling woman was leaning down trying to grab us all by the hair, while she'd dug her heels into the owl furiously, her red fiery eyes like coal embers staring at us. Then, when we'd reached a barbed-wire fence that had surrounded Ewart's land, the ram was butting us from behind, and the little man on board it was cursing and swearing profanities.

The saddled chickens were at our heels now, nipping at our legs, and the donkeys and sheep were also coming up fast, trying to fell us by nudging at our backs. "The fence! The fence!" my father had shouted, "Jump over the wire fence!" At the same time both of our fathers had tried to grab Peter's outstretched arms. Most of us had gotten over, but Peter had flown over our heads when the ram butted him in the posterior. He landed in a crumpled heap just in front of us. Finally we were clear, and when we'd reached the gate beside the Ewart's mansion the owl still came on, only to be met by Billy McCready, the Ewart's groundsman. He had two massive German Shepherd watchdogs in tow, or they had him in tow, both black, brown and tan coloured, but they pulled away from him, going backwards when the owl continued to swoop at us and the others chasing, and ran back into the darkness from the direction in which they'd came. McCready had beaten the owl off with his thick, blackthorn stick, while shining his torch into its eyes, which had made it retreat and fly back again.

The rest had gone quickly, as if they'd been picked out of the air, similar to a film projector in a cinema when the projectionist had suddenly switched off, leaving a blank screen, or scene, and I was waiting on us to shout, "We want our money back!"—as we did when that happened at the Saturday morning matinees at the Forum cinema in Ardoyne.

"That's the first time I've seen an owl attack a human!" Billy McCready had said, and when I looked at him up close I could see that he was a big, burly man. All of us would see him, dark-haired and broad shouldered, at the police station in front of our school. He'd double-jobbed, being a part-time policeman apart from his job on Ewart's land, and we would often see him at the barracks putting up or taking down the Union Jack flag, when a member of the Royal Family had had a death, birthday or a Coronation. "Were you doing a bit of rabbit lamping, lads? Or is that owl after you because you were trying to lamp it?" Usually, this big guy would turn a blind eye to us and our fathers doing a bit of hunting or fishing on Ewart's land if we were to give him a rabbit or trout to go with his dinner. "I came out when the electricity in the house failed; luckily for me the boss has gone overseas and the house is unoccupied. This isn't a single fuse blown, though, the entire house is in darkness, and the whole electricity box has blown... unusual, very unusual."

I was wondering why my father was prodding me in the back, he probably seeing that I was trying to interrupt the big fella; but probably he didn't want me to put my foot in it about the strange little people. But it had been too late, and the question just flowed out of my mouth.

"Mister... did you see, see that little evil woman on the owl's back? Or all the animals that had been chasing us, and the little saddles on their backs?" I was surprised because the big fella hadn't been surprised, or didn't laugh at me.

McCready studied me for a while before taking off his big, deerstalker hat. "Well... I'll be honest, son, I've seen some strange things as I patrolled this place, and one night, when I was coming back from the pub, I'd thought I'd seen a beautiful, red-haired girl, and she'd been wearing a wedding dress and a veil, and I thought that her and her husband had been fighting after her wedding that day, that she had second thoughts and had walked out on him! But although she'd looked sad enough, she'd sat at the side of the road to the house there, and was playing a musical instrument that I took to be an old-fashioned harp. But I think I had too much Guinness taken, and didn't know if I was imagining things or not." He paused, thoughtfully. "But I wouldn't be surprised at all, son, because lots of people in our village have seen strange things too, like a ghostly monk, and a highwayman who rides a red-eyed, demon horse. So I would be more open-minded about all that than the average person... and no, to be honest, I never seen, what did you call it, a little evil woman on the owl's back; but yes, I saw the white owl attacking you, no doubt about that, son! You know, lads, one night I was patrolling the avenue there one rainy night and guess what? I actually seen the monk everybody was talking about then, around fifteen years ago, during the Second World War. He walked down the avenue, you know, before turning up towards Mill Avenue, past old Jack's shop. He was completely silent, and as he walked along he had his hands stuffed up the arms of his robe. As I seen him, he appeared to have two holes in his eye sockets where his eyes should have been... scared me witless, I'll tell you! And I couldn't see his feet—he just drifted merrily along; unbelievable it was! He'd appeared to be looking for somebody, looking into bushes and over walls, and when I'd turned away to look for my dogs that had ran off, when I looked back he had just vanished, gone, like a puff of smoke! And guess what? The next day a young mother and her baby were pulled out of Bodel's dam there—you all know it, you fish in it—because her husband had been killed at Dunkirk, because when he'd left to go to war his missus was pregnant, and he never got to see his little baby. Sad... very, very sad, what? Since then, lads, a ghost of a young woman has been seen around here, and a little baby still has its arms wrapped around its mother's neck."

We'd just stood there open-mouthed, listening, and I was glad that we weren't imagining the things that were seen by us—we weren't just going mass mad. He would have to be believable, the big caretaker, holding employment such as his. He'd even mentioned the missing cows, which had probably been kidnapped from the land he was guarding, and he had been a part-time policeman as well.

Then McCready suddenly stepped forward, walking among us while shining his torch. "Nice lurcher lads," he said, "but do you usually put a saddle on him to ride him through the countryside while lamping for rabbits? Do you take him for a gallop instead of a race?"

Unknown to us, old Fearless, when he'd run off terrified, had returned after the little creatures had gone, silently walking up behind us. The little, green, velvet saddle had still been tied to his back, while little, golden bells had hung from the saddle all around its edges, and the reins had still been around its neck.

"No, not really, William," Jim's father had replied, "we always give the kids in the village a little treat now and again, and give them little rides around the village; it keeps them off the dangerous, main road. There's too many cars on the roads now, as you know, and I counted at least twelve this morning alone. We had him out with the kids during, the start of the weekend, but I'd forgotten to take his saddle off. We bought it from a fella who worked in a circus and trained miniature ponies."

"Tell you what, Jim," William had replied, "don't sell that little saddle there; those little, gold bells must be worth a fortune alone... that fella in the circus robbed himself blind!"

After tonight, I'd thought, all of us had been fools, and our luck couldn't hold out like this much longer.

Now we were to be saddled with another souvenir from our run-in with the evil little horrors, and had suffered nothing but bad luck since we'd picked up that little, fairy cobbler's shoe.

"Are you fellas going my way?" William had asked. "I'm going down to Jack's shop to buy a lot of fuse wire, an ordinary spool won't be enough, as the entire Ewart house's fuse box has been completely burned out. It's still only nine forty-five, and he'll still be open for another fifteen minutes yet."

Jim junior had tied the belt from his jeans around his dog's neck in case he ran off again, and held onto it like grim death. We hadn't got a good look at the little bells around Fearless' neck, and if they were gold, we would have another ancient relic to defend later on.

Chapter Thirteen

The Visit of the Monster called Grogoch

WHEN WE REACHED THE VILLAGE and Dickey's shop, the shop was in bedlam. Scores of people were clamouring for candles that Jack would occasionally stock for emergencies such as this. All the street lights in the village had inexplicably gone out, and when we'd looked around, all the homes on the main road's lights had also gone. All of Jack's customers had also been asking for fuse wire, and Jack himself had had two burning candles burning while stuck to his big, long, wide oak counter.

"There must have been a short-circuit around the main electricity transformer beside the underground reservoir, just above the bull field," Jack had theorised. "We had to shut the transformer off completely when the German bombers came over in '42, because some people had forgotten to turn their lights off." Lots of people, men, women and children, were running around the road, with some shining torches and with others cupping a hand around a candle flame trying to stop the slight breeze from blowing them out.

Car owners had positioned their vehicles in strategic places so that people could see what was going on, by idling their car engines and leaving their full-light beams on, to try to light up the entire village, main road and the side streets. The bars had been emptying quickly, the patrons walking up the road from the parochial hall and the other two licensed premises, while scores of people had walked down Ligoniel Hill, after the two bars up there had had to close because they, too, had been blacked-out.

"I hope one or two of the public house proprietors haven't been selling alcohol to teenagers again!" Billy McCready roared, "I'll get all the trouble of having to explain this, because the little brats short-circuited the transformer before when they threw beer all over the dynamo inside after they broke into it, two years ago!" But all five of us had known that brats had indeed short-circuited the electricity supply, but it hadn't been human brats as, at the same time, a patron of the parochial hall had told McCready that "not only had all the light bulbs blown, but all the fuse boxes had caught fire for no reason, as if there'd been a power surge and not a short-circuit of the system." Ewart's, Emerson's, Wolfhill and Glenbank mills had worked on with their night shifts there, as they had their own, diesel-run transformers.

Soon, word had spread that the problem had been so serious, because of the welfare of the younger children in the village, that the Electricity Board would be sending a team to repair the transformer and the damaged fuse boxes in the village; but it would take more than one team to complete the work, because the damage had been so severe. Then we were visited by a motorcycle policeman. We'd christened him Durango, after a well-known motorcycle racer who would race in the nearby circuit at Dundrod, where we'd all go to watch the races every August with our fathers during the school holidays.

"All people are to beware, or else stay indoors!" he yelled from his megaphone. "Most of the farm animals have escaped from the seven farms that have surrounded the village, and if any adult would like to volunteer to help round them up this would be very much appreciated!" This policeman had been our favourite cop: if he'd caught us playing cards or running a tossing school for coins he would ignore us, but when he'd seen the adults playing for paper money he would confiscate the money and give it to the wives or mothers. The women had done a secret deal with Durango when they'd asked him: "Don't allow our husbands or sons to fritter away our wages in gambling our housekeeping money, or drink it away," and he would always keep to his word and stop it.

Nobody got to bed that Saturday night, and instead of having to listen to the drunks fighting or singing on our streets as usual, we'd have to put up with stampeding farm animals all night. Goats, sheep, horses, cows and chickens were running around everywhere, and some people would be up all night until Sunday afternoon, until they'd finally managed to round the animals up.

Now we'd had a chance that Sunday to examine the little saddle that Jim's dog had failed to shake off. My father and me had called into Jim's house after dinner, and glad to say Jim's animals had been found on the Seven Mile Straight and rounded up, but their little saddles had disappeared. The animals had had a terrifying way about them, all of them running around and around in circles in their paddock, as if they'd been severely traumatised. They wouldn't eat or drink, according to Jim junior, and as we stood watching her, the nanny goat was running at the outside toilet wall and banging its head repeatedly.

The little saddle had looked beautiful though, when Jim senior had recovered it from the dog's shed, Jim trying to hide it from his wife the way my father had hidden the little shoe from my mother. The velvety-green saddle had two little leather pouches, one on each side, and when Jim opened the first pouch the little bells gave a beautiful, ringing sound. Jim withdrew a little square-shaped green bottle, and when he'd pulled the little cork out it had contained a white powder, like the talcum powder my mother had used on my little sister while changing her nappy.

"This must have been the potion that the ugly little woman had mixed with the little people's drinks," Jim senior had surmised, "and it's probably some kind of mind-altering drug... like the magic mushrooms that would make people mad when they'd eaten them, after thinking they were real mushrooms." Jim senior then poured a small drop onto his hand and tasting it with his tongue, before spitting it out, his face contorted. Jim junior then searched the other pouch, withdrawing a little, ancient, yellowed scroll, then carefully rolling it open slowly.

"This one's in Gaelic again," Jim senior said, "and I suppose you want me to translate this as well?"

My father and me had nodded, maybe with me thinking out loud, "Perhaps this is the treasure map that the highwayman had hidden, and which the little people found many years ago?" When we looked at it, it had black, squiggly writing, with a red surround, and I have to say it looked like Greek to me.

Jim senior studied it for a minute, shaking his head as if to say, "No, I don't want to read this." He looked up, shaking his head and said, "Are you sure you want me to translate this?" Receiving no reply, he went on: "Well... here goes, and I have to warn you beforehand, it's not nice, not nice at all! I'm not sure if I want to read this, honestly, and after I do, you can take what you want out of it and then make up your minds if you want to give the little shoe and this saddle back... and I don't know if somebody is joking here or not!" He then held up the little scroll and read:

> "May your chickens catch the foul-pest disease!
> May your cattle catch phosphorus disease!
> May those of you who read this go blind and never
> see your wife and children again!"

Then Jim senior had hesitated, handing the scroll to my father.

"But... but I can't translate this," my father had said, "because, unlike you, I never learned Gaelic at school... you'll have to finish it, Jim."

Jim senior took the scroll back reluctantly, starting to read it again slowly:

"May you be thrown over the Cavehill's cliffs!
Our curse on your village and may it never
know health nor happiness!
Evil! And a short life to you and yours!
May madness come to your tortured mind soon!
May the curse of curses follow you everywhere!
Since you stole our goods, we wish you torment
in Hades!"

"May you die without a priest being in attendance!
We pray for great sorrow on all your houses!
Oh Satan, our Lord and Master, and the great
oppressor of the lamb, protect us and keep this
carrion from us!
May your death come…"

"No!" Jim senior shouted, throwing the parchment to the ground, before taking a box of matches from his jeans pocket, lighting a match and setting the parchment on fire, so that it disappeared in a puff of green smoke. We could see that Jim senior and junior were both spooked, while Jim senior walked up and down the narrow paths between his four-section vegetable patch.

"You don't really believe all this hocus-pocus, Jim, do you?" my father said.

"Anyway, we need to go back to the mound to retrieve our tools, I mean, your tools?"

"Yes, we need to do that," Jim senior replied. "I will need them for work anyway... we have to put a stop to this now before somebody is seriously hurt, or even worse, killed! We'll return to the mound and retrieve the tools after they've managed to do the repairs on the fuse boxes, and suppose we leave this saddle and the shoe lying there for them to find, because I'd never forgive myself if anything serious were to happen! I'm worried about the kids in all this, not so much myself, and that warning on that scroll, 'Our curse on you, and bad health to you and your little ones'—that's all our little ones!"

"Well, at least let me test the bells on the saddle," my father argued. "I'll scrape them with my penknife, and if small slivers come off, then we'll know it's real gold. Then we can talk it over again.

"Then we could say that at least we were almost rich," my father said, scraping one of the little bells with his knife, "then we can leave the stuff back, the shoe at the ruins and the saddle in the canyon, how's that? And by the way, the bells were cast in gold, see?"—as tiny slivers of gold twinkled in his hand.

Jim senior nodded in agreement: but he hadn't worried when the evil little man had come to the yard wall of our house, I thought, but only when his dog had been kidnapped and because of that scroll with that list of curses written on it, and I'd been disappointed at his lack of courage, unlike my father.

Still, I'd thought that those little people had been psychic, and knew what would happen in the future. How did they know to leave that scroll in the saddle and that the dog would escape? And that we would argue among ourselves? King Cuchalliane wouldn't have known that we'd be going to the mound that night or that Jim's dog would enter that canyon, or did he? Or that that would force Jim junior to change his mind about holding on to the shoe, and leave it back? It had all been too much of a coincidence!

As Sunday had worn on, my father and Jim's had discussed some more about the leprechaun relics. The foray down into the tunnel at the mound would be cancelled for now, while we'd give the village a little while to return to normal. The workers from the Electricity Board had been slow, and had to go from house-to-house to fit brand new electricity fuse boxes and every street light, as all had been completely burned-out. The farmers had taken their power from the grid beside the underground reservoir as well, and they had to be connected first because they supplied milk and foodstuffs to shops in the area, and further afield. The workers would have to start at the bottom of the village, then work their way up, going into the little side streets, before ending at the outskirts and the outlying single houses and bungalows. We would have to wait a day or two to make our move, as the electric boxes in our homes would have to be completely replaced, because the houses had been almost a hundred years old, and the boxes were ancient, being built for the first electricity after gas lamps were abolished.

Although it had been just the end of October, the people who'd had barred electric fires would have to sit in the cold, as the great electricity invention had prompted them to brick up their fireplaces. Our fire and Jim's were open, and they would burn anything—coal, wood, slack, peat or Bakelite, and I could picture the people with the electric fires having to sit in their homes wrapped in their overcoats and other heavy clothing. To each rich house a little discomfort must fall! Bakelite had been plentiful in the village and it was free.

A local scrap-merchant, Jimmy O'Hara, who'd lived down the bottom of our street, would bring the wings, engines and fuselages of aircraft into the village on flat-backed lorries, where he would have them lifted off by a crane and deposited in a vast tract of land behind his house and down beside the river. We would play inside the pilot's cockpits, at being German and British airmen, but O'Hara, his sons and brothers had signed a contract with the Royal Air Force to dismantle airplanes that were used in the Korean War.

He would separate copper, brass and aluminium, and would leave the Bakelite stacked up for all the village to collect for fuel, for absolutely nothing, at the rear of his house, and we would stock up for the winter, depending on how many planes he had dismantled, and how often. The joke doing the rounds in our village, which was mixed-religion, was: that if black smoke had been seen pouring out of chimneys, then those houses were unemployed or were in receipt of Supplementary Benefit, and their kids got free dinners at school; but when grey or white smoke had risen from the chimneys, then they were the employed people. Also, when the white smoke came out, the rich people had elected a new Pope, or a Pope a day.

As night fell, most people had to retire to bed early, because their TV sets and radios had no power. As night fell, most people had retired to bed early, those with electricity fires, that was. The kids in both St Vincent's and Wolfhill had been sent work to stay at home, as there was no chance of the school fuse boxes being repaired in a single day; and as most of the teachers had lived in the village, they had to be at home when workers from the Board might visit their homes on Monday.

It was just after midnight, and my mother, brother and baby sister had gone to bed early. My father and me had sat at the blazing, Bakelite fire, while two flickering candles had sat on the fireboard.

My father had been straining his eyes, trying to get into a sports section of a Sunday newspaper, and I'd been reading the tail-end of my Topper comic. It had been quiet outside, deathly quiet, and unlike them, not even a single cat had been squealing as was normal on most nights. I was uneasy after our experiences over the weekend, and I was looking around the room nervously, watching the dark shapes on the sitting-room walls, caused by the candles and the multi-coloured flames that had rushed up our chimney, with a whoosh, from the crackling Bakelite.

All the flames were impressing onto the walls the climbing figures and strange forms, and now and again I would strain my ears in between the comics. All I'd heard was our family upstairs stirring, the odd cough, the odd nightmare, and a bump when something had fallen out of someone's bed. Sharp scraping sounds were coming from somewhere nearby, but that hadn't been unusual at all in our house. My father had a habit of putting a piece of bread inside a Wellington boot, then laying it down flat. Mice would then venture out from below the stairs, where the coal bunker had been. He would then give the mouse ten minutes or so, until he snatched the boot and clamped it closed tightly, and soon the mouse would run out of air and suffocate inside. I tried it one night, but when the mouse struggled to get out I panicked and stood on it, ruining a boot with the mouse's blood impossible to wash out, so my father had to go out and buy a new pair.

If my father had been a great, white hunter in Africa, he would have had the busts of Lions, tigers, rhinos and leopards on the walls behind, but instead, he was an Ulster hunter, and our sitting-room walls would have been mounted with two-hundred mice, mummy, daddy and baby ones. But lucky for us, there had been no plaques on the walls with rats' heads on them. They had been unable to breach the scullery door in the yard, because my father had screwed an entire tin sheet that was six feet long by four wide, over it. Suddenly, the windows of the scullery began to tremble, as if a moderate earthquake was about to kick off. A thin, squealing sound had rung out, that sounded like a cross between a moan of an owl and a wail of a young woman in distress.

Both my father and I had run upstairs, he grabbing the torch that had sat on the floor. My mother had been fast asleep in the front bedroom, and the Bakelite fire in the upstairs hearth was slowly burning out. My sister had been asleep in her cot in the middle room, and when we went to our room my little brother was also fast asleep. "Let's go up into your sister's room again," my father said, "it may be my imagination, but I thought I heard some animals running about, out in the back entry." In my sister's room my father had slowly withdrawn the face curtain over the window there, that had overlooked our yard wall.

I was at his right shoulder, then both of us recoiled in horror and disbelief. A sleek, jet-black horse had had its front legs up on our wall, and his head was looking over it. It had sulphuric, yellowed eyes and its long mane had been fluttering in the breeze, like an old, torn flag that had been left on its flagpole for much too long.

Then the horse snorted before lowering itself down and out of sight, only for a little, permitting a deformed man to spring up to land on top of the wall, he being hump-backed, red-eyed and yellowed, with an ugly face covered with warts and scabs. All this time my father had had the torch trained onto the scene, through the room window.

The midget wore the same dress as the other goblins from the bull field that other night, and now proceeded to hop, skip and to leap three feet into the air by turning completely over, before landing on his tiny feet again, like an acrobat, but fitter than any I'd even seen. The midget was laughing and cackling all the time while trying to hold his little top hat to his thick, long, red-haired head. "*Padraig a chara! Padraig a chara!*" it had chanted, just like the last time, but over and over this time. It behaved as if it could see us, although the torch was shining into its terrifying eyes, before a massive, black eagle, that I'd seen in American films, but weren't natural to Ireland, had settled just above the eaves of my room, vigorously flapping its massive wingspan, which must have been around six feet. The wake of its wings could be felt against the window of my sister's room, before little white pebbles would tinkle onto the windows and bounce off, landing in the yard below.

The little gorgon would then click his fingers and the pebbles would lift off the yard floor and into his hands, before he would toss them back up again. "Ramrod! Ramrod!" the little man called, and a massive, double-horned beast jumped up onto the wall, before jumping down again, then proceeded to batter the outer, back door where we would put our rubbish bin out, before clip-clopping back down the entry again, where the sound slowly faded out.

Then the little man waved an arm and the eagle flew off, disappearing over towards Divis Mountain. But he wasn't alone for very long: a blob had now joined him on the wall, which had materialised out of thin air. This being had looked to be half-beast, half-human, and the little man was patting the beast on the arm. "This is my friend the Grogoch, and although he has the power of invisibility, he allows you to see him tonight!" the little man had shouted up, speaking in English now, "because, because, if you will not return my goods to me, Grogoch will have you for dinner!

"You will not see him the next time, and wherever you go, my thieving humans, Grogoch may be standing beside you, and you will not know it! Your miserable lives for my shoe and my Queen's saddle, now! Put them from where you took them!"

I could feel my father shaking, and he was never afraid of anything in his life. But this strange creature, far more than the little man, had unnerved him.

Now the Grogoch was playing with the little man, running up and down our yard wall, trying to run right through the little man while he did somersaults trying to pretend to escape from his big, ugly friend. This creature had been taller than a greyback gorilla, but had red fur and it wore no clothes. Caked mud had covered the entire area of its body and his ears had been long and floppy, like a kangaroo's. It had a broad nose and wide nostrils that bellowed black steam all the time, and its eyes were like a crocodile's, only fiery red. Even from where we'd been standing, and the bedroom windows had been closed tight, this creature's stench was terrible. It had smelt like a dead sheep that we'd found lying at the bottom of the peak on the Cavehill mountain, and that had lain there for up to three weeks after falling over in the dark.

This creature had long, thick fingers, and long fingernails, and its toes and feet had been the same. A terrible thought had come to me: that day we'd been walking the barrel-sewer at the bottom of our street! Peter had been at the very last on our train going up there, and Peter had complained, and we'd seen the long scratch marks to verify it, that something had grabbed him, seventy feet under the ground. I wondered, was that this creature's home, the old sewer under Wolfhill mill?

My sister's bedroom door had opened slowly and squeakily, and when me and my father swung quickly around, he shone his torch in the tired face of my mother who'd been standing there in her nightdress. When we'd spun around again to look into the yard, the creatures had gone again, as if they had known that my mother had walked into the room without them seeing her, but probably sensing her presence.

"What's the matter, boys, what are you doing in here at this ungodly time of night? And Patrick... why are you not in bed for school in the morning? The Electricity Board men have the repairs finished... and the teachers sent up word today that they're back to normal tomorrow."

My mother, without knowing it, had got something right, the word *ungodly*. Whatever had been outside hadn't been send from Heaven, that was for sure.

"There's nothing wrong, Mary," my father had replied, "a mouse was trapped in the Wellington boot, but your man here panicked and opened the boot too soon, and the mouse was still alive and ran upstairs... we thought it ran into the baby's room, and we're in here looking for it. But it's all under control now, I killed it with my shoe and it won't be escaping anymore. Go back to bed love, we're coming now."

Chapter Fourteen

The Protective Ring of Fire

I WASN'T WORRIED ABOUT MY MOTHER and siblings now, because these creatures, while they had disappeared when one of them would show up, appeared to not want to hurt them, but I couldn't be completely sure if we were to hold on to their ancient relics for very much longer. The only one who'd appeared to have seen any of these creatures had been Ewart's gamekeeper and caretaker, Billy McCready, and he may be a good man to have on our side if we were to need his help in the very near future.

As I lay in bed an hour later, I'd been absolutely terrified, even when my father had left his torch with me. Every time I was able to drop off to sleep I would jump out of bed again, as if I were suffering a serious panic attack. The blind on our window, although just newly bought, would spring up by itself, and when I'd climbed out of bed to pull it down again, it would spring up again of its own free will, I think. I would stand at the side of the blind, peeking out at the yard wall all the time, swearing that I could see movement there, but most times it was just a prowling tomcat, looking for a partner or a juicy mouse.

That cat had lived up our street, and somebody once said that "if you saw mice then you would see no rats, and if you saw no mice you would see a cat," and my thinking was, that if you could see domestic cats, then I wouldn't see any monsters out on our yard wall or back entry.

"You did, didn't you?" Jim senior had asked when we'd gone down to his house that next night. "The visit from the ogres?"

"You too?" my father asked, "And the eagle? The Grogoch? That friggin' ram? And that nasty little man?"

"Affirmative!" Jim senior had replied, "But you left out that black stallion. That was some animal, but a devil animal, and that gorilla-like thing, the next time it has a bath it will be its first—it was reeking, stinking! And my dog has ran off again—it's probably reached Dublin by now where I bought it as a puppy; it has fled back to its old owner, and I don't blame it, even a little bit! That white-back gorilla up at Bellevue Zoo would look like a chimpanzee beside that thing."

"Did your wife and the rest of your family hear or see anything last night, Jim?"

"No, thank God," Jim junior replied, "but the wife got a terrible shock this morning when she saw the outside of the house! It has changed colour from whitewashed to rust-red! I had to tell her that a shower of rain early this morning had come down while the Gulf Stream blew sand up from the Sahara Desert! But you're right, these creatures only seem to show themselves to us and the three boys. Even Billy McCready saw that attacking white owl the other night, but unlike us, he never saw that little, Wicked Witch of the North wrapped around its neck!"

"That's because they're trying to discredit us," my father had replied. "They want people to think we're going nuts if we were to tell anybody this tall tale. But a few people do believe in all this. Well, what's our next move, Jim? Do you not think that we need more than a little more help now?"

"You mean something like an exorcism?" Jim senior asked. "Guns or explosives will have no effect on them... and who's going to exorcise the priest first?"

"We just can't leave the saddle and shoe lying anywhere, Jim. What would happen if somebody else picked them up and receives worse treatment than us? We should just leave the shoe back at the monastery and the saddle in the canyon. We could kill two birds with one stone then, if you'll excuse the pun!"

"Tell you what," Jim senior said, "let's return to the canyon tomorrow night and leave both curses, I mean articles, there... we could watch for a while, and if they don't show up we can hold a séance for an hour or two, but it won't be for faint hearts. We need to tell Peter to remain at home tomorrow night—remember what happened the last time?"

"What if they take their relics, then attack us for revenge?" I asked.

"Maybe not, not if we're ready for them," Jim senior replied. "We can use the Ring of Fire. This is a protection against evil and the occult. Once we have entered it nothing can break through its impregnable, invisible shield, not in a thousand years."

"Some of those creatures that we had seen looked more than a thousand years old," Jim junior added. "They can maybe wait for a thousand years, we can't! They would have all the time in the world for our fire to burn itself out—then we'd have to come out! What then?"

"Anyway," Jim senior said, "both of you lads can go into the church tomorrow after school and fill two glass bottles with Holy Water from the baptism font, because we have to try anything to get these evil little devils off our backs... all agreed?"

We nodded, sadly, because we couldn't keep the little, ancient relics.

After school the next day, Jim and I went to our chapel. We'd found a little castor oil bottle each in our houses the night before, and they gurgled noisily as we put them under the surface of the filled-to-the top, baptism font.

For good measure, we'd gone to the candle holder, where parishioners would put up candles to pray for a sick person, or a dead relative. Three old women had been praying there, where we'd pretended to pray, and when the old women walked away singly to line up to say the twelve Stations of the Cross, Jim and me had grabbed a dozen candles each and stuffed them into our schoolbags. If the Ring of Fire had managed to burn out before we escaped from the little monsters, these candles may just save our sinful lives.

When we'd left the chapel, I would have liked to have visited the old priest, Father Lynch, but our fathers had warned us last night: "Under no circumstances will you talk to anybody about this!" Then we'd gone home to prepare for tonight, the four of us agreeing to meet up at the old mound at 8 p.m. Once there, we could collect Jim senior's tools for work, although I wasn't banking on finding much of our sandwiches or sweets, as that area was filled with red squirrels, rabbits, crows, badgers and foxes.

We were rearing to go, my father and me being well covered with our combat coats and trousers, like soldiers, heavy, hiking boots and thick, black gloves. We'd used them to climb the Cavehill, Divis and Black Mountains, and for our toboggan in the heavy snow of 1957 when we'd been little tots. We were ready now, and if we were going to die tonight, it wouldn't be from the cold. Although my father had never mentioned it, as he hadn't been very religious, I sneaked upstairs to his room and pinched a little prayer that my mother had, with a little relic from Bernadette, the Patron Saint of France and Lourdes. My uncle Paddy had once owned it, before he died of fright, when he'd seen that old woman at Dickey's shop corner eight years beforehand. If anything of the occult was to happen, then I didn't want to die because of my father's atheism and a silly technicality.

After I'd arrived home, my father had already been to Dickey's shop where he'd bought four pints of paraffin oil fuel. We would often buy that fuel there, not only to start the light for our fire but to buy gallons of it for the bonfires in the 11th night of July, the anniversary of the Battle of the Boyne, and also the anniversary of Our Lady, the Virgin Mary, on the 15th of August every year. The dog still hadn't returned, after bolting, so we would have to use our own senses to detect anything out of the ordinary that night.

We would meet at the mound, then from there we would go to the bull field, leaving ourselves plenty of time to build the Ring of Fire. Jim senior would supply the dozen or so hessian rags from old hunting bags, before they'd left their house, while they would carry the hidden saddle in another old sack.

It had just became dark when my father and I had set off, and the little diamond-encrusted shoe was concealed in the inside pocket of his combat coat, the breast pocket. I'd be glad, as I knew my father wasn't, to see the last of it.

"That shoe could have become our legacy," my father lamented as we entered the lower reaches of Curtain's Avenue. "Just think," he complained again, "that little shoe could have been the making of our family; we could have been very rich, and the riches could have been passed on to your children and their children... but if it's not to be then it's not to be. When devils threaten us and we have no protection, then we have to bow down."

"Better to be dirt poor and to be alive than to be dead rich," I'd replied to him, "because if we'd kept that shoe and saddle, our kids and their kids would have been cursed for the rest of their miserable lives!"

We'd walked up past Jack's gravel path leading to his house, finally dropping into the little, steep grassy knoll and down beside the steel gate at the mound. The other two had already arrived, and both of them had been occupied, cutting up small bundles of hessian from two old sacks. They'd tied them all around with chicken wire and had dipped them into an old, two gallon, paint tin that they'd half-filled with paraffin. My and my father's paraffin supply would supplement the Ring of Fire once we'd lit it, and we could pour it onto the bundles of hessian to keep them burning. Jim senior's tools had still been lying there since Saturday night, although the eatables had been eaten, probably by the many animals that, as I had thought, would have run around there.

"I suggest," my father began, "that when we reach the canyon that Jim and me go down to inside there, while you boys keep watch. We'll leave the shoe and saddle beside one burning rag and light it. Hopefully the little devils will see them and take them away without having to come across us... Jim and me can return to the top here and watch with you. If they come along, we can then leg it out of here, and that will be the end of that!"

"Fair enough," Jim senior replied, "and I decided not to bring Peter along—he was more nervous than my dog the other night, and perhaps we may have to be quick when we have to run tonight!"

"And if these creatures don't show up... what do we do then, Jim?" my father enquired.

"Then we'll have to go down and wait," Jim senior replied. "Then we can build the Ring of Fire and sit in the middle of it, ready to light it if they do show up. These creatures may want to punish us in some way before they allow us to get on with our lives, and we've no other option." My father had nodded, with both of them getting the gear ready to make their way carefully down the side of the canyon.

Our fathers had left one torch with Jim junior and me. I had got an odd feeling that although the bull field and canyon was devoid of any kind of noise or movement, a shiver that had run up my back had warned me that we were being watched; but if they didn't show up at the canyon tonight, they may have attacked our house, and our families had been kept in the dark about all this.

Suddenly, the sounds of two dogs barking told us that Billy McCready was doing his rounds tonight, and his dogs must have sensed our presence in the bull field, but it had felt reassuring to know that somebody was close at hand, before the barking had stopped again.

Jim senior had left us his binoculars, and when we looked down we could see the two figures setting up the single paraffin bundle, leaving the saddle and shoe down beside it before a match had been struck that had lit the bundle. The dancing flame, although it was a good distance away, lit up the canyon, and although it hadn't been as bright as the two little people's beacons last week, the trees still appeared to be dancing and moving, like shadows, in tandem with the solitary, torch beam. The sky had been full of lead-coloured clouds tonight, and as a fresh wind was gathering from the north, I'd hoped that it wouldn't get much worse if we'd had to retreat to inside the circle.

The grunts and groans of our fathers had been getting closer as they'd climbed out of the canyon, for them to now join us, when we'd settled down behind a few clumps of thistles to watch and wait. The black smoke had wafted up to us, a putrid, rotting smell, as the bundle of hessian was flaring up, and it would be dying down again. That little fire had lasted for around half an hour now, and if the little devils hadn't shown up before it burned out, then our fathers couldn't climb up and down there for another eleven or twelve times.

As we'd watched and watched, Jim senior suddenly chuckled to himself with the three of us looking at him in the darkness, and although we could hardly see him, we thought that he may have been cracking up. "Don't mind me boys," he'd whispered, "I was just thinking that if these guys don't turn up tonight we'll have to leave the saddle here, and the shoe back at the monastery ruins... and the reason I was laughing was because—and Jim junior heard this—that little King... do you know what he shouted to us when he and his friends visited the other night?"

Both me and my father replied, "No, what did he shout at you the other night?" as a rabbit hopped over our legs and speedily sprinted off, making us jump.

"The little cur shouted in Gaelic, '*Go gcreime conna difrian do bhailFearge…*' In English, 'May the hounds of Hell gnaw at your manly parts!' He, he he! Then, before he'd hopped off with his Grogoch friend, he finished with, '*D'anan, don diabhal,*' meaning, 'Your soul to the Devil!' That little guy is really nasty! The Grogoch then hopped onto our house roof and defecated until it ran down the walls, front and rear. I tried to hose it off, but the wife seen it, all the streaks and stains, red, like blood, but I was able to, and Jim there, to clear the stench with a strong, disinfectant that I use to clean out our dog's shed, and that's always bad!"

Two hours must have passed as we lay there, and the homemade paraffin beacon of ours had burned out an hour ago. The only sound was from a family of badgers who'd came out to hunt for worms, the worms always emerging at night and attaching themselves to the grass. As we'd watched them through the binoculars and the dying embers of the beacon, they'd sniffed around the little shoe and saddle for a while, only moving on when they'd found out that they were uneatable.

Jim senior had amused himself by reading a little red book that he'd produced from his combat-jacket's inside pocket, at the same time reading it while he'd held his torch close to it so as not to give our positions away. A little, plastic-covered prayer had fallen out from between the book's pages, and Jim senior was quietly quoting from it, as we'd listened: "*Lignum sanctaecrisis defendat me a malls presentibus, Futuris, interioribus, and Jim, Jim junior, Peter, Eddie, Patrick, Omnes spiritus laudet Dominius Mosen Habent and prophetus. Exergat Deus and disipenture inimiciessus, Amen.*"

"What was that all about?" my father had asked. "Was that more of the Irish language?"

"No, father," I'd answered before Jim senior could get a chance, "I was an altar boy with Jim junior there, and both me and he used to say that language every week, during Mass… it's Latin!"

"And so was I," Jim senior had said, "in the same chapel too, Eddie, long before you moved up to the village from East Belfast and married Patrick's mother…"

"It means," I said, before Jim junior would get in first to show off, 'O Lord Jesus Christ, we beseech Thee, to preserve us, and all of our names, followed by, and all that we may possess, from the evil powers of spirits, wizards, demons, and this I will trust thou will do, by the same power as thou didst to cause the blind to see, the lame to walk, and they that were possessed with unclean spirits, amen!"

"We'll know if it works tonight or not," my father said, "if our backs are against the wall, provided the little fairies turn up, and that Grogoch stays away! His stink would kill you, never mind anything else that they'd do to us, there isn't a worse fate than to be stunk to death!"

I knew, somehow, that they'd turn up. They seemed to be well ahead of us. They'd known that the little shoe had been kept in our house, when the evil little man had visited us twice. They'd known that Jim's dog would be with us the other night, they having the saddle ready to strap onto its back, with the saddlebags containing that terrifying curse. But what had been keeping them tonight, or would they come on their own terms, and not on ours?

While both Jim junior and me had been sitting looking down through the binoculars, both of our fathers had risen to their feet, walking for a bit then sitting down again, twenty yards away from us. They'd been in a deep conversation, their voices rising then lowering. After ten minutes they had returned, sitting down beside us and putting their hands on our shoulders.

"Listen boys," Jim senior spoke first, "both of us think that our little adventure tonight may turn sour and may be just that bit little dangerous... for ten-year-olds. We've come to a decision... we know yours hearts are set on this, so one of us will take you down as far as Curtain's Avenue, and you can go on home from there. If your mothers ask about where we are, just tell them we've found a new batch of rabbit warrens, and we'll be out most of the night. The apparitions may not even come, and if that is the case, we will follow you down straight away, okay?"

"Not on your life!" Jim junior had said, raising his voice until his father put his finger over his lips, in case we'd been surprised by the evil others.

"We're not afraid, father," Jim junior had said. "If you're going to stay then so are we."

"Yes, so are we," I'd interrupted.

Both of our fathers had paced up and down then, looking at each other. "But are you sure, lads?" my father had asked. "If anything happens to you your mothers will never forgive us."

"Listen, father," I'd said, "if anything was to happen to you, our mothers wouldn't believe us about the little creatures... nobody in the village would believe us, except maybe Father Lynch and Billy McCready, and they wouldn't say anything, in case people thought they were nuts too! And don't worry, we're not as delicate as you think we are."

"Okay lads," Jim senior had replied, "but you must promise us, that if things get out of hand down below tonight, provided that the opposition shows up, we want both of you to stay close to us, very close!"

Then it was back to our sentry duties again, as the little, paraffin-soaked bundle was making its last gasp to stay alight.

"*Wee—aaaaaaaaa!*" The noise appeared to come from above our heads as we jumped to our feet.

"The torches! The torches!" my father had yelled.

"*Yaap! Yaap! Yaap!*" The shrill call had echoed all around the bull field and the canyon below.

"*Yee-ka-ka-ka-ka-ka-ka!*"

"I know what that is!" my father had shouted, "It's that massive, black eagle that landed on our back bedroom the other night! When the little gnome made a return visit with his friends!"

Our fathers were swinging the torches wildly, the beams going up towards the low clouds, as a massive, black eagle was flapping its wings so much that we could feel the downdraft. As a pair of large, yellow eyes had been glaring down at us, and as our fathers had shone the torches upwards, it had reminded me of that war film, 'The Dam Busters,' starring Richard Todd. Todd had played the part of Wing Commander Guy Gibson, when Lancaster bombers of the Royal Air Force were sent to bomb dams in Germany, in the Forum cinema during a Saturday morning matinee, as the eagle, like the planes then, was lit up by beams from the torches. The eagle had been diving lower and lower, almost striking us with its wings, as if it was trying to sweep us off the canyon's skyline and down, almost pushing us over.

"It's on! It's on!" my father had yelled, "Quick, grab all the tools and stuff and head down towards the canyon bottom, hurry! hurry!" But on the way, while we'd scampered down, Jim senior had tripped over a little bush in the darkness, passing us while he'd rolled himself up in a ball, reaching the bottom with a thump before we did. After Jim senior had recovered, he'd organised the Ring of Fire quickly, in a wide, twelve-foot circle. He'd built it around the saddle and little shoe, and a dozen, paraffin, rag-balls of hessian had been lain out, two feet apart.

Chapter Fifteen

Our Second Encounter with Abbot John

W **E SAT DOWN IN THE MIDDLE OF THE RING,** back-to-back, so that we could see anything approaching from all around us. The gigantic eagle had still hovered above our heads, while our fathers had opened the two paint tins, getting ready to top the rags up with more paraffin when they burned down low. We'd imagined shadows and shapes moving among the dozens of hawthorns on both sides of the canyon, as they'd danced all around in the glare of the flames. We thought we could see dozens of little people shapes darting to-and-fro. Suddenly, rabbits, badgers, foxes and other animals that had been sheltering under the trees had bolted from everywhere noisily, quickly disappearing over the brow of the canyon.

The eagle had still been trying to evade the long, light beams of the torches, as figures of little humans, a horse, ram, pigs, sheep and a dog, that had looked familiarly like Jim's lurcher, and the ugly and smelly bulky figure of what the little King had called the Grogoch—all sorts of shapes and forms—appeared, clambering down towards us, coming over the skyline of the canyon. Then Jim senior had handed me his torch; then, taking his little prayer book from inside his coat, amid the thick, acrid, black choking smoke of the Ring, began to read: "'*Liguam Sanctae crisis defendat me a malis presentibus, Futuris, interiorbus, and Jim, Jim, Eddie and Patrick Omnes spiritus laudet, Domonium Mosen Habert and prophetus… Exerget Deus and disipenture iminiciessus…* O Lord Jesus Christ we beseech you to preserve us, and that we may be protected from the evil powers of spirits, wizards and demons!… Thus we will trust thou will do, and by the same power as thou didst to cause the blind to see, the lame to walk, when they were possessed with unclean spirits, Amen!' Right, pray boys! Pray! Pray, then get behind us, now!"

The little queen and king were leading the ugly charge, the queen once again on Jim's dog's back, the king on his hare, while the same ugly people, as before, were riding sheep, the ram, pigs, donkeys and the goat. When they'd reached us, the Ring of Fire was doing its job, and the creatures rode around us instead of charging straight through it, reminding me of that western film 'Westward Ho The Wagons' in the matinee, at the forum cinema, when the Indians would ride around the wagon train without penetrating it.

"*Losea is do ort!*" the little king had growled, every time he would ride around us.

"That little monster is shouting in Gaelic," Jim senior began, "'Scorching and burning to you!' And 'Go mbeirean diabhailleis thu!— To hell with you!'"

The little king was trying to get closer to us as he'd gone around. "*D'anam don diabhal!*" he'd shouted, and he'd tried to spit on us. "And that one was, 'Your souls to the Devil!'" Jim senior had said, but the creatures didn't dare to attempt to break into the circle, yet.

"What's that coming down the canyon wall?" Jim junior had shouted, pointing. "Is that a horse and rider!" Our fathers had ignored the surrounding band for a minute, as they'd shone their torches in the direction of the new arrival. The sight had been spectacular but terrifying: the black, shiny horse had red, glaring eyes and a long mane, and when it had reached us it had stopped suddenly, rearing up. The rider was dressed in black, flowing robes, but its head wasn't on its shoulders; instead, it had hung from the side of the horse's saddle.

The dangling head had been cheese-coloured, and although the head had been detached from the body, the face had been smiling broadly, from ear to long ear, the ears like a rat's ears. Its large red eyes had darted from side-to-side, the horse still rearing up and sending black steam from its nostrils. All the while, the headless rider had been whipping the horse with a large, black whip, it becoming more and more maddening, its snorting sounding like a runaway locomotive now.

Suddenly without warning, the horse and rider had galloped off, running up the steep canyon as if they had been on level ground. *"Do chorp don diabhal!"* the little queen had growled again as she'd rode passed us, a look of terror on Jim's lurcher's face as she'd rode him. "That was, 'Your bodies to the devil!'" Jim had interpreted again.

"Quick! Throw the little saddle and shoe outside the Ring!" my father had shouted, even he becoming more terrified now. "Maybe they'll take them and clear off!" He then dived to the ground and grabbed both relics, then tossing them high outside the Ring; but the creatures just ignored them, riding over them roughshod. We may have realised then that they'd wanted us, not the relics!

"Damn v ort!" the little man on the ram had shouted, trying to reach inside the Ring to try to grab Jim junior or me, who'd been holding onto each other as if our lives had depended on it, and it did. "And that profanity is," Jim senior had said, "'Damnation to us!'" They'd been getting more daring now, coming closer... *"Mucha is ba ort!"* another little man riding a sheep had shouted. "That was 'Smothering and drowning to you!'" Jim senior had repeated.

"Go dtachta an diabhal! thu!" another evil midget shouted, from the back of a cow this time.

Suddenly, the riders had slackened off, slowing down and almost stopping, as the eagle still hovered above, with another creature on its back, as if acting as a spotter. Another figure had come sloping along, right up to the edge of the ring. This time it was a female creature, and she had been real ugly. She'd scales like a fish all over her body, pig-like features, long, pointed teeth and webbing between her hands and feet.

She had long scraggly, green hair that had looked like seaweed, as if she'd just walked up out of the sea, just standing there and staring in at us with round, fishlike eyes, and as she'd walked, water had been dripping off her unclothed body. After a while, she'd just walked off, disappearing up the side of the canyon. It had seemed, now, that everything was being thrown at us, and we'd wondered what terror would be coming at us next.

My friend Jim and I had sat in the middle of the Ring, our fingers over our eyes looking at the terror scene outside through our partly-parted fingers. Now and again, one of our fathers would run to the burning bundles of hessian, pouring more and more paraffin oil onto the flames, to stop the little creatures from entering, and for us to see more clearly if any more tricksters were coming our way. Something else ugly must have been on its way, because the little, riders were going into a more frenzied run now, shouting and cursing. I could hear both of our fathers gasping loudly, as my father had shouted, "Oh no, not again!" What had looked like a small, fluorescent cloud had drifted to the ground in front of us. She'd drifted right up to the Ring's border, another female, and she'd worn a white, shroud-like, flowing dress. The dress's flowing parts, just like Rosaleen's before, would fan out when caught by a light breeze, like washing hanging on a clothesline.

It had been terrifying although beautiful all the same, as she'd hovered about four feet off the ground in front of us. It had reminded me of the story of the Virgin of Fatima, where three young girls had been alleged to have seen the vision of the Virgin Mary beside a river in Portugal, at the turn of the twentieth century. She'd looked beautiful, until she'd opened her mouth, and her wail had been so piercing that the captured animals had stopped running around to look at her, starting again when the little people had beaten them with hawthorn sticks.

Then, as quickly as she'd appeared, she'd gone, in the blink of an eye, after calling us out of our Ring with a single, index finger, towards her—but none of us dared move. We never saw the Grogoch right away, until we smelt the rancid scent beforehand. It had stuck its arms into the Ring, its arms catching fire, but it had just laughed out loudly at us. If he could do that, it would only be a matter of time before he could push his rotten body inside, and be able to snatch us and pull out of there.

Then, as quickly as he'd appeared, he was gone again, after he'd grabbed Jim junior, but our fathers had beaten it off, and had grabbed him back. Our fathers had even thrown paraffin around him, setting him alight all over, but he was impervious to the flames and the pain.

Soon after, another creature had materialised. This had been a small, deformed goblin, who had stood and grunted at us. But this one had the power of speech, and he had horns where his ears should have been, with another two horns coming out of each side of his head, above the first two, and another larger and thicker horn sticking out of the top of its large, completely bald, bullet-shaped head. It had worn a long, green, scraggly gown down to its hairy ankles, its hands, feet and fingernails and toenails inches long. It also had a thin, red moustache and a goatee beard, and its green teeth had been pointed and rotted, as if they'd been worn down with a rasp. "*Go n-ithe an cat thu!*" it had stood and roared at us through the smoke and flames. "That's translated into English as 'May the cat eat you, and may the devil eat the cat!'" my father had said, picking up the Irish language at last in an odd sort of dangerous way.

This had become unbearable to my friend Jim and me, both of us getting ready to run outside the Ring in panic, but our fathers, seeing us as we'd moved, but grabbing both of us by the napes of our necks, pulled us further back into the Ring again. Then out of the blackness of the night with just an intermittent flash of the moon, as the sky had cleared again, everybody, including the monsters, had stopped and looked up into the sky, as a massive, airplane had flown overhead, landing somewhere with a deafening crash somewhere to the East of us.

"That was a B-17 American Bomber!" Jim senior had yelled, "but they went out of commission after the Second World War. O'Hara must have brought it in for scraping, but it must have overshot the runway at Nutt's Corner airport, ten miles away!"

But the torture hadn't stopped. "*A cruce salus! A cruce salus!*" the goblin had started again. It was now also reaching into the centre of the Ring with its long, hairy arms, as our fathers had been punching fresh air trying to beat if off, because it hadn't been solid. My father had looked at Jim senior oddly as the latest creature had just faded, before disappearing. "That was an odd thing to shout," Jim senior had remarked above his panic. "It means 'From the cross comes salvation!' Nothing like that would an evil entity say!"

This shout in Latin had brought the creatures into a more frenzied state, and now they were moving in on us in force. "*A cruce salus!*" The shout had gone up again, loudly echoing right along the canyon, but louder this time. Then the voice had boomed out even louder again, and even the evil ones had stopped dead in their tracks, staring up at the skyline at the top of the canyon. "*Pater, pater pater Noster! Noster Noster Noster, aia aia aia Jesus! Christus. Messyas. Emmanuel, soter, Sabaoth, Elohim-on-a-donay. Tetra grammaton! Ag. Pantlon-reaton. Agies. Jasper, Melchor-Balthasot, Amen!*"

"How did you do that again without moving your lips, Jim? Are you a ventriloquist?" my father had asked Jim senior.

"No... that wasn't me, definitely not me... am I going mad or what?" Jim senior had replied, all our eyes darting all around the canyon at the little, evil ones.

"No! It was him!" Jim junior had shouted, pointing up at the skyline of the canyon, where a fluorescent figure had stood looking down at the manic scene, his arms outstretched, and it had looked like the ghostly monk that the Ewart's gamekeeper, Billy Mc Cready, had described to us, the monk Abbot John.

"What is he shouting, Jim?" my father had asked Jim senior.

"Latin again... and he's shouting at the evil ones: 'And by the power of our Lord Jesus Christ and his heavenly angels, being our Redeemer and Saviour, from all witchcraft and from assaults of the devil... we beseech you to preserve us and all that we possess, from the power of all evil beings, spirits and wizards, past and present, to come outward and inward. Amen!"

Suddenly my father looked round, at the other side of the canyon this time. The clouds had cleared a little, and through the clouds the moon was able to sneak through the clouds as well, to have a look. Suddenly, another horse and rider had appeared, the horse rearing on its hind legs. To the rider's right, three canine-like animals had stared down at us as well, two adults and their cub, their heads lowered, watching us. Then their heads rose towards the moon: *"A-whooooo..! A-whooooo..!"*— their howling echoing all along the canyon.

The little evil ones had just froze, as another twelve figures walked up and stood beside three canines, some of them putting their hands on the canines' shoulders and patting them. The canines had been wolves, long-dead for at least two-hundred-and-fifty years, while the twelve humans had been dressed in American airmen's uniforms, in light khaki, with each wearing a peaked, khaki cap. The twelve men had waved down at us, before turning and walking away, as the wolves had followed them out of sight, their *"A-whoooos!"* as a signal that they may not ever return to our village again. Then a choking cloud of dust had gathered, as the observing horseman and his mount charged down the side of the canyon wall. The rider had a blazing, amber lantern in one hand, and a sword in the other. As we watched in absolute shock, we'd thought that another monster had returned to finish us off, as he'd drawn nearer and nearer, almost on top of us now.

"My God!" my father yelled out, "it's the ghost of Naois O'Haughan, and he's heading for the little people!"

All the evil ones had stopped dead in their tracks, while their mounts of various animals had reared up and had thrown the evil ones up into the air, like a rodeo show, before the evil people landed on the ground around us with a loud thump. The remaining monsters had disappeared in clouds of red smoke, while most of the little ones ran in all directions, with some of them running into the solid rocks of the canyon's sides, disappearing as if there had been a secret, invisible door there.

The king and queen have been dodging and diving from the horseman's sword, even running under the black horse, while O'Haughan had looked magnificent with a piece of black cloth pulled up to his eyes, his three-cornered hat, his pistols by his side, and his shimmering, black clothing glistening in the moon's glare. "Stand and deliver!" he'd shouted out, "Not your money or your ill-gotten and accursed treasures, just your miserable, demonic lives!"

"*Wee-aaaaaaaa!*" The eagle, that had been hovering over our heads all the while, had swooped down, while the highwayman had swung his sword to try to bring it down, the black eagle now snatching the little king and queen in his massive talons before lifting off skyward. The little people had put their little, long-nailed, webbed fingers deep into the eagle's wings, and they had gone, and when we'd looked around after watching the eagle climbing, the highwayman had been riding up the side of the canyon.

He'd stopped at the top, before the horse had rose up on its hind legs, the highwayman waving back at us, with his three-cornered hat in his hand; then he was gone, over the rise.

All four of us had stood there, staring at each other, the attacks ending just as quickly as they'd began. Jim's now saddleless lurcher had been standing licking his hand, as we'd sat down in the middle of the ring, exhausted. I couldn't help myself as I burst into a fit of nervous laughter. My father's and the two Jims' faces had reminded me of those fellas on that Saturday night cabaret show, 'The Black and White Minstrels', as all you could see were the whites of their eyes. Their faces, and presumably, mine, had been completely blackened, as if we'd all fallen down a chimney, and when my father and the others had seen my joke, they ran their hands over their faces and laughed hysterically, too.

The silence all around us had been deafening, as if nothing had happened at all. The canyon had been completely still now, except for the thick, black smoke that swirled all around us. Thankful, as we saw when we shone the torches around the outside of the Ring, the little, shoe and saddle had gone.

"And what about those American airmen, the three ghostly wolves and especially that magnificent spectacle, Naois O'Haughan the Highwayman... who the hell will believe all this?" my father had said, looking like he'd been in an extreme state of delayed shock.

"And that monk..." Jim senior had said. "Where do they all go with the little evil, people? Probably back to hell!"

"*Abitt excessit evas it, erupit!*"

"You did that again, Jim!" my father shouted at Jim senior. "You said that without moving your lips!"

"No, I didn't utter a word," Jim senior had replied, "honestly!"

"*Abiit excessit, evas it erupit!*" We'd all jumped to our feet, Jim's dog whimpering and running around in circles, wildly. We'd realised then that another presence had been within our Ring, although we still couldn't see it. "That voice, that voice in Latin," Jim senior had translated, "it just said, 'He has left, absconded, escaped and disappeared'—but where is he that speaks?"

"*Abyssus abyssum invocat!*" We'd all look around us again, becoming more afraid now, as if the evil people had called up a ghostly monk to give us a false sense of security, before snatching us, as the Ring's fire had been dying out. "It said, 'Hell calls hell, one misstep leads to another!'" Jim had repeated, shrugging his shoulders now, at a loss, like the rest of us, as to where the voice was coming from. Then, as if by magic, we'd all sprung back when a brown-clad figure had suddenly materialised before us, a monk wearing a long, brown habit, his waist tied around tightly with a white rope, like the skipping rope used by the girl in our street. A hood was pulled up around his head, and for the first time, we'd probably been the only ones in nearly a hundred years to see the monk's features. He had sported a little, white, goatee beard, and had piercing, lit-up blue eyes. He'd just stared at us and said quietly: "*Auxilio ab alto... Annuit coeptis.*"

"That, translated, means 'By help from on high' and 'God has favoured us,'" Jim senior had whispered.

"*Ave atque vale, Amor sincitom nia,*" the monk had said again.

"He just said, 'Hail and farewell... love conquers all'—and I think he's going now," Jim senior had whispered again.

"*Agenda astetnum vale... Satanas Apage,*" the monk said.

"He just said, 'Things to be done... farewell forever... Satan, gone!'"

Then the monk pointed at his chest with a skeletal finger before pointing in the direction of the moon. "*Agnus Dei!*"

"And that was 'The lamb of God'—but where did he go? Can any of you see him now? Where did he go to?"

"Probably to his home in the sky," my father had said. "His job's done... this was probably why he'd hung around for so long."

We'd noticed Jim's lurcher running all around the canyon, his nose to the ground, sniffing; when he'd returned wagging his tail furiously we'd known that the canyon had been cleansed. Jim senior had gathered up his tools, the spades, pick and hacksaw, before we'd set off climbing up the steep canyon, exhausted and unbelieving what we'd just witnessed. We'd sat down when we'd reached the summit, and while we'd shone our torches into the darkness the rabbits, badgers, foxes and other animals had been returning to their homes, as if they'd known that the evil ones had gone...

As we'd looked across our valley, Napoleon's Nose on top of Cavehill, and Belfast Castle just below that, had been looking over Belfast Lough, as a light mist was drifting up the Lough from the Irish Sea. I'd wondered about the twelve American airmen who'd died on the Cavehill, over twelve years ago, and after tonight they must have been wandering these hills for all that time. They'd tragically died fighting for us, and now they'd turned up again tonight to fight for us again, people that we'd have been proud to meet. And our own ancient countrymen, the monk and the highwayman, and the little, evil ones, and even the last wolves to be killed in Ireland. I would have liked to have met them again to thank them, except the evil ones.

We'd left the bull field and made our way down past the ancient mound, with the steel, entrance padlock almost sawed through. I wondered if we'd ever be back there again, as I'd felt that the highwayman's treasure had been within touching distance. At least we'd known that Naois O'Haughan's spirit had never left this area, because he would always watch over his treasure. I had a feeling that our paths would cross again, but would he be as mad at us, like the little evil people were, if we'd found his treasure?

We'd reached Curtain's Avenue, and since leaving the bull field we'd not uttered a word to each other, still been in severe shock.

"No luck lamping tonight lads?" the voice of the gamekeeper Billy McCready had come from out of the darkness.

"Not a thing, Billy, not a friggin' thing!" my father had replied. "Not even a single bunny rabbit."

"Yes," Billy McCready had replied, "very quiet tonight, except for one thing though. Did any of you hear that massive roar of an airplane, a Second World War airplane?

"It had been flying far too low probably because of the encroaching mist. It appeared to be in trouble, but just before I left the house there, there was nothing on the radio news. I wonder if he'd landed all right. Strange, that! And what are you wearing black polish on your faces for, lads... did you not know that camouflage against rabbits doesn't work? They scent you, you know!"

My father and me, and Jim junior and his father, had parted ways at the bottom of Curtain's Avenue, promising to meet up later the next day, or Jim and me at school.

It was midnight when we reached home. The cuckoo clock had sounded as usual, but my mother and siblings had been in bed, placing the wire fire guard there before they'd went. Before my mother had gone to bed she'd left us a still warm casserole on the top of the oven. When we'd sat down, my father and me had been eating slowly, as if with our nervous exhaustion we couldn't get the food to swallow.

"We should have asked Naois O'Haughan tonight where his treasure was hidden," I'd said by way of a joke. My father looked at me as if I'd had two heads instead of one.

"What, son?" he'd said, jumping up, but quietening down again in case my mother had heard him. "Did you not get enough for one night? One month?" he whispered now, looking utterly disgusted with our experience.

"But the metal-detector," I'd argued, "We've used it only once and that underground tunnel that leads from the mound to the underground chamber below the monastery ruins... this could be where the highwayman may have hidden his booty. It would be daft to just give up now!"

"Metal-detector! Metal-detector!" my father had raved, almost pulling his hair out. "I'll show you metal-detector!" my father shouted, forgetting that people might have heard him at the top of the street, never mind my mother and siblings upstairs.

Suddenly my father jumped up from his armchair, going to the coal-bunker under the stairs and rummaging, until he'd emerged again, his face red with rage. He'd brought out the metal-detector where we'd stored it, heading for the scullery before throwing open the back door leading to the yard. I'd followed him out, just in time to see him lifting the bin lid before dumping the metal-detector into the bin with a loud clunk.

After an hour or so, when he'd quietened down, he'd risen from his chair and stuck his head under the water tap of our Belfast sink and scrubbed his face, followed by me doing the same, before my mother would see us in the morning. "I'm away to my bed now," he'd said wearily. "Don't forget to switch off the lights, the radio... and put the fireguard over the fire."

I'd waited another half-an-hour or so until I'd head no movement coming from my father's and mother's room, when I'd stood at the bottom of the stairs listening. I'd carefully opened the back door, trying not to make it squeak, like the rats would squeak sometimes, when I'd lain in bed listening to them.

When I'd gone out into the yard, my first reaction was to look up at the yard wall, not believing that I wouldn't see that evil little king again, before going to the bin and lifting the metal-detector out again. When I'd retrieved it and cleaned it down with a towel, I'd sneaked upstairs with it, finding an old, duffle-coat that my father had discarded. Little George had been sound asleep, when I'd carefully wrapped the coat around the detector... before hiding it below my bed. There was one thing that I'd known... I would never stop looking for the highwayman's treasure, and I might just be able to spot the lovely Rosaleen again and listen to that beautiful singing voice. I'd look forward to that very much.

Chapter Sixteen

The Secret, Underground Tunnel

AFTER OUR TERRIFYING MISADVENTURE in the autumn, we'd not experienced anything unusual, except for the time when we would help the local farmers to bring in their harvests, when a scarecrow, in the middle of one of their fields, had mysteriously moved to the end of the field under its own power, then had settled there, until it had moved back again. All three of us, Peter, Jim and me had witnessed it, while the farmer and his wife, who'd been working beside us, had sworn that the scarecrow hadn't moved at all from its original spot.

It had now been approaching Christmas, and Peter's father had been released from prison. As usual, before the Christmas holidays, our three fathers would pack their cases and go to Dublin or over to England to look for work, to get money to buy our food and Christmas presents. This time a construction firm called Wimpey had advertised for workers for overseas, and our fathers would go to Birmingham, in the English midlands, to start work in a place called the Bullring in Birmingham city centre.

My father hadn't liked England very much when he'd worked over there before, for the same construction firm, telling my mother once that the English workers would make fun of the Irish. They would sing a song to the tune of Rule Britannia, and would sing a song called, the W...I...M...P...E...Y... song, and would sing, "We-Import-More-Paddies-Every-Year!" Since our fathers had gone away, all three of us could do as we'd liked, more or less, except to play truant from school, but we'd liked a smoke at the street corner on the quiet.

Before they'd gone away, our fathers had expressly warned us about going treasure hunting again on our own, but this warning hadn't stopped us from pitching our tent at the summit at Cavehill, Divis or the Black Mountains, in all weathers. We'd never set eyes on the evil little ones again, although we'd been out hunting with our father's hunting ferret, Fearless and the union bag nets for the entrances to the rabbit warren exits and entrances, after the ferret had been sent in.

"Whatever happened to that metal- detector that your father bought you?" Peter whispered in class one day. "I'd heard my father being told by your father that he'd thrown it into the bin, and now it's probably buried under tons of rubbish on the shore of Belfast Lough, where they're reclaiming the land from the sea. But you still have it, haven't you?" Peter had now looked even funnier, because he'd been into his fifth pair of spectacles, and now he'd been wearing another brand new pair, but this time with the glasses tied around his ears.

Peter, on his own, had made an optician very rich at his shop in Belfast's Royal Avenue, the main city, shopping centre, buying a new pair, on average, every four weeks. When he'd usually lost his glasses, he would buy a new pair to look for them, and so it went on and on. But Peter had reminded me: I hadn't forgotten my metal-detector, and I'd been secretly waiting for our fathers to go abroad. While my father had still been at home, I'd always kept the battery charged, coming downstairs in the early hours while everybody else had been in bed, then coming down again to take the charger out of the plug and hiding it below my bed just before they'd gotten up.

I'd never intended to give up so easily in looking for Naois O'Haughan's treasure, and once our fathers had been well-settled into England, I would persuade Peter and Jim to tackle that underground tunnel that had led from the mound to under old Jack's house and into the monastery ruins' underground chamber, with me. Over the weeks, while we'd been out hunting, we'd always checked out the heavy padlock on the steel door at the entrance to the mound. Nothing had been disturbed, and things had been as we'd left them, with the padlock sawed almost all the whole way through. It would only take a tiny effort now to finish it.

"What do both of you think?" I'd asked my friends sitting on each side of me. "Are you game enough to try again... searching for the highwayman's treasure, I mean?"

Old eagle eye, Mister Murray, was watching us over his spectacles as he sat at his desk, before rising and walking up and down between us, as we'd been under his strict instructions to copy down the questions on the blackboard for our homework, about the Battle of Hastings in 1066.

"Jim, we'd need your father's hacksaw," I'd said, as soon as the teacher had returned to his desk. "We would need to cut the rest of the way through the padlock, about a quarter of an inch. Could you get it?"

"Not the hacksaw," Jim had replied. "My father has it with him in England, along with the rest of his tools, but I can get a blade that he left behind. It will cut through if we put a piece of cloth around it, to save us from cutting our fingers."

"And Fearless... should we bring Fearless?" Peter had interrupted, "Seeing that the little ones don't want to ride him like a horse again? Now that they've gone?"

I shook my head. What would happen if the tunnel ran beside, or through, old Jack's cellar? And if the dog heard him through the wall it would only start barking, alerting the old man? "Better that the three of us go in alone," I replied to Peter. "If the dog started scraping or barking old Jack would just hear us, and if he doesn't shoot us he'd send for the police, and we'd be charged with trespassing... and you would end up in your father's old cell in Crumlin Road prison," I'd joked.

"Anyway, Peter," Jim had interrupted, "what would happen if we saw the lovely Rosaleen again and she'd started singing and playing her harp again? Your dog would go nuts!" That was our next plan: we would saw through the rest of the padlock next Saturday, when Jack would be in his shop late again. We'd planned to bring a spade to dig our way out, if there'd been a cave-in, and the dozen or so candles that we'd borrowed seven or eight weeks before, from the chapel's altar.

Once inside the tunnel, we could light a candle and leave it sitting, each ten yards apart, as the tunnel was around a hundred yards long, to find our way out again, if we'd been successful and had found the highwayman's loot at last. Although we'd liked Abbot John, we'd hoped that he wouldn't be there when we'd reached the underground chamber. He had been friendly, but when he'd just disappeared like that it had unnerved us all, although he'd meant well. We could hardly understand English, never mind Latin or Gaelic, if he and Rosaleen had suddenly popped up and had babbled away to us.

Hopefully there wouldn't be a sudden, cave-in, as we would be there for years without anybody knowing where we'd gone, because our mothers, under strict instructions from our fathers, had warned us to tell them nothing about our exploits, in case they'd worried too much about our welfare. We'd leave from Jim's house on Sunday evening, after we'd put our own tools together, Jim's polecat ferret, the hacksaw blade, a box of matches, our holy candles and our torches. We would also bring half a dozen rabbit warren nets, to deceive anybody, especially the Grand Master of the Atlantean Federation, Matt Collins, if they'd wanted to nosey about where we'd be going, and also our wellington boots and waterproof overcoats.

We'd also bring a spade, just in case the tunnel would cave in on us. Our hills had always been the first stop for heavy rains, because of the never-ending north wind that blew, even in the summertime, and at times, after the rain, the torrents of water would charge through our village's six or seven rivers that had fed the three mills in the area. Most times they would have burst their banks, and because there was a river that had always ran alongside the old monastery ruins, the water was bound to have seeped into the tunnel.

Even an underground reservoir had been formed, just above the bull field, and the village would use its freshwater supply often, from a sunken pipe and water tap. Just to make sure, I would write a note to my mother, telling her where we'd been going, and I would leave it below my pillow on Sunday afternoon after returning from church. If nothing happened to us, then I would return home on Sunday evening and destroy the note.

We would also bring a spool of catgut, fishing line, two hundred yards long. We would tie this to the ferret's collar, and if there was a cave-in, we could send the ferret to look for a way out if we'd been trapped. After our dinner we'd set off, careful to approach Curtain's Avenue from the direction of Bodel's Dam. Old Jack wouldn't see us then, as if we'd approached from our house on Mill Avenue we would have passed Jack's shop window, and he'd missed nothing.

It had been around 7 p.m., and the dam's surrounds seemed spookier than usual tonight, probably because no adults had been with us in the pitch darkness. The only noises we could hear was from the humming of the spinning and weaving machines, coming from the interior of the mill and the nightshift machine operators there. We'd reached a little, white, pebble-covered path that looked into the beautiful well-groomed gardens of the Ewart mansion. Then we could hear another familiar noise in the distance, from whence we'd come. It had been old Fearless, pining after Peter as much as Jim. Fearless had taken to Peter and Peter to him, because both had recognised the stupidity in each other. Thankfully, Jim had chained him firmly to his yard wall, but Peter had wanted to return and release the dog.

But Fearless had now started a chorus of dog barking, and even the German Shepherd dogs behind the Ewart house had started barking and howling, as well as the rest of the dogs in the village. There had been no sign of the gamekeeper, as Billy McCready liked to go out drinking like everybody else, on a weekend.

Now we'd reached the top of Curtain's Avenue, and had stopped just outside the main, steel gate to the front of the mansion. While looking all the way down the avenue, we could see old Jack entering the path of his house, the outside light at the front of his house shining onto him. He was dressed in his Sunday best, probably having been out all day to visit his wife's grave, something he would do most Sundays.

"Excuse me, excuse me... could you tell me when the next tram is coming through the village?"

All three of us had stopped dead in our tracks, trying to look at each other's lips to work out which one of us had said that.

"Excuse me... excuse me... could you tell me what time the next tram is at?"

Now I could feel the hairs and goosebumps standing up all over my body. The low voice had been that of a young girl, but as yet we could see no-one else on the avenue. We'd tried to get our eyes accustomed to the pitch darkness, looking intently into the vacant nothingness.

Then, we could just make out a slight figure of a girl in her teens walking, or was she floating, towards us, with long, light hair? She had one arm outstretched towards us, while her other arm had grasped something to her breasts tightly. "Sorry miss," I'd replied trembling, "but the trams went out of commission up here around seven or eight years ago... are you sure you don't mean when is the next bus due up to the terminus? I think it's every hour; the next is at eight o' clock, and if you hurry you will catch it."

The girl was almost up to us now, and strangely, although it hadn't rained for two days, the water was dripping off her... and her baby... who'd been almost choking her with its arms tightly around her neck, and the baby was crying uncontrollably, as if it had been afraid that we'd take it off its mother. Although the torches had been shining right into her eyes, she'd never blinked once, and the baby had been dripping wet too. The girl and the baby had edged much closer to us now, while looking intently into our faces. "Excuse me... could you please tell me what time the next tram is coming through the village... I want to go down to Belfast to see my husband," the young girl had kept repeating, as all three of us had slowly backed away from her and the child, terrified.

I'd remembered, vividly, when the trams had been introduced into our village. That was before I'd even started primary school, and they had been replaced by London-type, red, double-decker buses. The trams had run on electricity, and the overhead cables would be connected to double arms that had protruded from the roof of the buses. Sparks would fly when the buses would start up or slow down, and when the trolley buses had been taken off the roads our fathers had made a fortune.

They'd climbed up the connecting poles at the side of the road, cutting down the electric cables with hacksaws, then selling the copper cables to O'Hara, the scrap merchant, and the red buses had diesel engines. Then all three of us appeared to read each other's minds... and took off in a stampede of panic, down towards the ancient mound fifty yards away, with Peter falling over a stump of a tree that had been cut down two years before.

When we'd stopped to help him, we'd shone our torches to where the girl and baby had been exactly, but there had been no-one there, as if there'd been nobody there in the first place. We'd stopped at the sloping, small, grassy knoll at the entrance to the mound, and had flopped down onto the ground.

"Jesus Christ!" Jim shouted, "What the hell was that, that is all I want to know, what the hell was it?"

"But I didn't see anything," Peter had said, "I only heard one of you asking what time the next tram was coming up the road at, and you were having me on again—we use buses now... did you think I'd fall for that one? And you're supposed to be my friends!"

Both Jim and I had laughed nervously, both at the apparition and its baby nearly frightening us to death, but at the same time I'd felt awfully sorry for the girl and her child, saying an Our Father and three Hail Marys for them under my uncontrollable breath. But old Fearless and the German dogs must have sensed something, and as we lay there we'd shone both torches up towards to where the apparitions had been, especially around the trees in case they'd been still loitering there.

"Shall we call this off?" Jim had moaned. "Would it be better if we went home again now... because if this is what we're in for we'll not last the rest of the friggin' night!" Jim's voice had been hoarse with shock, as if his mouth had been stuffed with sawdust, and as if he'd been ready to burst into tears.

"Maybe both of you were just imagining things," Peter proffered. "It's getting very windy and those rose bushes beside the mansion were blowing and swirling all over the place, and their whistling scared the hell out of me!"

What Peter had just said was exactly what my father had said to me a few months ago, when that evil, little leprechaun sat on our yard wall and had taunted me, until it had happened to himself. I'd known that when I'd seen that girl and her baby that it had been the girl who had killed herself and her baby, because her husband had been killed during the withdrawal from Dunkirk during the Second World War.

"Let's list what we've brought with us," I'd suggested, when all of us had calmed down and before we'd break into the underground tunnel without something that we may have left behind.

"Candles... torches... matches... spade... ferret in the sack... fishing line..." Jim had reeled off quickly.

"And our cigarettes. I've brought us twenty Woodbine," Peter said, it being obvious that his father was back to his old habits again.

"All present and correct sir!" Jim had clicked his heels together and had saluted me, giving me the impression that because the tools had been mostly Jim's then he should have been giving the orders.

I'd laughed under my breath at Peter, who'd stood there like the Grim Reaper, holding onto his new spectacles, although he'd tied them to his head and eyes with two elastic bands. Then I'd handed Peter a torch to keep him occupied, telling him to "shine it onto the padlock so that we could finish what Jim's father almost did, sawed clean through it." But the torch's beam had been flying all over the place in Peter's extreme nervousness, like a lighthouse beam, on the move all the time.

I'd sawed at the padlock bar vigorously, the sparks flying all over the place, with some landing on my hair that had left it smelling like a burning mattress. "Done it! That's it!" I'd shouted, my hands and fingers sore and hot. I'd not bothered to bring my metal-detector with me tonight: if there'd been anything underground then we would have found it without having to dig. But if we'd failed to find anything tonight, I was intending to go to the main library on Belfast's Royal Avenue, where I would be able to obtain an old map of our area from nearly two hundred years ago. It had taken all three of us all of our strength to push the heavily creaking door inwards, just as Peter was about to tumble forward, head first, us not knowing that the drop inside the door was steep, where the steps ran downwards.

A heavy, musky smell had hit us in the face when we'd stood on the first two steps, as if, and it had probably been true, we'd been the first humans to set foot in there for generations. The tunnel had been around five feet from steps to ceiling, and around four feet wide, and when we'd shone our torches inside, the multiple steps had gone down and down, as if they'd be leading to hell itself.

The steps had been shored up with thick shards of wood, like a shortened version of railway sleepers, that had probably been hewn out of the branches of the many oak trees that had grown on the avenue for two or three hundred years, when the hills around Belfast had been covered in forest, and thick mud sods had been stuffed between each backed-up sleeper. Thick, wooden planks had also shored the roof, and ran for a yard or so along the ceiling.

The *drip, drip, drip* of water droplets had sent a deep echo all along and down the tunnel shaft, the water perforating through the earthen roof of the tunnel, while the tunnel had appeared to have no end at all. "Get a candle out of your rucksack, Jim," I'd ordered again, "and before you light it, close the steel door behind us, in case the draft blows the candle out. Don't worry, we can't be closed in, there's nothing here to lock the door with, from the outside. Put it on the second step away from the door, then others every ten yards or so. That way we'll be able to find our bearings and the way back out again."

"If the candles run out before we reach the end of the tunnel, our torches will see us right through to the end... either way we'll be all right for light and sight." As we'd inched downwards, the ferret was trying to burst out of the sack that Jim had been carrying, the ferret probably hearing what we were—rats squeaking and running all over the tunnel. Dozens of bats had also been hanging around, their toenails clinging to the roof, as now and again one or two at a time would detach themselves, then flying off in the opposite direction from where we'd entered. I'd wondered how the bats and rats had been able to enter this place, it being closed to almost airtight for donkey's years and more.

"Oh no, not again!" Jim had whispered, after he'd volunteered to take the lead. "*Shoosh... shoosh*, did you not hear that noise close by?" Jim had said, but Peter had let go of the back of my coat, looking over my shoulder at Jim.

"Now don't be starting that again," Peter had protested. "Do you think I'm stupid?"

We didn't want to answer Peter's question in case we'd hurt his feelings.

"No! No!" Jim had said, "I can hear that singing voice just ahead there, do you not hear it? How did they get into the tunnel ahead of us if the steel door has just been opened for the first time in over a hundred years?"

"Probably how the lovely Rosaleen had got in," I'd replied, "through that crevice when Rosaleen went down... in other words, the voices are probably more ghosts."

"Stuff this for a game of Scrabble!" Peter whimpered, "I'm getting out of here now, right now! Are any of you coming back to the entrance with me?"

"And how do you propose to go back, Peter?" Jim had asked. "This place is like the narrow, storm drain that runs under Wolfhill mill. We can't turn around, and could you walk uphill backwards? I can't! Let's go on. Maybe, as you said, Peter, it's just the wind whistling through the tunnel, like the trees. We'll only worry when somebody approaches us in here and asks us what time the last bus goes into Belfast city centre... he, he, he."

Up until now, we'd left at least eight lit candles behind us: we'd climbed down into the tunnel for at least seventy or eighty yards, and it was possible that we'd underestimated the length of that tunnel. One good think about it was it had been getting higher and wider, and more fresh air had blown into our faces from far below.

"I told you lads, can you not hear the music above us there?" Jim had said, breaking the silence. "Can you not hear the musical instruments and the female singing?"

We'd stopped and had listened intently to the music coming from above, wondering if Rosaleen had returned.

"How come the female voice is singing that pop song, 'Lipstick On Your Collar' by Connie Francis?" I'd asked. "And that musical backing—that's a guitar, not a harp!"

"That's because it *is* Connie Francis... and she is singing 'Lipstick On Your Collar, Told a Tale On You, You,' and that's Jack's radio playing above us up there: we're directly under his house now," Jim had said, "or maybe Rosaleen has gotten a recording contract with RCA Records, the Recording Company of America."

As we'd moved further along the tunnel now, after coming to the end of the steps, we'd been on flat, damp ground, and while we'd used all our candles to mark our way back out again, we'd now be depending on our torches as we'd be going deeper and deeper into the chamber. Soon we'd came upon what we'd thought had been box-shaped entrances, that had ran at least seven feet into the sides of the tunnel. They'd been old tombs, and three feet square, marble slabs had been sitting on the ground beside each one, on their sides, with foreign names on them that we'd taken to be the dead monks' names in Latin.

When we'd shone our torches into the tombs, we'd then pulled out old strands of human hair with our spade, and what had looked two or three human teeth, and pieces of brown cloth. The dead monks had obviously been moved, probably to hallowed ground, before the monastery had been finally closed down.

Chapter Seventeen

The Devil Worshippers and the Treasure Map

"IT SOUNDS LIKE OLD JACK'S DIALLED** into another radio station," Jim had surmised. "It seems as if he's listening to a radio church service now." As we'd walked further on, we could see that the chamber had widened out so much that it was now nine feet from floor to ceiling, and around eight feet wide. Peter had suddenly squealed as the biggest spider we'd ever seen had dropped down on a web strand from the ceiling, landing on the nape of his neck before he'd swiped it off and stamped on it.

"Hell! That's a service all right," I'd whispered, "and it's not coming from above, or from Jack's house, it's coming from directly in front of us, as if the ghosts of the monks are holding a ghostly Mass... do you hear that friggin' chanting?"

The chants appeared to be emanating from another chamber connected to the one that we'd been walking along, and some flickering lights were intermittently flashing from within it.

This tunnel had been much longer than a hundred yards, and where the lights had been coming from a half opened, steel door had been the centre of the noises and lights. Some kind of movement had been going on, as well as five of six muffled voices, and we'd crept up as quietly as possible. We'd peered into this other chamber and we'd jumped back in horror, as a group of adults had been dressed in long, white garments like sheets over their heads, that covered their entire bodies, right down to the soggy ground.

"Jesus!" Peter had whispered, grabbing both me and Peter, "these fellas look like those people from Alabama, in the southern states of the USA, who stand before a burning cross and hang black people! The clue... the clue ...?"

"The Ku Klux Klan you mean, Jim," I'd corrected him. "I've seen their kind in my father's political newspaper, *The United Irishman*... real bad guys, and their lynching is called after an Irishman called Lynch, too, who'd owned a cattle ranch in the American West, and he'd hanged a rustler for stealing his cattle and that name stuck, the lynching name." It seemed to get more bizarre as we surveyed this new, square-shaped chamber. It had looked a lot like our chapel at Saint Vincent's, but underground, that the monks of old had probably used when the upper floors had begun to collapse, or when they'd been in hiding, and may have forgotten to dismantle when it had closed down. The beautiful, white-marbled altar had sat in the middle of the chamber, but instead of a white, altar cloth, the cloth had been of a black satin material that had draped right down to the floor, like loose curtains.

Three burning torched each had hung from four walls, a total of twelve, that had been made out of broom handles, and, like our Ring of Fire months ago, the burning parts had consisted of old sacking tied up with steel wire. As well as wearing long, white robes that had reached the ground and their feet, each person had worn a black, tall, pointed hat, like dunce's caps, but what was more sinister was the holes that were cut out of the black satin masks, that had completely covered their faces, where the eyes, noses and mouths would be.

On their backs had been a map that had looked like a map of Ireland, but had had the words written on them, 'The Lords Of Atlantis'.

"Oh no!" I'd whispered to Peter and Jim, "Surely these fruit cakes weren't Matt Collins, the Grand Master of the Ancient Order of the Atlanteans and his nutty friends? And Matt was probably one of the nuts hidden under one of those masks." I'd felt a heavy tug on the hood of my coat.

"Let's get the frig out of here!" Peter had whispered, now shaking and getting ready to run off.

"No!" Jim had said, "Don't move! If we switch the torches back on again they'll see us... and maybe all three of us will be sacrificed on top of their altar there!"

Now Jim's comments had got me thinking: sacrificed to who or what? We'd heard about the devil worshippers who operated on the Cavehill mountain, for years, and I'd wondered, if this had been true, in which case perhaps these nuts had been the culprits all along?

I didn't have to wait long for my wondering: one of the comical-looking fellas had stepped forward from the main group, then, walking up to the altar he reached down and pulled a large, hundredweight-sized, black satin sack from beneath the altar cloth. He produced six, golden-coloured, tall, candlesticks and six thick, black candles, walking over and lighting one of them from the light of one of the blazing torches on the wall, before returning to the altar and lighting the other five. Then they'd all gathered around the altar, the main one, or boss, who produced a black scroll from under his vestment. When he'd opened the scroll out, the language that he spoke was unmistakable this time, not Gaelic or Latin, but English.

"Satan," he'd started, before all three of us had recoiled in horror. "Satan, guide your followers here who attend to you tonight, and come and take your place at the altar among us here." After a moment of silence the voice boomed: "Take your place at this unholy altar and join us in this mortal realm. You have a place of great love and respect among your followers here, on behalf of the Ancient Order of the Atlanteans!"

"I've had enough," Peter had whispered, "let's get out of here before Old Nick shows up!"

But now we'd been even too terrified to even breathe loudly, never mind trying to escape from this place; but I'd still hoped that our fathers had been with us tonight. If we'd stayed we may have been in trouble, and if we'd given ourselves away we'd still have been in trouble.

As we'd looked on at this surreal scene, we'd not known if all the nuts had been men, or if some women had been with them. Another of the men or women had then stopped watching the speech maker, then went back to the black sack and rummaged through it carefully. We'd been horrified again when he'd pulled out a human skull and a set of bones, placing them on top of the altar carefully, presumably for their occult operations.

"May these offerings bring you to our presence tonight," the main man had said, "as you have brought great darkness and great evil into our once miserable Christian lives, filled by idolatry and untruthful Catholic, and Protestant, Hebrew priests!"

"Do not forget your servants who walk beside YOU in your darkness, beloved one," the black-and-white-garbed man had said, "and lend to us your never-ending, truthful life! We feel the need for everlasting life, and your guidance that we may live and dwell with you for all eternity!"

These guys were probably the ones, I'd thought, who'd been breaking into churches to steal candlesticks, and wine and communion chalices all over the country. Some of these holy instruments had been used in occult ceremonies on the Cavehill mountain above Belfast, and it had been so bad once that churches had to close and people couldn't pray inside them, unless a service had been taking place and lots of people had been around. Even the bodies of newly-died children, it had been said once, had been dug up from their graves just hours after they'd been buried. This had been done by the occultists because the babies' blood would still not have coagulated, and the blood had been drained from them for sacrifices, and even animals were killed and drained for that very same reason.

Incredibly, my fears had been realised when another of the masked people had gone to the sack, this time producing a golden chalice and a crucifix that had been turned upside-down, with Christ still hanging on it, and this chalice had looked similar to one that had probably been stolen to order, in the USA, and had been shown on the TV. This chalice had looked to be gold-plated, and beautiful, green emerald jewels had gone all around the equator part of it.

Another of the ghouls had gone through another door that we'd not came through, it being in the far side of the chamber, and hadn't walked past us from the little, steel door that we'd entered from. This ghoul had, when he'd returned, been carrying a large, green, glass decanter, similar to one that would have contained a chemical, like acid. When he'd pulled the cork, he'd poured a thick, red liquid into the chalice, that had appeared to send the rest into a frenzy, and when he'd put the chalice down beside the skull, the bones had been arranged into a cross, or the pirate sign, the skull and bones.

"Satan! You live forever!" all the people had shouted together now, while they'd all held their arms aloft, just like Abbot John, when he'd saved us from the little, evil ones. "As long as we follow you, the lord Satan, we shall live forever and ever, amen!" they'd shouted again. "We are here to share our lives with you, lord, and we open our hearts to you! We will never abandon you, and we shall share our lives with you forever!"

One of the ghouls then lifted the chalice to his mouth, then sipped the contents, passing it around the rest in an anti-clockwise fashion, all of them drinking thirstily from it before wiping their mouths. "It is with great joy that we welcome the great one," they'd started again, "and we offer the bones of the highwayman, Naois O' Haughan, down to you. We call on the great ones—the sun, the moon, to deliver the great Satan to us, to give us his dark blessings. We call on the air, the wind, the little, creatures of the night, and we bring this human child's blood for you, and for you to witness! Host of host, king of kings, lord of wisdom, you who know all, while waiting at the crossroads for us all, the night is yours, the time is near, oldest ancient god... give us strength so that we may arise anew and reborn! Receive the highwayman's head, and also his flintlock pistols, his saddle, sword and lantern, and his garb, with our further blessing! Ready are your faithful servants that await your unholy blessings!"

If I could believe what we'd been hearing now, everything that had belonged to the highwayman had been here all along! But the treasure—where had the treasure gone if the human ghouls hadn't got their blood-stained hands on it? Did these people find the highwayman's grave first and bring the remains here, or were the remains always here?

And Rosaleen? Where had Rosaleen gone to? Did she just hang around the old ruins here just to watch over the bones of Naois? Was the treasure buried somewhere else around our village, so that it would never be discovered again, ever? Without a map? Perhaps the treasure had been in that black sack there, and the Atlanteans had decided to wait to present it to Old Nick last?

Now I could hear Peter's teeth rattling again, and his bones had been rattling again, too. If the Atlanteans had heard him shaking they would have offered him up, or down, where the devil was.

Our long-time-dead friend, the highwayman, had saved our lives three months ago; now we had to stand and watch as his remains were being defiled, and we couldn't do anything at all about it! Jim had been in front of me, I'd been behind him and Peter had almost been in the back pocket of my jeans, when we'd all jumped again.

"You live!" all of the men had chanted together, "And we open our hearts to you, our great, dark master... and you shall never die!"

"We would even sacrifice the lives of our families for you, and your presence will even swim in the air of the earth's atmosphere... now, come to us, come to us! We will never abandon you, ever! Come to us so that you may know and love us, come, come now!"

Jim had cursed out loud when he'd dropped his torch, with the torch switching itself on when it had struck the ground, sending wild beams into the eyes of the devil worshippers. Suddenly, all of the men swivelled their heads around in our direction, then made a mad scramble towards us, looking like they'd wanted to tear us to pieces, like a pack of Rottweiler dogs. We all ran in panic in the direction in which we'd came, making for the safety of the steps and the open door of the mound.

Peter, as usual, had slipped and had fallen, as when we'd helped him to his feet the men had almost been right up to us, shouting and cursing.

Suddenly, a voice that had echoed all around the chamber, but hadn't come from the evil ones or us, grew louder.

"I am Satan... I come from the realms of the dead... I have taken my proper seat among my followers, now come back to this chamber, for you are all under arrest!"

A flood of uniformed men, policemen, entered the chamber, led by the gamekeeper, Billy McCready!

He, too, had been wearing his black, policeman's uniform, while, by now, all the members of the Ancient Order of the Atlanteans had been wrestled to the ground and handcuffed, and disrobed. Matt Collins had stood there with his head bowed; then he was led away, chained to another policeman.

"Are you young fellas all right?" Billy McCready had asked, "We've been watching this gang of loony bins for two years now, but we could never pin them down, until tonight, that is! I'm sorry that I had to tell you lies about the so-called ghosts—there are none, and no ghostly monk; no ghostly girl and her child, and no red-haired girl singing with a guitar out on the avenue! Ghosts don't exist, you understand this lads, right?"

"But," Jim had asked, "how did you get inside the underground chamber? You never came past us and we came in through the little gate at the mound." At the same time I pointed towards the steps and the pyramid of still, half-lit candles that had looked like a Christmas tree in the murky darkness.

"No," Billy had replied, "we'd always known that the little door was there, but we'd thought that it had still been padlocked, until one of my men saw you tonight, cutting the padlock, but we'd came in the way the devil worshippers came in, so as not to give the game away. They came in through a manhole cover that had been lifted up beside the bus terminus, and they'd waded along an ancient sewer that the monks had built, and into the chamber. I'm not a Catholic lads," Billy went on, "but these monks were great construction workers and they should be commended... they invented wine too, you know, thanks be to God!"

As we went into the chamber where the altar had been, we could see policemen putting all the evidence back into the black, satin sack, with one of them putting his finger into the chalice and tasting its contents, his face contorting. "Blood!" he'd shouted to his boss. "It's friggin' blood!"

"Listen, you boys go on home now and we'll take these freaks back out through the sewer again; we've got transport waiting for them on Ligoniel Hill. If they have done what I think they've done—grave-robbing, thefts of sacred articles from churches and threatening to do you boys harm... not to mention trespassing onto listed and private land, like you did!—then they'll be in prison for a long time."

"Maybe Matt Collins there will get your father's old cell, Peter?" the policeman had laughed out loud, "for the parrots that he sold me and the judge, remember?"

But all three of us had doubled over in laughter as well, but not about Peter's father getting caught for selling the exotic and ordinary domestic birds. "No ghostly monk; no ghostly girl and her child; no highwayman and no Rosaleen singing, with her red hair hanging down, out at Curtain's Avenue, eh?" I'd asked.

"No, nothing," Billy had replied, removing his black, peaked cap and scratching his head. "And who's Rosaleen?" He shook his head. "Anyway, I had to keep you all away from here some way, knowing and all these arrests were to be made soon."

But I could swear that Billy had given us a wink. We'd been making our way back up the steps, able to use our torches to see where we'd been going this time.

"Oh lads!" Billy had shouted after us as we'd made it halfway up the steps. "While coming into the chamber from the old sewer, I'd found this old telescope leather case—do you want to have it, since you'd found nothing during your treasure hunting? It just may be worth something, and, at least, you could always say that you got something from your treasure hunting."

When Billy had walked away from us, he'd put his torch under his big chin, and while he'd contorted his face, he'd gone "Boo!" at us, laughing. "By the way boys," he'd turned to us again, "you won't be able to return here again... we've asked old Jack's permission to allow us to bring in concrete lorries to fill this chamber in; that way none of you boys, or anybody else, for that matter, will be hurt, or worse, inside here again. Goodnight lads, now off you go."

When we'd reached the top of the steps, a policeman had been standing waiting for us as we'd squeezed through the little, steel door, and when we'd gone outside the policeman had replaced the sawn padlock with a newer, stronger one, then walked down Curtain's Avenue to join his friends in the village, just in front of us. Our adventures at the old monastery had been over, and as we'd reached the main village street we could see three police cars sitting on the hill, the policemen putting their captives inside them, while the white-clad prisoners had looked sorrowful, Matt Collins looking down at us as if to say, "*You* caused our downfall!"

Jim, after checking his ferret and his belongings in his own sack, had said, "We'll head on home now, me and Peter, and we'll see you at school in the morning," before they'd started off down the road. I'd shouted after them: "Listen, when our fathers return home next week, I'll get them to check it out if this telescope case is worth anything... all right? Thirty-three per cent each?" Then they'd waved and had quickly disappeared. We'd had enough excitement tonight to do us for a year, but, as I'd passed old, Jack's shop, I'd no doubt that Matt Collins, with their occultism, had called up the little, evil people, and their minions.

My grandmother had always said, before she'd gone to Heaven, "Never have anything to do with evil people, who would blaspheme, play with Ouija boards and upside-down, crucifixes—it will all come to no good, no good at all. They will bring you nothing but tragedy, nothing but bad luck."

Then I'd wondered: how did Billy McCready know that we'd been treasure hunting? If he'd been watching the old, monastery ruins, then surely he would have seen us that first and second night, when Rosaleen had showed up with her harp, playing and singing? There'd been more to Billy than had met our eyes, and why did he give us this telescope case?

I'd reached home at around eleven o'clock. My brother and sister had been in bed, and my mother had sat at the fire knitting, in my father's armchair, as she'd always knitted us our pullovers, and had even made me and little George school satchels out of a pair of denim jeans. I'd kept the telescope case hidden, in case she'd seen it, up inside my pullover, because my father had said, "Don't tell your mother anything, in case you worry her." But my mother hadn't been stupid, and had been very intelligent. She must have sensed something.

She'd given me my supper, then going to the front and back doors, ensuring that they were locked for the night, she said, "When you've eaten that supper, Patrick, make sure that all the lights are out and the fireguard is over the hearth; then get to bed for school in the morning." She went upstairs, where I'd heard her looking in on my siblings before entering her own room.

Then I'd pulled the telescope case up from my jean's belt, looking it over before going into the scullery to fetch a large, serrated knife that my mother had kept for cutting up vegetables.

But it had still bugged me, as I'd wrestled with the telescope lid cover, whether my mother had known or not, and whether she had an inkling of our having had a run-in with the little, evil people. She would find out soon enough, when the rumour had gone around the village, and the country, about what Matt Collins and his evil friends had been getting up to, and he, and probably the rest, when we'd found out who they'd been, had been close neighbours of ours. But it would have been better if she'd never known that we'd been in that underground chamber at the monastery tonight.

The police wouldn't be calling us as witnesses, because the crazy gang had, with the evidence on them, been caught red-handed. And something had told me to look more closely at that telescope box; and when I'd forced the lid off, that had probably been on there for two hundred years, I'd turned it upside down, after looking inside it under the light bulb in the sitting-room.

There had been some dampness and a little water inside the box, as I'd carefully pulled out a yellowed and damp scroll, or piece of parchment, that had been stuck to one of the sides. I'd been astounded, because it had been an old map, and as I dried it at the fire, and it had dried out, I could see the writing on it: Naois O'Haughan 1712 AD. If this had been the highwayman's map, then we'd spelt his surname wrong all along, as there had been an 'i' in it.

When I'd looked more closely at it, there had been letters of the alphabet, twenty-two of them, and beside then were small x's. Our village, although not seen as present day, had been there, as well as all the surrounding areas and dams, including the Black, Divis and Cavehill Mountains. Where 'A' had been marked out with a cross I'd figured that to be around Curtain's Avenue, before there'd even been such a place. 'B' had been marked with an 'X', and that had been Squire's Hill, beside Bodel's Dam. 'C' had been on top of the Cavehill itself, and 'D' had been where the Flush Road was now, Naois O'Haughan's old, ancestral home. 'E' had been marked out with an 'X' where a little, natural quarry was, just above Kennedy's Race, and 'F' had been on the old, Budore Road that was still there today. 'G' had been Carnmoney Cemetery, where Peter, Jim and me had tried to find the highwayman's grave in September, and 'H' had been where the BBC aerial was, on top of Black Mountain. 'I' had been at McArt's Fort, at the bottom of the cliffs at Cavehill, and 'J' had been on the south bank of Kennedy's Race itself.

'K' had been marked out at the Bottom Dam, that had just started to feed the newly-erected Wolfhill mill, and 'L' had been marked-out at the former McElwan's hill, to the north of the Hightown road. 'M' had been marked, also with an 'X', and that was shown situated at the south of the Hightown Road, and 'N' had been marked at in a field to the south of Wolfhill Road, just above Top Dam, another that had fed Wolfhill mill. 'O' had also been shown at the foot of the Black Mountain, just two miles from our village, and 'P' had been at Wolfhill Quarry, just above our village.

'Q' had been marked at a field to the north of the Hightown Road, and 'R' had been marked at the top of the bull field, where we'd had all the trouble with the little evil people, while 'S' had been marked at a little, artificial waterfall, at the stream on the Wolfhill Road. 'T' had been marked out at the Ballyhill Road, one mile from our village, on the road to Nutt's Corner Airport, where the stagecoaches would either pass through our village or the Main Line to Antrim town. 'U' had been marked at Ben Madigan Heights, were Bellevue Zoo had been situated now, and finally, 'V' had been marked at Mill Avenue, beside our street, where locals had chopped down the fairy, hawthorn tree, just seven or eight years ago.

I'd thought that our treasure hunt had ended, but it had looked more and more if it was just beginning. I would hide the little treasure map after showing it to my friends Peter and Jim, and when our fathers would return from England, it had looked all the more possible now that we'd all be very rich. I'd still have my metal-detector at the ready, the battery fully-charged up, and afterwards, when my father had a chance to view this map, he would be glad that I'd retrieved it from the rubbish bin, after he'd lost his temper and had dropped it in there.

Hopefully we could start searching again in the spring, and I would get a pencil in school tomorrow and a page of tracing paper to highlight the map a little stronger, for that original map could be very valuable because of its vintage age. The lineage of the map had faded over the years, both with the water and green mould, but I would bring it back to life again. Then I would be ready to go to visit the last resting place of that elusive highwayman, Naois O'Haughian—after I'd asked the policeman, Billy McCready, where they had laid Naois, finally to rest in peace.

Chapter Eighteen

We Resume our Search at New Locations

OUR THREE FATHERS HAD RETURNED FROM ENGLAND in January, and we had begun our search again. We'd started to the north of our village this time, working our way back to the west. They'd taken the ancient, telescope case to the Ulster museum in Cultra, where the curator had sent it to "their main office at the British Museum in London for a thorough examination" while we'd waited at home in anticipation.

Later, he had informed us by letter that "we'd have to wait for months because we were at the bottom of the list as one of the artefacts, dozens actually, had been articles like coinage, shields, swords, and body armour," that "had been found in a field by a farmer who'd ploughed his land months before, in East Anglia, and it had been

thought had belonged to Hereward the Wake, a great English king."
We'd attempted to search some of the sites marked on the
highwayman's old map, during January and February, but we'd gotten
nowhere because of the cold, icy ground during the heavy snow that
winter.

We stupidly had searched the high ground first along all the ridges of
the mountains, up hills and down valleys, all six of us, and old Faithful,
Peter's brindle lurcher, hadn't liked the cold at all. We'd left crater-like
holes all over the terrain, starting from McArt's Fort at Cavehill right
through to the Black Mountain. Although we'd tried to keep prying eyes
away from us as we'd searched, local people had been suspicious of our
every move after our terrifying adventure with the devil worshippers,
and had probably thought that we'd been involved, and they'd been very
wary of people, especially us, going around and digging up things. We'd
hidden our metal-detector, pick and shovel, in an old sack, while we'd
left the badger cage out in the open for people to see. We'd put all our
tools into an old pram that we'd found in a rubbish dump and had
removed the wheels, axles and trusses and had made it a homemade
toboggan sledge to pull along in the heavy snowfall. Later, our three
fathers had narrowed our search down to the few places that we'd never
searched yet, and where the highwayman may have had a safe house
around the bottom of the Black mountain adjacent to the Wofhill road,
where it was thought he and his band of outlaws may have hidden,
before they were caught and hanged at Carrickfergus Castle in County
Antrim.

During the winter, we'd used old tennis racquets as snowshoes as
we'd searched, although old Fearless was so lazy that he'd sat on the
pram as we'd pushed along. Then, the fields, forests, rivers and
mountains had looked like a winter scene from Siberia in Russia instead
of Ireland, but April and Easter were just around the corner thankfully, a
time of renewal, a new awakening, and Pentecost, after Jesus had been
scourged before he was finally cruelly crucified after he'd been called
an imposter.

It was beginning to get much warmer now, and flowers like daisies,
daffodils and tulips were trying to force themselves through the hard
permafrost soil, and were succeeding. The real harbingers of spring, the

swallows, corncrake and cuckoo had been returning from their summer holidays in South Africa. My father would laugh out loud, and would retort: "I'll bet you when these birds returned home and flew over where we've been digging, they'd think they were flying over Europe after the war, or the moon, with all the craters where we've been digging!"

But we all knew that nobody would fly over the moon, ever, because the moon was too far away and anyway, they could never build a petrol tank big enough to reach there. And after our terrifying experience last year, with the evil little people and their monster friends, we never did see those terrible paranormal sights again. My father had said this was "because of Abbot John, the monk, who'd exorcised and banished them forever." But I hadn't been too sure of that. A cold, cold chill had run up my spine when I'd remembered those little, ungodly men and women, especially that smelly Grogoch. Somehow, I'd thought that we'd all cross their haunting paths once again, some dark night.

We were off school for a week during the Easter holiday, and our fathers had suggested that we "keep the metal-detector battery charged up" as we would be going treasure hunting again, any time soon. All six of us had sat in Peter's shed where his old dog Fearless usually slept, but not before Peter had thoroughly disinfected it. We'd gone over the highwayman's old map frantically, dozens of times, with pinpoint accuracy, careful not to crumple it because it was so delicate. But now we'd hidden it, beneath my bed at home in Finlay Street, because it had been so valuable, and anyway, I'd brought a few sheets of tracing paper home before Christmas from school to heavily outline it.

Even if we'd managed not to find anything, at least the map, with its age and all, may have been worth a lot of money to the Ulster Museum. We'd been very careful not to let anybody else see it until we'd known, once and for all, that the treasure was there or it wasn't. Now there was just one 'X' left to search, at the side of the river, further up Kennedy's Race, beside the natural waterfall.

"Let's see now," my father had said, going over the map with his index finger as we all looked over his shoulders in anticipation. "We'd started at Carnmoney Hill... worked our way through all of Cavehill... on to Squire's Hill... across to Wolfhill Quarry, where their watchmen never stopped telling us to clear off." Then Jim's father took up the map, twisting it round and round and upside down, setting it down again on the child's cot mattress where Fearless slept at night.

"We've also searched Forthriver," Jim's father said, "then Colinglen... Divis Mountain, then Black Mountain, and all we're left with is indeed Kennedy's Race, when I then took my turn at the new, traced map, turning it upside down and inside out, afraid we'd missed some important place.

"Yes," I proffered, "we haven't yet tried the artificial waterfall at the end of Kennedy's Race."

"I just can't see it being there," Jim's father said. "Naois O'Haughian was operating around the turn of the eighteenth century; that waterfall wasn't built until the mid-eighteenth century or a bit later, by the mill owners, or up to the eighteen sixties or seventies, so that's definitely out."

Suddenly Jim's father grabbed the map and stuffed it under his denim jacket, as an almighty bang was made on the outside of the dog's corrugated metal shed, causing us all to rise to our feet and bang our head on the ceiling of that confined space. Then Peter's nanny goat stuck her head into the inside the door, looking all around as if to say, what are you all doing in here?" And that's the place we haven't yet marked-out, Peter himself said, after the goat had backed away from the door and had settled down again.

"Yes, if we turn right at the artificial waterfall and wade right on, follow the river for about a mile, we'll come to the natural waterfall," Jim junior had said. "That's where Patrick, Peter and I go fishing sometimes tickling for trout, and the pool below the fall is around four feet deep; better not fall in, because it's fast-flowing and very dangerous."

True enough, I'd thought, when we did go up there to fish I remember the remains and foundations of an old, hundreds of years old house beside the waterfall, and if the highwayman did have a safe house to hide in, then this could have been the place, well out of the way and isolated.

"Well, this could be our last throw of the dice," my father had said. "If the treasure isn't here it isn't anywhere; we must have torn up half of the countryside in the last few months." He was thoughtful for a moment, then continued: "Listen, tomorrow is Sunday, and Sunday is the quietest day of the week; if they're not at church, they'll be at the pubs, so we'll have a free rein to search in peace."

We'd decided to gather all our tools at around five-thirty, when it would be just getting to twilight and then full darkness. "During this time," my grandmother used to say to me before she died of cancer last year, "the spirits come into our world and while our faculties and strength decline theirs get stronger."

At least the ghouls and evil little people that we'd encountered during our treasure hunt last summer, I thought, would never leave their haunting grounds at Curtain's Avenue and the old monastery, and as for that great, smelly and ugly Grogoch, that creature had come straight from hell—hopefully it had gone home, never to return. And that talking white owl—owls never leave the place of their birth or their original surroundings—so hopefully we'll get a free run to complete our treasure hunt, then return to normal, maybe, just maybe, very rich.

After supper, all six of us met again in Peter's father's shed, to have a quick equipment check. The metal-detector had been fully-charged and operational when I'd tested it on old Fearless' metal-stud collar. Again we suddenly hit the floor, when a loud metallic thump echoed through the shed, the noise running down the high river bank at the end of the garden and into the small canyon where the river ran through to its long journey from Kennedy's Race to the River Lagan that meandered through Belfast, and then on into Belfast Lough and finally the Irish Sea.

I was wakened from my dreaming when, again, the goat stuck its head through the door angrily, its yellow eyes shining like beacons. We'd all looked at each other in shock.

"I hope this isn't a portent of what's to come?" Jim senior said, a worried look on his big ruddy face.

"Yes," my father had agreed, "the last time we saw that angry look on her face it was being chased and ridden by the little, evil people up in the bull field last year while another hung onto the white owl's neck!"

We'd been spooked again, when the old, teacup-reading witch who lived in Wolfhill Lane, had told Jim's Peter's and my mother that the hills around our village, in the same area where we'd be heading for tonight, were known to be a strange place. There were men, women and children who'd been seen and heard in the hills, between the Black and Wolfhill Mountains. Our headmaster had touched on that when he was giving us a lecture for our history thesis, but we'd thought he'd been mischievous while attempting to stop us from going up there, while we'd played truant from school when the summer weather had been too warm to sit all day in the classrooms.

According to him, "the countryside around Belfast had seen scenes of utter horror. A million people had died of starvation while another four million had left Ireland because of a horrible famine." We'd always listened intently, especially when he'd came to the gory bits, when he'd said that "two hundred thousand small farms were wiped out, forcing hundreds of thousands of people to attempt to make their way to the population centres, in the hope of attaining food to feed their starving and emaciated children." The famine had started in 1845 and had lasted to 1849, he'd said. "A lot of them had suffered premature deaths before their journey's end on the outskirts of our village," he'd concluded. I'd imagined these poor, wretched people, starving after having to walk for days and even weeks, eating anything at hand, like nettles and grass, the poisonous berries from the trees, while the good blackberries wouldn't have been enough to save their miserable lives. A lot of them had died of diseases like cholera and dysentery.

According to our ancestors, "wails and screams could be heard around these hills, in the still of the night," but this catastrophe could have been prevented, and although the potato crop had failed, there was plenty of livestock that was exported to Britain, but the poor people hadn't the money to buy it. Even to this day, when farmers would come to the village to buy supplies in the shops, they would often narrate how sometimes the farmers would have to chase off "raggedly dressed people who'd been trying to steal their chickens and other small livestock," and when they'd caught up with them the people had just disappeared in front of their eyes "as if they'd fallen into a deep hole in the ground when it had unexpectedly opened up."

Gypsies or travellers had been known to camp on their lands with their multi-coloured, horse-drawn wagons, but the gypsies had "never been seen during these forages for food, and the farmers had been vexed trying to understand who these strange beings were."

I was a little wary, because this was the place where we'd carried out our last treasure hunt, and although none of us realised it, Jim's father had, after Peter's goat had battered the dog's shed, as if to say, this is a warning.

After dinner on Sunday night, we'd all called down to Peter's shed again. I'd hidden my metal-detector in an old army coat, while our fathers had stuffed two Hessians sacks with our hunting tools, a heavy metal bar that would usually be used to dig into a badger set, our two polecat ferrets for night hunting for rabbits, the badger cage, two spades for digging out the ferrets if they'd decided to stay in the rabbit warren if they'd killed and had decided to stay in the rabbit warren for the night. We'd also been suitably stocked up with a bag of unpeeled potatoes, six tins of beans, half a loaf, a box of matches, two petrol lighters and my penknife, and six tin plates and six tin cups.

We'd reached the artificial waterfall around an hour later, after we'd followed the path at Kennedy's Race. It was just reaching twilight, and although the sun had set it had become chillier as a stiff, north-east wind swirled down the valley and up our jean's trouser legs. The ice age millions of years ago, along with the fast-flowing river between the Black and Wolfhill Mountains, had formed a deep, canyon into the soil and rocks at the bottom of the mountains, around seventy feet deep.

A small forest of willow trees had risen on each side of the fast-flowing river, the trees almost strangled by thick beds of reeds and water cress, and we'd be having some of that with our potatoes later if we'd needed to stay out there all night. We'd been lucky tonight: usually when we'd gone out bailiffs would follow or stop us, asking us where we were going, and what we were doing?

It would be even more obvious after this week, because young grouse and pheasant had been stolen from cages in the nearby, big houses on the village outskirts, by poachers; but they were missing tonight, both bailiffs and poachers, and my father had remarked: "They're probably in the pub together, splitting their ill-gotten gains." I'd shone a torch down into the deep, dark water of the deep waterfall pool, the rush of water tumbling over its summit noisily like a steam train.

We'd fished that pool below with our fathers for three years, and in its depths lived a monster trout that my father had christened Albert Einstein. We could never catch it, with nets, hooks or gaffs, and my father had remarked, "Einstein may have been the most intelligent in the world but he had a serious rival in that fish!" Nothing could tempt Albert Trout out of the depths of that pool, and my father was exasperated one day when he had Albert on his hook, only for the fish to wriggle off again. "Long runs the fox until it's caught!" he'd screamed, not realising that Albert was a fish.

Chapter Nineteen

Eureka! We Find the Mother Lode

"LISTEN! LISTEN!" PETER SENIOR WHISPERED, as we'd stood at the summit of the artificial waterfall looking down into the fast-flowing torrent of water in our Wellington boots.

"I don't hear anything, save the waterfall," my father said, looking around at the rest of us.

"The silence... can you hear the silence?" my father had added. "The birds are nesting this time of the year and are supposed to be feeding their young; no badgers or foxes out foraging for food... and not even a slight breeze swaying the bushes. It's as if very nature itself is observing us."

Peter senior had spooked us that much that my friends Jim, Peter and me edged closer together, huddling in a bunch.

"And your friggin' lurcher there on the mountainside isn't helping us either," Jim senior had said. "Do you hear him howling there on the hillside? He's scaring everything on the mountain shitless, the friggin' mutt!"

"Wait a minute," Peter senior said, "that's not old Fearless... he's standing right behind the lads there, trembling. Look for yourselves! Right there!"

Jim junior swung his torch around and flicked it on, us following his blinding beam. Sure enough, the brindle had been cowering behind us, his head down and whimpering softly, his eyes bulging in his eye-sockets with extreme fright.

"Then what the hell was that growling and howling if it wasn't your dog?" Jim senior had asked. "No, don't tell me, that was that family of three wolves that had died on this mountain, right?"

"Do... do... you all think we should go on?" Peter junior asked, taking off his glasses and rubbing them clean with the end of his pullover, then stepping back about six feet when I had to grab him as he almost went over the waterfall.

"Now calm down, calm down," my father had said. "That was probably just Fraser the farmer's sheepdogs; their senses are so acute they probably heard us before we heard them. Let's get on and see if we can get home again before the end of the night. We don't want to hang around this mountain for longer than we have to."

But I wasn't so sure, after I'd told my father about the little, evil king of the leprechauns. He hadn't believed me then, but animals can sense things, even fear in humans, and Peter's goat didn't go loco for nothing.

But my father could sense my worry. "Listen son, lightning doesn't strike in the same place twice, and what happened in the village last year—that won't return; the old monk, Abbot John, saw to that... he's watching over us now, even as we walk in this river. Let's get on... the time's flying, and I want to get home tonight like the rest of you, to my own warm bed."

We started off again, splashing as we got deeper and deeper into the little valley, the water now and again overlapping the tops of my Wellingtons and soaking my socks.

Now, to unsettle us even more, a light, wispy mist was slowly drifting and descending down towards us, from the grassy knolls at the summits of the Wolfhill and Black Mountains, drifting down to each side of the river like thick, grey fingers. On a night like this I could imagine the highwayman getting himself ready to hold up the stagecoach on the Hightown Road, with a flintlock pistol in one hand and a lit lantern in the other, swinging it to-and-fro.

What had been a clear night on Divis Mountain in the distance had been engulfed by the mist, and even the one-hundred-feet high BBC TV mast, with its ten strobe lights to warn aircraft, had been engulfed by the gathering mist that had been turning into thick fog now. Now I'd wondered if the ghost of Archie McGrath, the RAF flying Officer, was abroad on that lonely mountain tonight where he'd died so tragically in June 1937.

"Did you all know," Peter's father had said, "that loads of sheep have been found on these slopes over the years, dead, and the sheep had appeared to have all their blood drained from their bodies?"

We'd all tried to look at what the slopes had held tonight, but the mist was enveloping everything around us, and we couldn't even see the mountain tops any more. "Maybe Count Dracula had emigrated from Transylvania in Rumania, but I've never seen a castle on these mountains before," Peter junior had replied. Now Peter senior had spooked us again.

As we'd waded further up the deepening river, the water had been getting colder, while old Fearless had decided that he'd had enough of this and had decided to leave the river and to walk alongside us on the rocky shore where there had been just enough room for an animal. Peter junior had been to the left of us, and now and again he would clean his spectacles with the end of his pullover when they'd steamed up with the mist again. Suddenly Peter junior had stopped as we'd walked on, leaving him slightly behind. He'd started to wave his arms.

"Get away! Get away!" he'd yelled, pointing to the trees to our right. "Get away! Get away!" he began again, pulling his coat over his head to hide.

Alarmed, we'd all stopped to let Peter junior catch up.

"Peter! Peter!" his father shouted out, "What the frig's wrong with you, kid? Are you having waking nightmares again?"

Then, as if by a signal, old Fearless had bolted from the thick cover of the trees, diving into the water head first and running behind us, terrified.

"What's that, what the hell's that?" my father had shouted out when he looked in the direction from where Fearless had ran from. We quickly looked in the direction where my father had been frantically pointing, and we couldn't believe our eyes. A young woman had stood in a small clearing at the edge of the forest near the river. She'd been tightly holding a baby, a baby that hadn't been making any noise at all and had appeared to be white and lifeless. The woman had worn a black shawl around her head and shoulders and her ragged white dress had stretched to her ankles, it being ragged at the edges as if she'd dragged herself through a thorny bed of blackthorn bushes.

"Oh my God!" Peter senior had shouted, "it's the Blessed Virgin Mary and the baby Jesus!"

As I'd looked on, I'd thought I'd seen figures in the mist and thought I'd been imagining things, like you do when you see faces in wallpaper or carpets, if you imagined long enough. Although I was terrified, I'd known, after our experiences last year, that this was no Virgin and baby Jesus, and we wouldn't get rich either by opening a holy picture or rosary bead shop on these slopes.

While the woman had cradled the baby with her right arm, the left hand was outstretched, and it held a little bowl, like an alms bowl, that the poor would use in India while begging. Her lips were moving but nothing was coming out, at first. The little baby had been wrapped in a dirty, white baby blanket, and the child's face, like the mother's, was pure white like snow, and both their faces were thin and skeletal. As she'd drawn closer to us she'd appeared to walk into the river, but seemed to walk on the water, like Jesus at the Red Sea before he was crucified.

When we'd shone our torches in the pair's direction we'd all blessed ourselves, sensing that this had something to do with the Irish Famine of 1845 to 1849. "Glory be to the Father, son, and Holy Ghost, Amen," my father had said, and we watched intently as the woman and child backed away into the little forest again, without looking round to see where they were going. Both torches were full on the tragic pair now, and we had gasped when we saw that the pair hadn't any eyes in their sockets, just what had seemed to be deep, black holes. The baby never had stirred even once.

Finally they'd gone, as if there'd been a light bulb that had been switched off quickly. Shocked, we'd waded ashore to another little clearing in the forest and rocks a little way ahead. We'd flopped down in unison like crumpled heaps. "Jesus Christ!" my father had said, "we'll never get peace from these spirits that are trying to stop us from finding anything... it would make anybody go onto the real liquid spirits and drink yourself to death!"

After all the excitement Peter senior had seemed nonchalant as if this wasn't real, or somebody was carrying on, and playing a trick on us for a laugh. But he'd been in prison last year, and hadn't experienced what we'd had. My friends, Peter, Jim and me had sat there, legs crossed, while my friends had been frantically shining the torches into the trees, where the long shadows were scaring us just as much as the girl and the baby, while our fathers had gone over our equipment to ensure that we'd lost none in the mad stampede.

Jim senior had been the unelected leader of our group, because of his knowledge of different languages and customs, and he'd finally spoke: "Listen, everybody, we've two options here—either we return from where we've come or we go on ahead, and finish this for good. What do you all say?" Old Fearless had just lain outstretched in front of us, his head resting between his legs, his paws covering his eyes, he was so frightened.

"Jim?" my father had said to his friend Jim Senior, "You heard something being said back there, didn't you? I could see it in your mannerism. That girl was trying to speak, wasn't she?"

"Yes," Jim Senior replied, "but I didn't want to spook the rest of you about what I'd heard, but since you asked, and I'd known what she'd meant... I learned the history of this place and it wasn't very cheering. She was distressed."

Jim senior had gone on: "I thought she'd said, distinctly, 'We'd only asked for food and they sent us soldiers instead.'"

"We could see that she was distressed, Jim," Peter's father had said, "and that baby looked dead. What do you think she was doing up here in these hills at this time of the night? Do you think she was a farmer's wife or daughter?"

"No," Jim had replied, "she wasn't anything belonging to a farmer, a present-day farmer, at any rate. And as she was backing away back into the bushes she had repeated it: 'We'd only asked for food but they sent soldiers instead.' Tragic, really tragic. And all of you were there, you saw that her and the baby were emaciated, and before they'd died they'd probably lived on wild blackberries, turnips, rotten cabbages and rotten potatoes. Stinging nettles even, and it was called the Black Forty-Seven. The dead were buried without coffins, just a few inches below the ground, that had been dug-up by dogs and rats and the bodies eaten. There were tens of thousands of unmarked graves, and it wouldn't surprise me if such graves were prevalent in these hills."

"There's one sure thing, father," Jim junior had said, "there's no friggin' way I'm going back down the way we came, and as the cliffs are far too steep to climb in the dark, we'd just as well move on the waterfall, light a fire, and make our way down again in the daylight!"

We'd all nodded our heads in agreement, and even the dog had nodded its tail in agreement.

Around half an hour later, we'd reached the high natural waterfall, to be met by a wall of white spray and water, the roar like a steam train on a quiet Sunday going past a graveyard. After shining the torches for ten minutes we'd found the old ruins and foundations of the hundreds-of-years-old house, what could have been possibly one of, or the main, safe house of Naois O'Haughian.

We put our equipment down beside what would have been the front door and sitting-room, leaving it there, then went off to forage for twigs and small branches for our fire, while Fearless had decided to lie down there and watch our equipment. We'd decided to stay in two groups, my friends Jim, Peter and me, while our fathers had gone up to higher ground to find the dry twigs and firewood, each group with a torch.

The lads and me had decided to do some night fishing for mountain trout. Luckily for us we'd brought some catgut fishing line, wrapped around a small bobbin, six hooks stored in a matchbox, and some worms what we'd dug up today, in a baked beans tin. I'd carefully dropped the threaded hook into the deep, dark water, wrapping the end of the line around a large stone that we'd dislodged, leaving the deadline tackle on the waterfall bed overnight. Hopefully a big, mountain trout would be on the hook at first light, that would be an addition to our roasted potatoes and beans. I'd looked down to the edge of the pool where I'd dislodged the stone, and seen something as shiny as gold, under the glare of the torch. I'd called my friends over excitedly, my friends and our fathers dropping the twigs and branches that they'd gathered.

"It's a box!" I'd shouted out loudly, "a little, silver box with odd designs all over it! Like a cigarette box!"

Our fathers had almost jumped on top of me, perhaps thinking from a distance that the phantoms had paid us another visit, Jim senior almost snatching the box from my hands.

"This is amazing!" he'd shouted, "it looks like silver all right... but it's not a cigarette case, far from it; it's a snuff box and in great condition." He passed the little box to my father who rubbed it up and down his jean's trouser leg. Each of us had gotten a look, while rubbing it against our clothes excitedly, as if expecting a Genie to burst through its little cover.

My father had taken a little, Swiss penknife from his coat, carefully going around the groove at the top where the little lid would appear to be, scraping the dirt and grime away frantically, slowly forcing it open. Inside had concealed a little portrait, of a young girl who had dark hair down to her shoulders, who had worn a pair of chandelier earrings, and a pearl necklace around her neck, the little portrait measuring two inches by two inches.

Underneath the portrait was a lock of somebody's dark hair, probably her own, and stuck to the lid of the snuff box was a little, gold coin, with writing going all the way around it, in Latin, '*Nummorum Femulas*', which meant, according to Jim senior, "The servant of the coinage." We'd all dropped to our knees simultaneously, as if we were those birds who could turn in a flash, dozens of them together, frantically parting the rest of the stones at the edge of the pool, not minding that we were under a continuous spray of water that had soaked us through to the skin. All of us then frantically clawed at the rest of the stones at the edge of the shallow part of the pool, now going further in wading, until we'd found something when we'd put the torches under the water. Then we'd found old farthings and halfpennies, until Jim junior had cried out: "Impossible! This just can't be!" When we'd all waded out of the pool we'd gathered around Jim junior, wondering why he was making such a fuss over old, almost worthless, coins.

Then he'd held another coin up into the air, above the flashlight, turning and twisting it, and at one point putting it between his teeth and biting it. It was obvious that this was a gold coin; then, laughing hysterically and sinking to his knees, he cried, "My God! A piece of eight, a piece of eight, similar to the one we found at the old monastery, but that was gold while this one is silver!" When Jim junior had passed it around us, we'd each examined it, seeing a cross on one side, and a stamped portrait of a perceived Spanish king. The king had long, flowing hair, the date, 1556, and the words in Latin again: 'Plus Ultra'—"The Pillars of Hercules, and that King was Charles V of Spain," Jim senior had remarked.

"I've got another bad feeling about this one," my father had said. "Could this be the really last hiding place of the highwayman and not the old, monastery after all? Is it possible that these creatures knew we were coming here tonight, and sent that girl and baby to scare us off, the way they did last year?"

"That may be so," Peter senior spoke up, "I don't know about coins or treasure, but tell me how the hell did English coins and Spanish coins end up in the same small place? How did the highwayman get his hands on Spanish coins when he held up English stagecoaches?"

Chapter Twenty

We Encounter Strange, Ancient People

"**T**HE ONLY EXPLANATION I CAN THINK OF** for that one, is the Spanish Armada of 1588!" Jim senior had replied. "They set off to invade England then, but in a short battle the English had routed them. To avoid total destruction, the Armada made for the west coast of Ireland, but ran into a severe gale off the County Mayo coast. These Spanish ships were destroyed and the majority of the crews and sailors were drowned. The coins had probably been part of the soldiers' and sailors' pay, but they never got to spend it. Twenty-four Spanish ships were destroyed on the sharp reefs, and just one, the *Gerona*, made it up to Killybegs in Donegal for repairs."

"And if I remember my history correctly," my father had interrupted, "another fierce gale had blown up and the *Gerona* was driven ashore at Lacada Point, right? Near Dunluce Castle? Not far from the Giant's Causeway? Thirteen hundred sailors and soldiers lost their lives and the *Gerona* had been captained by Don Alonzo de Martinez Leiva, and the old legends of Ireland often repeated that the leprechauns were able to salvage old treasure chests and that they had stripped the soldiers of their armour and arms!

"The chests had contained great treasures, such as gold salamanders inlaid with diamonds and emeralds, plus gold and silver coins, holy gold crosses, silver and gold salvers, all belonging to King Philip the V of Spain?"

We'd all marvelled at Jim senior and my father and their knowledge of Irish history, but Jim senior had been far superior in his widespread knowledge to anybody else I knew. I'd pinched myself, and my friends Jim and Peter had pinched each other... gold and silver coins? Gold salamanders? Gold, holy crosses? Gold and silver salvers? Gold jewellery, inlayed with diamonds and rubies? We'd all been very shocked at the size of it all, and it had been mind-blowing, our ecstasy finally being interrupted by Peter's father: "We can't do much more here tonight, and I suggest we bed down, light a fire, and get the beans and potatoes into the embers of the fire... better to wait until the cold light of morning when we'll be able to see our way into the pool more clearly. It's as dark as coal in there in the night."

The valley had still been strangely quiet, as we'd built a tall fire, dropping our potatoes into the centre of it, then opening the six half-tins of beans with my penknife, leaving them at the side until the fire had ignited properly. We never slept much, busily rubbing the coins with dirt to put a sheen on them—thirty-seven low value English coins, two Spanish, silver, pieces of eight and a silver, English snuffbox.

It had been 3 a.m. when we'd finished the burnishing, and we'd taken turns at watching, two at a time, while the rest of us had tried to sleep in our excitement, but without much luck, and our food just wouldn't settle in our nervous stomachs.

Still, despite all that, sound sleep could never be had, with the noise of the water crashing over the fall. The sheepdogs were as restless as they were earlier, and their incessant howling must have lasted all night. I'd been delegated, along with my friend Peter's father, to take the 5:30 a.m. to 7 a.m. watch, and time had flown as the first light had broken from the direction of the Cavehill in the east, while we'd shaken the rest of the gang to get up. Unusually, the usual Dawn Chorus had failed to materialise, and it was as if some avian disease had struck all the birds down.

When dawn had broken, I'd half-expected to see a war party of Red Indians rushing out of the small forest behind and in front us, like in the matinee shows at the Forum cinema in nearby Ardoyne, at the Saturday morning matinee where we'd pay a sixpence admittance fee. Old Fearless had ran off again, like he did when danger threatened last year, but there was no danger to be seen after last night, and he'd probably headed up to the grassy knolls at the foot of the mountains to search for himself for an early morning, unsuspecting rabbit. But he appeared to be near, his sudden incessant barking coming from somewhere very close, as it echoed around the deep canyon. We'd decided to investigate the deep pool further, forming a human assembly line, handing each other rocks that we'd carefully and watchfully removed from the edge of the pool.

When I'd checked my dead fishing line from the night before, the worm had still been attached to the hook, and even the trout had failed to show up as well.

"Fearless! Fearless!" Peter junior had shouted out, his hands cupping his mouth, when suddenly, Fearless had suddenly emerged from behind the waterfall before darting back into it again, his tail wagging furiously. We'd stuffed the copper coins into the empty bean tins, and the silver coins and the snuffbox into one of the sacks, preparing to move over to the ruins of the old house with the metal-detector, but now Fearless had been onto something even more pressing.

"I've seen old adventure films," my father had said, "especially 'Treasure Island', were the pirates led by Long John silver had hidden treasure behind a waterfall on an island in the Caribbean, and, I wonder... ?"

We'd known what was going through his mind that led all of us for a mad dash to find a way in behind the waterfall, and if the dog could find a way in, then so could we.

There had only been enough room for us to crawl under the waterfall, and as we went in on our hands and knees, we'd still gotten a severe soaking as the water bounced off our heads and shoulders. We'd found a blocked up depression behind the waterfall, and the floor below us had been artificially laid, with flat rocks and some kind of cement mixture to keep the rocks firmly in place, like an old, Roman, stone road. What had looked like a vertical stone wall had also been built up behind the waterfall, about three or four feet behind the flow. It had appeared to be covering a natural cave entrance, again with great precision and skill, again with some kind of cement holding it all together tightly, except for a hole, two-foot in circumference, and probably the place where Fearless had been scraping at, detecting probably a rabbit or some other small animal that had run into there to escape while we'd been sleeping.

"Hand me that torch," Peter senior had said. "It's my turn to muck in now, and keep that bloody dog back out of the way! I'll stick my head inside, and have a look to see what's on the other side, if anything, while at the same time Jim and Patrick's father there can chip away at the sides of the opening... hopefully we can get enough room to crawl inside."

"A musty smell," my father had said, "a very musty smell, like rum or some kind of alcohol throughout the inside," he being now half in and half out of the rapidly widening gap, pulling out thick beams of wood that had been used as a barricade, as well as stones and rocks.

"Right," Peter's father had said, "and cobwebs, lots of thick cobwebs, as if there has been nobody here for donkey's years, if there's been anybody here in the first place!" They'd shouted louder and louder, to try to drown out the crashing of the waterfall. "Is it just possible," my father had said to Jim senior, "that this waterfall is nothing more than an artificial one to divert the water down into our village, where it operated the waterwheels at the three mills down there?"

"We're looking in the wrong place, and our answer may be under the foundations of that old house to the right of us... that looks like a more promising place."

"That may be possible," Jim senior had replied, "but what are the coins that we found doing in this pool behind us? They appear to have been washed out of the cave there, and down through that little stream, running out of the gap below us here, when water sunk after rainfall, into an underground river."

A very loud noise like a collapsing of old, crumbling rocks resonated throughout the cave, as if the whole place was about to collapse, as we'd feverishly dislodged more and more rocks and old timbers. Before long we would be able to stand up and walk into that damp, dank place.

Then another obstacle had appeared behind the artificially-built stone wall, when a loud, dull sound had been heard when Jim senior had struck something directly behind the now demolished wall, and when we'd shone both torches in that direction and the new obstacle could be seen—a row of vertical wooden strips like railway sleepers, again fastened with a cement-like substance. "Looks like those stakes the US Army had used to build their forts in the old Wild West, for protection against the native Americans," my father had said when he'd crawled between Jim senior's legs to have a closer look.

The noise of the iron bar against the new barrier sent deep echoes further into the cave. Whoever had built this had made sure it had been built to last. Jim senior had been working at a frenetic rate, and was worn out, leading my father and Peter senior to take over for a while, hammering and hacking at the obstacle. Now they were almost through; then, without warning, both of them had jumped back in panic, almost falling back under the waterfall's heavy flow and into the pool.

"God almighty!" my father had yelled, "where the torch's beam landed inside we'd both seen a pair of horrible, yellow eyes staring back at us—they were more terrified than we were! What the hell was it?"

"*Woof! Woof! Woof!*" came the familiar sound of old Fearless, from inside the cave, who must have crawled through the small hole at the base of the cave wall, getting stuck in an old barrel that we'd seen. He'd been stuck in there, head first. We would have to get into the cave and rescue him ourselves before he'd suffocated, because by the time one of us had run back down into the village to report it, any rescue service or fire brigade would take hours to reach us on this mountain. Anyway, if the main treasure trove had been in this cave we wouldn't want anybody to know about it before we'd retrieved it and had safely delivered it to the Ulster Museum for our, hopefully, massive reward.

Another loud, dull rumble had come from inside the cave, that had sounded like the beginnings of an earthquake, and we had to get the dog out sooner rather than later.

The dog had started barking in a muffled bark again. "Nice dog! Nice dog!" a voice had shouted, or two voices this time, trying to reassure Fearless again, but this time followed by low, childish chuckles. "I told you before, boys, we have to get inside to rescue him— he can't hear you from out here," my father had said, but it had been useless trying to tell him that it wasn't us talking to the dog, because he wouldn't believe us.

And none of the three of us had been ventriloquists, for the voices came from *inside* the cave, not outside. Our fathers had dug and dug for at least another hour, until, finally, the second, wooden blockade had been demolished, and then we'd all crawled in, one at a time, up to where the dog's legs had been wriggling and dangling in the stale, airless place. The cave had been around thirty feet long and around ten feet wide, and a little waterfall had ran down the walls, down the middle of the cave, exiting where we'd came in.

This cavern had strongly resembled the old monastery underground vault, minus the steep steps, although six wooden torches had been dug into crevices in the cave's walls, although the leather-looking material that was the flaming part at the top had appeared to have burned out years ago. Old green moss and damp lichen were stuck to the cave walls, and the old barrel that Fearless had been jammed into had fallen on its side, after he'd struggled frantically, with Fearless' head looking at us while his tail and rear end had stuck out of the rear of the barrel.

My father had suddenly stopped in his crawl. "Metal! Lots of metal of some sort!" he cried out, leaping further in as if he'd found a gold mine. He'd tapped the metal that had been protruding from the ground, the blow sounding like a church bell pealing in that enclosed space.

"And more! Much more!" Peter senior had shouted, slamming the metal with the flat of the spade.

"It looks like military uniforms or that sort of paraphernalia... but how the hell did this stuff end up here? And no, this just isn't possible, this stuff is at least a thousand miles from where it should be... Spain! Spanish military stuff!" We'd all kicked away old leather clothes and animal skins, hides and old rags.

"This is, my friends," Jim senior had gasped, "body armour and the remains of military uniforms from sixteenth century Spain, unmistakable!"

But there were no remains of human skeletons anywhere, just old, animal bones like badgers, rabbits and other small animals, and what looked like the bones of very large dogs, probably Irish Wolfhounds, the biggest known dogs in the world. But they must have gotten into the cave when they were pups, seeing that gap at the bottom of the cave wall was around two feet by two feet in circumference. "Strange that," Jim senior said, "unless there's another way in here that we can't see."

"Or maybe wolves?" my father had surmised. "The last wolves in Ireland were killed around this area—could the remains be them? That howling last night had to be heard to be believed, and we all heard it all night and it wasn't any farmer's sheepdogs; they haven't got the range or the voice box. That howling was a big bad omen in itself."

Our fathers had concentrated the torches in the direction of the pile of bones.

We'd all dropped to our knees simultaneously after we'd moved the barrel, when we'd spotted something silver—like glistening metal—with the torches' beams.

"Go and get your metal-detector, son, and run it over the ground here, quickly now!" my father had ordered, and I had been out and back in there again in thirty seconds.

"Eureka! A watch!" Peter senior had yelled. A gold, pocket watch with a short, gold chain hanging from it... and it had a tortoiseshell ampule inlaid with gold, shiny gold! "Quick son, crawl outside too and bring the sack in; all these things will need to be separated in case we're mixed up. This is dynamite!"

"This stuff had to belong to the highwayman!" Jim senior had remarked. "Who else could have put it here, hidden carefully inside a mountain like this?"

"And more friggin' stuff!" Peter senior had shouted, probably thinking that this loot had been much better than the stuff he'd gone to prison for, when he'd stolen the hot cigarettes, shoes and exotic birds when he'd worked down in Belfast docks.

"Necklaces!" he'd repeated, "and plenty of them—and gold ones at that! And gold earrings... diamond necklaces with rows and rows of emeralds, white diamonds attached to them. This friggin' place is a virtual Aladdin's cave, and some! And diamond-set bows and brooches, with tightly wound gold wirework... and look! More emeralds! And rubies and sapphires with other precious stones, amethyst chartreuse, coral ivory, pearls and white imperial, pink topazes!"

We'd laughed out loud, because Peter senior had known his jewels. Before he'd been arrested he'd been a fence or a middleman for criminal gangs all over Ireland, and all we'd needed to be found now would be exotic birds like parrots to make his day. The hum of the metal-detector permeated the entire cave in that very enclosed space, that had now sounded even louder than the cascading tons and tons of mountain water, made even heavier by the winter's snow thaw, as it smacked down onto the waterfall's pool.

"Dig here!" I'd shouted excitedly, "Lots of metal here, just under the damp surface," while the other five had sunk to their knees, digging with their hands or any sharp instrument they could get their grubby hands on.

"This might be the mother lode!" Jim senior had yelled, probably after watching too many Western or cowboy films. "It's a friggin' Morion!" Jim senior yelled again, although I'd not known what a friggin' Morion was, but when he'd yanked it from the ground we could see it had been an old helmet that the Spanish had worn when they'd gone to South America in 1492 to colonize it.

What had remained of a short, baggy, leather jerkin had also been unearthed, red and yellow-coloured, and what had looked like a burnished, silver breastplate of armour, and the ragged remains of baggy, leather trousers, and Moorish-type knee-length leather boots.

"Jesus!" my father had said, as he pulled from the ground what had looked like an old fashioned crossbow, its butt eaten away with time and dampness, a faded, red sash and a rapier, plus a little, faded, red nightcap.

We'd dug for hours and hours, and were becoming hungry, and soon we'd go outside and relight the fire and roast what had remained of our potatoes, and eat our extra supplies of chocolate and potato crisps. Our tally had amounted to the jewellery, coins, both English, fifty now, and Spanish, five little leather purses containing silver coins that must have been the soldiers' and sailors' wages which, unfortunately, the soldiers and sailors had not been able to spend. Still, there hadn't been any human bones found at all, and all this Spanish paraphernalia was hard to understand, and how it came to be in a sealed cave, just a few miles outside Belfast, in the year 1956...

"Stash all the loot against the far wall at the rear of the cave," Jim senior had ordered. "That way we can hide it until we leave with it when it gets dark again. It might happen that a farmer may come along and claim the loot for himself, while it's on his land, but if we get it to the Ulster Museum first, he will have to split it fifty-fifty, as Treasure Trove. We can store it in Peter's shed." The flags we'd found had been faded but still beautiful; the flag of Burgundy, a plain, white background with the inscription in red, 'Ave Gratis Pienna', the Virgin Mary, on one side, the other side in blue, showing Christ crucified.

We'd also found a mounted standard, dated 1503, with a green background and a black eagle painted on it.

Another faded cloth showed a beautiful, yellow castle on a red background, and another with lions painted on a white background. But we'd been particularly wary of ten barrels of what had said "gunpowder" in Spanish, under an old, tarpaulin part of a sail, and our fathers had declined to smoke. It may have been wet or damp after all those years, but they weren't sure.

The air had been thick, damp and oppressive inside the cave, us deciding to leave for a while to catch gulps of fresh, mountain air, but still getting a severe soaking as we'd inched from behind the waterfall, to rest in the old, ancient house foundations, where the fire had still been smouldering when we'd stocked it up with fresh kindling to get it going for tea. We'd watched the outline of the black mountain in particular, darting our gaze to the summit, where soldiers had been stationed to guard the BBC transmitter for years, in case of political emergency and bomb attacks.

"Nice dog! Nice dog! Go now!" the little voices had sounded as if from behind the waterfall at the cave's entrance where we'd dug it away, and again our fathers had stared at us, us shrugging our shoulders again as if to say, not us, maybe the woman and her child we'd seen last night, further down the river.

"Return to the cave lads, and see what's going on there; somebody is after our loot and is playing a game on us... a game that we can't lose this time."

My friends and I had sidled towards the cave entrance between the sheer rocks and the waterfall itself, with Jim and Peter junior in front of me, careful not to get more soaked than we were.

"And when you go into the cave again," my father had shouted after us, "don't set off a spark beside the kegs marked *polvora*... that is Spanish for gunpowder! If that goes off we'll be the second people to fly to the moon, after H. G. Wells!"

Jim junior had been the first in, and the first quickly back out again, with Peter junior sidling out afterwards, dropping his spectacles into the deep pool, as expected, as we'd nicknamed Peter Glassless.

"Run! Run like the clappers!" Jim junior had shouted, "I just seen a little, ragged-clothed, eight or nine year old boy and girl just standing at the mouth of the cave there, and their voices together had shouted, above the roar of the waterfall: 'Leave! You all have to leave here now...!' And the boy had a lit torch in his hand, waving it back and forth!"

I'd almost fallen into the pool when Fearless had sped past me, almost knocking me off my feet.

"You have to leave this place now!" the boy's voice had boomed out in echo, sounding more like a grown man instead of an eight or nine year old.

I'd stood there frozen to the spot, lifting my head nervously in the direction of the voice, and my heart had skipped ten beats, not one.

"You have to leave this place!" the voice had repeated. Two little figures had stood there, luminous, but transparent as well, as I could see the rocks behind through them. Both of them had appeared to be emaciated, and where their eyes should have been had just been black eye sockets. The boy and girl had been like skeletons, and the little girl had been chewing on what had appeared to be grass and watercress.

The boy's trousers had been ragged and torn, up to his knees, like the trousers people may have worn during the Irish Famine on photographs I'd seen at our history lesson at school, while his once white nightshirt had been torn and filthy, his dark hair now a mess of dirt and knots.

Suddenly, as I'd stood transfixed staring at the children, a loud rumble had appeared to come from within the cave, and little orbs of light and light streaks had floated out of the cave's entrance, lighting up the back of the falling water and the damp rock wall behind it. Beautiful red, green and blue lights. Strong hands had then grabbed me by the shoulders, as my father and I fell backwards, and out of the waterfall's range, both of us landing in a crumpled heap among the rest of our gang, in the old, derelict ruins of the house.

"Run, run like hell!" my father had shouted, while the other boys had told their fathers of the strange spectres behind the waterfall. Our long, loping strides had brought us down to where we'd seen the woman and child last night, but we'd left all our tools and the metal-detector inside the cave, along with our long, sought-after treasure, and had wanted to go back but my father had stopped us. Then, like the sound of an earthquake, only twenty times worse, a massive bang had echoed down the river valley, sending us diving into the river as massive lumps of rock had fallen into the river beside us.

It had been similar to multiple explosions in Wolfhill Quarry, far above us again, when they'd detonated their explosive charges every Saturday, to loosen the solid rocks there to be used for major road works on Ireland's roads. For the first time since we'd entered this river valley, the birds, foxes, rabbits and hares had broken cover, running past us in a panic, with birds flying into trees, and each other, before crashing into the ground and river beside us. We'd needed to get to higher ground to see what had been going on, crawling up the sheer rocks by holding onto the trees that had grown outward, inching ever so slowly to the top, exhausted and wondering what had hit us.

Finally, we'd reached the summit of the Wolfhill Mountain, flopping down beside each other, glad that we'd all been in one piece.

"Who the hell were those two little kids?" I said, "I wonder if they were killed?"

"Killed?" Jim senior had replied, "I think they were dead a long time, around a hundred and ten years dead... two, or should I say, four of the Famine dead; I think they were all the same family and had wandered around here for all that time, ending up living in the cave."

"Then how did they get inside that cave? If they were inside it all that time?" Peter senior had asked.

"Remember the spectres we experienced last year?" Jim senior had replied. "They could walk through walls, and if they could do it then, so could that poor, starving Famine family. Either way, they must have been the guardians of that place, employed by the leprechauns from last year."

"Nobody was supposed to get their hands on that treasure and nobody did," Jim senior said, sullenly.

Peter senior had whistled, then had laughed: "Speak for yourself, Jim, but I'm glad to prove you wrong for once... you may know four languages, but I know all about pickpockets!" Peter senior began holding up some trinkets and still chuckling. "One gold and diamond encrusted salamander... twelve silver, Spanish coins... a certain, silver snuffbox... a set of chandelier earrings and matching necklace, and this will buy us lots more equipment for our next treasure hunt, even better and newer than the stuff we'd lost, and with lots of money left over for our own, personal, lucrative use. Where did you say that the next treasure map was located?"

"Great!" my father had said, "but that waterfall that was once down there is now a dam, and getting bigger all the time... the waterfall as we knew it has completely gone. Let's get the hell out of here and straight home. I could eat an elephant!"

As we'd crawled up along a hedgerow on our hands and knees, looking back down into the river valley, a plume of thick, white smoke, like that when the atomic bombs had gone off at Hiroshima and Nagasaki during the Second World War, began to smother the valley below. As we watched we saw a swarm of British soldiers running down the Black mountain to investigate the massive blast, probably thinking that the BBC transmitter had been under attack by the Russians.

THE END

Lightning Source UK Ltd.
Milton Keynes UK

172229UK00001B/16/P